Requiem at the
Refuge

Also by Sister Carol Anne O'Marie

Death Takes Up a Collection
Advent of Dying
The Missing Madonna
Murder in Ordinary Time
Death of an Angel

Requiem at the Refuge

❦❦❦

Sister Carol Anne O'Marie

Thomas Dunne Books
St. Martin's Minotaur
New York

THOMAS DUNNE BOOKS
An Imprint of St. Martin's Press

ISBN 0-312-20906-1

First Edition: March 2000

10 9 8 7 6 5 4 3 2 1

To the women of A Friendly Place,
who have taught me so much
about courage and optimism

Requiem at the Refuge

Saturday, August 15

❦❦

Feast of the Assumption of Mary

When Sister Cecilia, president of Mount St. Francis College, missed morning Mass, Sister Therese was very concerned. Once Father Adams had left the altar, Therese, who preferred her name pronounced "trays," turned to face the handful of nuns who still remained in the pews.

"She never misses morning Mass," Therese's whisper reverberated through the chapel. "Especially on a Holy Day of Obligation."

"It's not a Holy Day if it falls on Saturday or Monday," old Sister Donata corrected. "They're changing everything," she lamented.

"That is not my point," Therese hissed. "My point is Cecilia must be sick."

"Why don't you go to her room and check?" Sister Mary Helen asked sensibly. Not that she would want anyone checking on her, particularly if she'd overslept.

"Let Anne go," old Donata grumbled. "She has the youngest legs." This, of course, was true. Sister Anne had just recently celebrated her thirtieth birthday.

Therese would have none of it. "I will go," she said with a sniff and rose from her pew.

Beside her, Mary Helen heard her friend Sister Eileen sigh. "Poor Cecilia has every reason to be tired," she whispered, "what with this business of getting ready to open school. If you ask me, it's more work than being in school."

Eileen stopped short. Therese had reappeared, her face the color of codfish.

"Dead! She's dead!" Therese rasped, scarcely able to get her tongue around the words. Her bright sparrow eyes were riveted on Mary Helen. "Cecilia is dead!" Therese sputtered before her ragged sob tore through the shocked silence of the chapel.

Sister Mary Helen felt her heart thumping. *Please, Lord, not murder!* She held her breath. In the distance, foghorns wailed, warning San Franciscans that they were in for another dripping summer day.

"What happened?" Old Donata cupped her hand behind her good ear.

Therese hiccuped in a valiant effort to control herself. "Cecilia is dead," she repeated. "She must have died in her sleep."

Oddly relieved, Mary Helen hurried from the chapel to the nearest phone to call 911 while Eileen went for the priest.

After a quick breakfast, the nuns, still in shock, divided into groups and shot into action. Fortunately, they still had two weeks before the opening of the fall semester. It would take at least one of those weeks to prepare a proper funeral for Cecilia. After all, this was the first time in the long history of Mount St. Francis College that an acting president had died in office.

Before noon they had contacted Sister Cecilia's relatives

and friends, the college faculty and staff, the Superior General, the Archbishop, and any other dignitaries that they thought should know. Finally they prepared the death notice for the *Chronicle*.

Surely, they reasoned, they would have to wait two or three days for the official coroner's report, although the paramedics assured them that Cecilia had died of a heart attack. Odd that Sister Cecilia, who had always seemed so strong and steadfast, had a weak heart.

More to keep from thinking about the tragedy than any-thing else, the nuns spent the afternoon on the details of death. They notified McAvoy and O'Hara's Mortuary and decided on an appropriate burial suit, her good navy blue wool, of course, with a lace-trimmed white blouse. Then they arranged for a fitting wake with refreshments, planned the funeral Mass, put the program into the computer, chose the eulogist, scheduled the burial at the Order's plot at Holy Cross, and organized the reception after the cemetery.

As the day wore on, they became more and more deter-mined to have a requiem worthy of the president of San Fran-cisco's only Catholic women's college. They even made up the beds in the convent's spare rooms for overnight visitors. Surely there would be a crowd.

Late Saturday evening, after a light supper, they checked off the last detail. Satisfied that all was in order, the nuns col-lapsed into the comfortable chairs in the community room. Most eyes were glazed.

Therese put her long, narrow feet up on a hassock. "Poor Cecilia," she said. "I guess you could say she died with her boots on."

"Actually, she died with her bed booties on," old Donata commented, seeming not to notice Therese's flaming face. "I knit them for her."

3

Since she retired, old Donata had honed her knack for driving Therese crazy into a fine art. If Mary Helen didn't know better, she'd suspect Donata of practicing.

The sharp ring of the telephone pierced the tension. "I guess the word is out," Sister Anne groaned and pushed herself up from her chair. "It's going to be a very long week."

"It's a lovely feast day to die on, anyway," Sister Ursula said piously. "To ascend into heaven on the same day as Our Blessed Mother did."

"Unless you're the one who is doing the ascending," Donata snapped.

Another uncomfortable quiet filled the room.

Eileen, who had little tolerance for awkward silences, glanced around. "You all look exhausted," she said, wagging her head. "As they say back home, 'It is well that misfortunes come one by one and not all together.' "

"You're right about that," Sister Ursula agreed.

Mary Helen studied Eileen in amazement. She was more convinced than ever that her friend made up these Irish proverbs on demand, although Eileen adamantly denied it.

Furthermore, it had always been Mary Helen's experience that misfortunes came in threes. Now was not the time, however, to say so. Now was the time for each of them to go to her own room and have a good cry.

Saturday, August 22

❧❧❧

Feast of the Queenship of Mary

Sister Cecilia's Requiem Mass and her burial ran as smoothly as a large funeral can. It was a simple and dignified celebration of the woman's life befitting all that she had accomplished in her own simple and dignified way.

Even the weather cooperated. The morning fog burned off quickly, leaving San Francisco sun-bright and crisp. The sky formed a quiet blue dome over Mount St. Francis College while in the distance white sailboats bobbed on the bay.

Thick borders of vanilla impatiens punctuated with purple stalks of society garlic lined the driveway. A fresh green apron of lawn in front of the main building made a fitting welcome mat for the hordes of mourners who solemnly trekked up the hill to the college chapel.

The gardener had remembered to turn off the automatic sprinkler. The eulogist kept her remarks short and real. The choir sang even better than usual, and all day long Sister

5

Ursula resisted the temptation to say that it was a lovely feast day on which to be buried, although it was.

Late Saturday evening, when the final well-wisher had gone home, the nuns gathered, once again, in the community room. Down the hall, the washing machine swished with the last of the visitors' sheets and towels.

"I wish Cecilia was here," Donata said. "I'd love to know how she liked it."

"She is here in spirit," Ursula said piously. Her cheeks colored. The words seemed to have just slipped from her mouth.

Donata glared, her hearing remarkably improved. "I know that," she grumbled. "I'm just curious about how she liked it."

"I'm sure she liked it very much." Sister Therese appeared in the doorway wheeling a cart filled with several half-empty wine bottles, cans of beer and soft drinks, a little brandy for Donata's bad heart, ice, a small stack of napkins, and plastic glasses.

Sister Anne followed close behind with two heaping bowls of popcorn.

"Furthermore, I'm sure Sister Cecilia would want us to relax and toast her." Therese's dark eyes darted around the room daring anyone to contradict her. For once, she received no argument.

❧❧❧

Glad to be alone at last, Sister Mary Helen shut her bedroom door firmly behind her. With relief, she kicked off her good shoes and threw her good suit over the back of the desk chair, promising herself that she'd hang it up before she left her room in the morning. Once in bed, she tried to get into a new murder mystery, but her eyelids refused to stay open, even for that.

It had been a very long day and a longer week. Yet Mary

Helen felt a good tired, the one that comes from a job well done. It was the least that Cecilia deserved after all she'd done for the college and for the Order.

A cool breeze from the raised window made Mary Helen's room a perfect sleeping temperature. The hum of traffic along Turk Street was steady and, in its familiar way, soothing. Faintly she heard the convent telephone. Thank goodness someone picked up on the second ring.

What now? she wondered. Even drowsy, she felt that nagging sense of dread. *Good news never comes this late at night,* she thought, too weary to be really anxious. Tomorrow morning would be time enough for any more misfortunes.

❧❧❧

Sister Mary Helen was just drifting off when she heard the noise. At first, she wasn't sure what it was . . . *Peck, peck, peck.* Was it a bird or a tree branch against the convent wall?

As the sound grew more steady and persistent, she realized that it was a knuckle against her bedroom door.

"Come in!" she called without even opening her eyes.

"It's Molly," the voice said, and Mary Helen recognized the soft brogue of her friend Sister Eileen.

"What's Molly?" Mary Helen asked, snapping on the bed lamp.

Eileen's round face was ashen, and her eyes were filling with tears. "It's my sister, Molly. Bad news."

"Come in. Sit down." Mary Helen swung her feet out of bed and felt for her glasses on the nightstand. "What happened?"

"They called from home," Eileen began, perching on the edge of Mary Helen's easy chair. "Molly has cancer."

Quickly the story tumbled out. Sister Eileen's youngest sister, Molly—actually her only living sibling—had been diagnosed with terminal cancer. Molly, who had never married,

7

still lived in the family home in the small town of Ballygloo-nen in Galway.

It was one of Eileen's nephews who had called, asking if she could come home just for a time to care for Molly. The family had met and none of them were able. Yet no one wanted to turn Auntie Molly over to the care of strangers.

They wondered if, just maybe, Sister Eileen could come home for a few months. Surely it wouldn't be more than a few months.

"Give me a day or two to see what I can arrange," Eileen had said, although she suspected there would be no problem. For the last few years, although the college library staff had been extremely deferential, her work was really volunteer.

"Head librarian emeritus," young Anne called her. Not that Eileen ever complained. In fact, she often said that she liked the freedom, and *emeritus* had a nicer ring to it than *retired*.

The Superior General would easily grant her the permission to go. In fact, under the circumstances, the Superior would most likely encourage her to.

"What I really need," Eileen admitted, wiping her eyes, "is a day or two to get used to the idea of leaving San Francisco and moving back to Ireland."

Sister Mary Helen shivered. Suddenly her bedroom seemed cold. A siren from a police car screamed on its way up the Masonic Street hill, setting off a chorus of barking dogs. Over the din, the moan of a foghorn floated in from the Golden Gate. Without warning, Mary Helen felt as lonely as it sounded.

Friday, August 28

❧❧

Feast of Saint Augustine, Bishop and Doctor

Today was the day Sister Mary Helen had tried all week not to think about. Today was the day Sister Eileen was leaving for Ireland.

As Eileen had suspected, the Superior General did encourage her to go home. "A short sabbatical," she had called it, "to minister to your family."

Preparation for the trip had gone smoothly. Eileen's passport, the one she'd used when Mary Helen and she went on their pilgrimage to Spain, was still valid. Packing clothes was no problem, since Ireland and San Francisco could have much the same weather in the summertime.

The head librarian had seemed genuinely sorry to lose Eileen, promising to save her volunteer job. The nuns had given her a surprise bon voyage party and insisted that they would keep her bedroom "as is" until her return. "I'll even dust it," Anne had joked, knowing what a tidy paws Eileen was.

The only thing that both old nuns found difficult during the week had been keeping up a cheerful front. *The less said, the better*, Mary Helen thought, sitting on Eileen's black suitcase while she snapped it shut.

From the expression on her friend's face Mary Helen knew that she, too, was fighting with her feelings and losing the battle.

"I'll miss you something terrible, old dear," Eileen said quietly.

"Me, too," was all Mary Helen trusted herself to say. Now was no time to get sloppy. They still had the ride to the airport.

Thank goodness Anne was driving them. Mary Helen wasn't sure she could cope with both her emotions and the late-afternoon traffic. Anne could be trusted to keep the conversation light.

Two hours before the flight, the three nuns stood in the British Airways line making small talk with one another and the passengers on either side. Slowly the queue snaked toward the counter where a perky young attendant in a smart red, white, and blue print dress checked Eileen's ticket and luggage.

"You don't need to stay," Eileen said, boarding pass in hand. "I know you've things to do, and I'm all set."

Mary Helen felt the lump in her throat swell. She shook her head, not trusting herself to speak. Good-byes were like a little bit of dying.

"We'll see you safely on board," Anne insisted.

"I'll be fine." Eileen's eyes were filling.

"Are you sure you want us to leave you?" Anne asked.

The appearance of an alumna of the college, Marilyn— Mary Helen couldn't remember her married name—saved them from any further discussion on whether to go or to stay.

Marilyn worked for British Airways. "Please, Sisters, come up to the executive lounge," she insisted. "It's much more comfortable up there, and I'd love to treat you to a cup of coffee and a snack."

Silently they rode the small padded elevator to the lounge. As Marilyn had promised, it was much more comfortable than the public waiting area. Actually, it was elegant, with sofas and easy chairs and plenty of space to spread out.

Before she was paged, Marilyn managed to serve their coffee and fill the low table in front of the sofa with cheese and crackers, scones, butter and jam, small mints, pretzels, and a bowl of mixed nuts. "Enjoy!" she called cheerfully.

Mary Helen watched Eileen nibble on a cashew. How she was going to miss her dear old friend! Over the years, their lives had become so entwined, their friendship so genuine and simple. Mary Helen was going to miss Eileen always being there, not so much for the things they talked about, but for the things they no longer needed to say.

When Eileen's flight was called, Mary Helen was relieved. She'd always found that the best way to do something painful was to do it quickly.

At the security gate, they stopped. "Visitors go no further," the uniformed woman checking tickets informed them, all business.

"I guess this is really it," Anne said.

Smiling, Mary Helen locked Eileen in a tight hug. "Take care of yourself, old friend," she whispered as they rocked back and forth.

"You, too," Eileen said, her voice thick.

"Write," Mary Helen said.

Eileen just nodded.

"Or call."

Eileen nodded again and gave a final hug. In an instant, she disappeared down the long hall.

For the first time, Mary Helen noticed other passengers

swarming around them. All apparently were headed for the British Airways flight.

Men in dress suits carrying laptop computers mingled with college students with backpacks and ski jackets. A freckle-faced youth with a lilting brogue was obviously on his way home, as was a tired looking woman in a sweat suit leading a cranky toddler by the hand. Behind her was a corps of African men dressed in long brightly colored silk robes, hand-tooled leather sandals, and Rolex watches. Absentmindedly Mary Helen turned to ask Eileen what country she thought the Africans might be from.

When she did, Eileen was not there. All that had replaced her was a strange ache in Mary Helen's throat.

The ride back to Mount St. Francis College was slow and silent. Anne flipped on the news and traffic station, and Mary Helen closed her eyes and pretended to listen.

Between the report of the impending BART strike, which threatened to leave ten thousand commuters without transportation, and the latest on the new Forty-niners football stadium, one of Eileen's "old sayings" popped crazily into Mary Helen's head.

Actually, it was what Eileen had said on the day Cecilia died: "It is well that misfortunes come one by one and not all together."

Even as she said it, Mary Helen had wanted to correct her. In her experience troubles came in threes. Unfortunately, she had the sinking feeling that she was being proven correct. Wasn't Molly's cancer necessitating Eileen's departure easily trouble number two? What, she wondered, would be the third one? She didn't have to wait long to find out.

When Sister Mary Helen and Sister Anne arrived back at the college the nuns were still in the dining room. The meal itself was over, but the tension in the room let them know that something else was definitely on the burner.

Without thinking, Mary Helen looked for Eileen to find out what was up. She remembered with a sudden thud in her stomach that Eileen was gone.

"Let me get us something to eat," Anne offered as Mary Helen sank into the nearest chair. "You try to find out what's happening."

Mary Helen didn't even need to ask. Ursula came right over. "I am so glad you're back," she said. "We just heard who has been appointed to take Cecilia's place as president," she added, her neck and cheeks flaming with excitement.

Ursula took a deep breath. This was going to be a long story.

"The Superior General called with the news. We will get it in an official letter, of course, but she wanted us to hear it before anyone else did, and we heard it from them. Therese answered the phone."

"Who is it?" Mary Helen blurted out, unable to control her patience for any more of Ursula's preamble.

Ursula looked shocked. "Who? What do you mean, who? Didn't I just tell you?" She looked so positive that she had, Mary Helen didn't have the heart to contradict her. "Like I said, it's Patricia. She'll be here from Los Angeles next week."

Mary Helen was dumbstruck. Ursula waited a minute for a reaction, but when none came, she spotted a lively discussion across the room and excused herself to join it.

Sister Patricia! Mary Helen couldn't believe it. Patricia! It couldn't be! If Donata rather than Therese had answered the phone, Mary Helen would have demanded a call back. With her hearing, Donata could have easily misunderstood, but not

Therese. Sister Therese would never mix up a message that important.

So it was true, which baffled Mary Helen still further. Why would the General pick Patricia, of all people? Not that there was anything actually wrong with the woman. Patricia was young, but not too young, smart, and efficient. She was even tall and square, and with her full head of prematurely white hair she looked as distinguished as a college president should look.

Patricia had administered several small institutions of the Order with good results and, in general, was well thought of by the civic community, if they thought of her at all. In Mary Helen's opinion, the problem was that Patricia, through no fault of her own, mind you, had one fatal flaw. The woman had little or no sense of humor. How, Mary Helen wondered, could anyone run anything, let alone anything as big and complex as Mount St. Francis College, without a sense of humor? By comparison, the Israelites' making bricks without straw was a piece of cake.

Anne returned, balancing two plates of vegetable lasagna with green salad. Obviously Mary Helen was eating healthy tonight, like it or not.

"Thank you," she managed, glad to see Therese following her with a tray of crunchy sour dough bread, butter, and two glasses of red wine.

"The condemned might as well eat a hearty meal," she said, leaving as quickly as she'd come.

"Now, what did that mean?" Mary Helen asked, piercing the lasagna with her fork. Steam rose up like an erupting volcano, fogging her bifocals, so she sipped her wine instead.

"Rumors! Nothing but unfounded rumors," Anne said peevishly. "The news service of the weak."

"Clever," Mary Helen said, impressed.

Anne shrugged. *"Reader's Digest,"* she admitted.

Old Donata, who was never hampered by the lack of foundations for her facts, grunted as she settled into the unoccupied chair at the end of the table.

"I guess it's all over for you," Donata said, nervously fingering the handle of her cane.

"All over for me? Why do you say that?" Mary Helen asked, fighting down a feeling of uneasiness. She blew on a forkful of hot lasagna. A person could starve to death before the cheese cooled enough to be eatable.

"We're not getting a death sentence," she told Donata, sounding much more blasé than she felt. "We're just getting a new college president."

"Haven't you heard?" Donata's eyes twinkled with delight at being the bearer of bad news.

"Heard what?"

"This new one—"

"Patricia, you mean?"

"Whoever. They call her Queen of the Clean Sweep."

"Who calls her that?"

Donata's hearing must have failed again, since she didn't answer. She simply shook her head sorrowfully and repeated, "Queen of the Clean Sweep."

"What exactly does that mean?" Mary Helen asked loudly.

"It means that wherever she goes she brings in new blood. Would you like me to cite some examples?"

Spare me the chapter and verse, Mary Helen thought, shaking her head.

Donata pursed her lips, clearly ready to deal the death blow. "She brings in new YOUNG blood." The *young* was in capital letters, and she paused to let the implication sink in. "She'll do it nicely, of course, but she'll do it. Before you can say, 'Jesus, Mary, and Joseph,' you'll be out of that Development Office and knitting bed booties with me." She gave Mary Helen a doleful look. "And, as I remember, Mary Helen, you're not too good with your hands."

Mary Helen felt her blood pressure rising. She was just about to snap back that she could crochet a wicked afghan if she had a mind to, which, of course, she didn't, when Anne interrupted.

"This is nothing but pure speculation," Anne said. "I refuse to spend energy worrying about something that may never happen."

"Easy for you to say." Donata narrowed her eyes. "You're young and besides, you're not at the college anymore. You simply live in the convent. This really won't affect you."

Old Donata had a point. Before beginning the previous school year, Sister Anne had felt an overwhelming call to work with the homeless women in downtown San Francisco. "Women are the most vulnerable people on the streets," Anne had said, and Mary Helen didn't doubt her for a minute. With the blessings of the Superior General and the well-wishes of the Sisters at the college, Anne had left her position as campus minister and founded a daytime drop-in shelter. She named her place the Refuge.

"What a nice name," Mary Helen remembered remarking at the time. "After Our Lady of Refuge from the litany?"

Anne had looked blank.

"The litany? The litany of the Blessed Mother?" Mary Helen repeated, hoping to land on common ground.

Although there was a flicker of recognition, Anne shook her head.

"Why *did* you name your shelter the Refuge?" Mary Helen asked, feeling sure she'd missed some recent church movement or some new saint.

"Because *retreat* sounded too religious and quiet for what I wanted. *Shelter* was too cold. *Sanctuary* was already taken.

Refuge means help and comfort and a place of safety, which was exactly what I hoped for. So I called it *the Refuge*."

At the time Mary Helen had smiled. *Whatever happened to the custom of giving our works religious names, like St. Joseph's or Seton Hospital or, for heaven's sake, Mount St. Francis College itself? It was a way of putting them under the special patronage of the particular namesake.*

"And you never even thought of Our Lady of Refuge?" Mary Helen asked.

When Anne shook her head Mary Helen knew she was looking straight into the face of a generation gap.

❦❦❦

As soon as she had finished eating, Sister Anne excused herself, sure that she wouldn't be missed. All the other nuns were too preoccupied with Sister Patricia and the changes her arrival might make in their lives.

Anne paused in the hall outside the dining room. It was too early to go to bed, but the thought of sitting in the community room listening to another "Patricia" story was more than she could handle. Besides, the lasagna weighed like a boulder in the pit of her stomach. What she needed was a walk!

Grabbing her windbreaker, Anne ducked out the side door into the parking lot. Except for a few cars, which belonged to the kitchen crew, the place was nearly deserted. A far cry from what it would be when the school term began. She started down the middle of the driveway. Soon it would be worth your life to try to walk anywhere on this road.

Anne took a deep breath. The air was tangy and cool, with just a hint of the wet fog that was banked beyond the Golden Gate, waiting to roll in and cover the bridge.

As she walked, a breeze rattled the leaves of the eucalyptus trees and moved through Anne's short dark hair. She detoured

17

around one corner of the main college building and took a half-hidden path that wound its way into a wooded area along the side of the hill. Scotch pine and acacia mixed with the juniper, fern, and ice plant to give it a country feeling. If one really tried, it was almost possible to block out the sounds of traffic on busy Turk Street.

Anne moved quickly along the path. It felt good to stretch her legs and swing her arms. Stones crunched under the soles of her tennis shoes. She listened for the sounds of small birds and squirrels settling in for the night.

Before she knew it, she'd reached the clearing where a concrete bench had been placed in memory of some early benefactor. Stuffing her hands into her jacket pockets, Sister Anne perched on the edge of the cold bench. She looked out over the city. "Best view in town," Sister Mary Helen had called the spot. Anne suspected she might be right.

Below Anne the City Hall, even the skyscrapers, looked dwarfed. The rolling Oakland hills and Berkeley's campanile seemed like miniatures, the boats like children's toys bobbing in the bay. The lights outlining the Bay Bridge gave it all a fairylike feel.

From this height everything below looked so beautiful, so dreamlike, but Anne knew better. Just beyond the bright lights of the luxury hotels was another world. A world where babies cried and men fought and women sold themselves for food and drugs.

While Anne sat safely on this secluded hillside, Peanuts and Crazy Alice and Venus scrounged for dinner and a place to sleep. They'd be glad to see her tomorrow morning when she opened the Refuge. They'd swarm in with all the others for coffee and rolls and hot showers.

It was the end of the month. Anne shivered. The worst time to be homeless. They would be out of money and out of friends to borrow from. Anne tried to shrug off the sadness she sometimes felt. Being overwhelmed and depressed didn't help anyone, least of all the women to whom she ministered.

She had been at the Refuge for nearly a year, but it had taken her only a few weeks to realize that she could not solve the problems. At first she'd become angry and frustrated. Slowly she was realizing that all she could do each day was be there with a little help and a lot of compassion.

Tomorrow—she stared up to the sky, ashen gray and gold, in the twilight. The moon was just becoming visible. Tomorrow dozens of women would descend upon the Refuge anxious to have their most basic needs met. And she would try her best to meet them.

Sometimes, late at night, Anne worried about where the money would come from. The shelter operated on a shoestring. Even so, too often even the shoestring got a little threadbare. But then a small miracle would happen: a hundred dollars here, a shipment of toilet paper there, a carton of toothbrushes. Anne was beginning to count on these miracles for the everyday existence of the Refuge. So far, she had never been disappointed.

Her most pressing need at the moment was for volunteers. The summer vacation months had decimated her regulars. Anne sighed. *Everyone needs a vacation, even volunteers!*

Only faithful Betsy had continued to come every week. Anne smiled at the thought of short, solid Betsy. She was the wife of a prominent attorney in the city. Dressing as she did in old blue jeans and a sweatshirt, Betsy never seemed quite the image of a powerful man's wife.

She was a powerfully good volunteer, however, and Anne needed more like her. She had published her need in several parish bulletins, but so far, she had no takers. She'd just have to count on another miracle.

Deep shadows covered the hillside. The distinct aroma of fog-wet trees filled the air. Anne pushed herself up from the bench. She had better make her way back to the convent before it was too dark to see the trail. She'd put her problems in God's hands, where they belonged.

"Providence will rise before the sun," some wise saint or other had said. Anne was banking on it.

❧❧❧❧

After dinner Sister Mary Helen was exhausted. She could scarcely keep her eyes open during a game of *Scrabble* in the community room. The summer reruns were on the television, and any conversation at all was centered on Sister Patricia and what she might do at the college. By nine o'clock, Mary Helen had enough. Excusing herself, she went to her room. A few pages of her latest murder mystery and she'd be fast asleep. At least she thought she'd be.

Unfortunately, when she clicked off the bed lamp her mind clicked on, inventing, as it did, the most desperate scenarios: Sister Patricia, politely but firmly, asking her to leave the Development Office; endlessly knitting booties with Sister Donata while her aging mind drew little blanks with names and places.

She twisted in her bed, thinking of the never-ending stories she'd have to endure about "the good old days," stories that left no one really yearning, or even willing, to go back to them.

Before long, her nightgown was wound around her like a shroud. The only sensible thing seemed to be to straighten it out, lie still, and attack the problem head-on.

The lonely sound of a jet on its late-night flight over the Pacific reminded her of Eileen. How she missed her friend!

If Eileen were here, by now they would have, at least, the thread of a plan. But Eileen wasn't here. And a long night of wishing wouldn't change a thing. She could almost hear her friend saying in that soft brogue of hers, "If wishes were horses, this entire hill would be full of manure."

Sister Mary Helen stared at her ceiling. Distant headlights made odd shapes and shadows appear, then disappear as quickly as they had come.

It seemed as if days, not hours, had passed since she'd put her friend on the plane—days since Father Adams had said morning Mass and given his five-minute homily on Saint Augustine. Mary Helen's eyes burned. She closed them.

Now, there was a real character, she thought. Augustine, not Father Adams, although he, too, had his moments.

Augustine was a notorious sinner who drove his sainted, if nagging, mother, Monica, to a life of tears and prayers. What made Augustine a saint, of course, was his unlikely conversion. He had changed his life completely. God had used Monica and the bishop, Ambrose, as instruments, instruments of His grace.

Just as God still uses instruments to get His work done on earth, Mary Helen mused. She tried not to think of Sister Patricia's appointment to the college and the obvious conclusion she would come to if she let herself.

"I don't want to retire, Lord," she spoke aloud in the still room. "I'm not ready to retire. You know that. What do You want me to do? Anything but retire and knit," she coaxed.

No answer came. Only the familiar phrases from Augustine's famous *Confessions* rose from somewhere deep in her memory: "O Beauty of ancient days, yet ever new! . . . You called, and shouted, and burst my deafness. You flashed and shone and scattered my blindness. . . . You touched me, and I burned for your peace."

Sunday, August 30

❧❧❧

Twenty-second Sunday in Ordinary Time

S ister Mary Helen had thought that yesterday was the longest day that she ever lived. That is, until today. Sunday was just dragging by, one slow minute at a time, giving new meaning to Eileen's old saying "as long as a wet Sunday."

For the first time in her memory, she wished that Father Adams had given a longer homily. Anything to make the morning pass.

This wasn't like her. Usually there wasn't enough time in the day to do everything she wanted to do. Not knowing exactly what that was might be the problem.

She checked her w ristwatch. Two-thirty, at last. All the nuns were meeting in the community room to greet the new president, scheduled to arrive at three. She had better hurry if she wanted to get a soft seat. She started down the deserted convent hall.

All day yesterday, she had gone back and forth on the question of retiring, until she had almost yearned for the time in religious life when the Superior gave the orders and the Sisters obeyed. Almost! Of course, life had been simpler then and if things didn't work out, you always had someone to blame it on.

She turned the corner. An excited mumble floated down the hall from the community room. Apparently some of the other Sisters were as eager as she was to get a good seat.

Near the doorway, Sister Mary Helen paused. Her mind still churned with indecision. In less than half an hour, Patricia would arrive. Mary Helen must decide whether to act or to be acted upon.

In all fairness, the Development Office needed new blood. Mary Helen knew that. Maybe even young blood, though she hated to admit it. A younger person might have more in common with younger alums.

Besides, Mary Helen's faithful secretary, Shirley, was making "quitting" noises. Her husband had recently retired and was urging her to travel with him. What would she do without Shirley? She'd never be able to keep all the details straight. And that computer! The very thought of conquering the computer left her with lacteous legs.

Next Wednesday, Sister Patricia would preside at the convocation of the administration, faculty, and staff. She would kick off the school year with her State of the College message. Then, right after Labor Day, college classes would begin.

Actually, Mary Helen felt sorry for the poor thing. She couldn't imagine anyone taking over this enormous institution on such short notice.

It was really poor planning. Not that Cecilia had any hand in planning when to die. May she rest in peace! *Most likely, that is exactly what she is doing at this very moment,* Mary Helen thought. *Resting in a well-deserved peace, while the rest of us stew.*

All weekend the community had been in a frenzy preparing

for the arrival of the new president. Therese had taken the helm. And, if the truth be known, they were all getting a little seasick.

Patricia's bedroom and convent office were polished to a high shine. Mary Helen was amazed that Therese managed to get the curtains and drapes cleaned on such short notice.

Sister Donata was the leading organizer of this afternoon's reception. With a great deal of help from nuns with younger legs, she had put together what seemed to be something between high tea and happy hour. *Perfect,* Mary Helen thought. *Something for everyone!*

Sister Anne, who closed her Refuge on Sundays, rushed past with a bouquet of Mylar balloons filled with helium. **Welcome!** they all proclaimed in bold purple letters.

The Sisters milled around, speaking now in hushed tones. In this room full of nuns, despite what Father Adams had said in his brief homily, Mary Helen felt oddly alone.

"Appreciation and respect for others attunes our ears to pay attention to their wisdom and advice," he had said, commenting on the first reading from the Book of Sirach.

This afternoon, she'd settle for just one person's wisdom and advice—Eileen's. The now-familiar dry ache of missing her friend swelled in her throat.

Her more sensible self reminded her that not even Eileen could tell her what to do. She could simply lob the decision back into Mary Helen's court, where it belonged—in Mary Helen's court.

Lost in thought, she found a vacant seat at the end of the sofa and sank into it without realizing that Anne was next to her.

"A penny for your thoughts," Anne whispered.

"These are fifty-cent thoughts," Mary Helen snapped, then wished she hadn't. Anne could never let a remark like that go by.

As Mary Helen suspected, Anne jumped on it. "I've been wondering what was wrong with you," she said, studying Mary Helen's face until the old nun began to feel like a hair in someone's soup. "You haven't seemed yourself in days. Are you all right?"

Mary Helen made a pretense of not hearing the question. Actually, she was struggling to keep her peace. As good as Anne was, what did she know about getting old? At thirty how could she understand the turmoil of an almost eighty-year-old woman who still feels thirty inside?

"It's more than Eileen's going, isn't it?" Anne was undaunted. "It's Patricia's coming, too. Am I right? You've heard the rumors about her getting rid of all the older faculty and staff."

Behind her round, wire-rimmed spectacles, Anne's hazel eyes flashed with indignation. "And it's probably true, too," she said, her lips forming a small pout. She patted Mary Helen's arm. "Let's beat her to the punch. Quit and come volunteer at the Refuge."

"Leave the college?"

"You can live here like I do and minister there."

At first, Mary Helen wasn't sure that she'd heard correctly. Did Anne say quit and work at the Refuge? She had considered quitting and retiring, of course. But quit and start a new career at her age? Regardless of how young she felt, she knew she was—as they say—"over the hill."

The idea was bizarre and risky. Mary Helen felt an unexpected shiver of excitement. All her life, she'd taken risks. Why stop now when age made it easier? After all, at almost eighty what had she to lose?

A tendril of doubt crept into her mind. The whole notion was not only bizarre and risky but also impractical. She was just about to dismiss it when a small inner voice urged, *But it sounds like fun!*

What if she'd never really talked to a homeless person except to say, "How do?" Not that it mattered. People are people after all.

"She's here," Anne interrupted Mary Helen's thoughts. Therese stood at the community room door with Sister Patricia in tow.

A tall, square woman, Patricia's businesslike body all but filled the doorway. Her startlingly white hair was freshly permed, her black wool suit pressed to perfection. Flat-heeled black suede pumps turned out a little from the strain of supporting beefy legs. Her face was expressionless, except for her wide forced smile. Only her darting dark eyes betrayed her uneasiness.

Again Mary Helen felt a pang of sympathy for the new leader. *Not an easy task*, she thought, *but I can make it easier. Tomorrow morning, I can make an appointment, march into her office, resign, and retire. Then help Anne at the Refuge.*

Retire to the Refuge! she thought crazily. *Now, that has a very nice ring to it.*

❧❧❧

As soon as the words left her mouth, Anne could have bitten her tongue. What was she thinking of? Sister Mary Helen at the Refuge!

How could she have been so imprudent? How could she expect a woman of Mary Helen's age, so used to academia, to adjust to the Refuge? Why, the language alone could put her into cardiac arrest.

Just because I like the old gal doesn't mean that she can do the job, Anne chided herself. Although, she had to admit, it helped.

And, in the few minutes since she'd mentioned it, the strained expression on Mary Helen's face had eased. The determined set of her chin was back, and the old spark was returning to her eyes.

Most likely she'll never take me up on my offer, Anne thought hopefully. *But at least she knows she's wanted. Maybe my invitation wasn't so imprudent as it was providential. With God there are no slips of the lip*, she thought complacently. *And you never are really sure of what She has in mind.*

Monday, August 31

❦❦❦

Feast of Saint Aidan of Lindisfarne, Bishop

Sister Mary Helen rose early. She had spent a restless night rehearsing, not so much what she'd say to Sister Patricia, but how she'd say it. Sometimes her explanation sounded too long and circuitous; other times, too short, almost curt. For some reason, it never sounded just right.

Toward morning she had begun to wonder if there was a right way to say, "I quit," although with every rehearsal her choice of the Refuge seemed more reasonable.

Finally dawn broke over the East Bay hills. When she went downstairs, she was happy to discover that some other early riser had brewed a pot of strong coffee.

Waiting for her toast to pop, Mary Helen was struck with the ordinariness of the morning that would literally change the direction of her life. Important decisions are never accompanied by flashes of lightning. She knew that, but this morning the college wasn't even covered in fog that could lift symbolically. The August sky was blue and cloudless. The hill was so silent that the chirping of the early birds rose in a crescendo. *Poor worms,* she thought in unexpected sympathy.

She checked the clock on the kitchen wall. It was only six o'clock. Morning prayers and Mass were on a vacation schedule until after Labor Day, which meant that the nuns would assemble in chapel at seven-forty-five. Figuring in time for breakfast and to make her bed and brush her teeth, Patricia should be at her desk by nine-thirty.

In three and one-half hours, Sister Mary Helen's resignation would be an accomplished fact. She was wondering how best to break the news to Shirley when she became aware of another person entering the kitchenette.

Fully expecting it to be Therese, always up before the sun, she was surprised at the appearance of none other than Patricia herself. Patricia appeared just as surprised to see her.

"Good morning, Sister," Patricia mumbled.

"How do," Mary Helen answered quietly.

Patricia didn't look as if she could handle too loud or too long a greeting. Actually, she looked as though she hadn't slept at all last night. She clutched her blue chenille bathrobe to her throat. Her white hair was crushed and her eyes red-rimmed and bloodshot. The skin on her face was drawn so tight that, at first glance, she reminded Mary Helen of a snapping turtle.

"Coffee?" Mary Helen offered.

Sister Patricia nodded. "Black, please."

"Toast?"

Another nod.

"Thank you," Patricia whispered hoarsely when Mary Helen set the cup and plate before her.

"Everything will be all right," Mary Helen said, feeling a sudden empathy for the woman, who appeared so capable.

"You have a very good group to work with here. Cecilia did a fine job. Everything will be in order, I'm sure."

Patricia gave a weak smile. "Thank you. I know you're right. But at the moment, it all seems so overwhelming. Everything happened so quickly.

"When the Superior General asked me to take the presidency, I should have given it more thought. I guess I was flattered by her confidence in me." Patricia hesitated, obviously unaccustomed to letting even this much vulnerability show.

"And she has every right to have confidence in you. You are a very capable woman." Mary Helen stopped, unable to go further. Patricia was capable, not that she approved of all her methods. All the empathy in the world wouldn't make Mary Helen say that she did.

"I'm sure you're aware they call me Queen of the Clean Sweep," Patricia blurted out.

Mary Helen nodded, surprised that Patricia was aware of it, too. Although having a nickname was one form of acceptance.

"Yesterday afternoon, when I saw the number of Senior Sisters on the staff—" All at once, she clamped her lips shut, realizing, no doubt, that she was speaking to one of those Seniors.

At least she has the good grace to blush, Mary Helen thought, watching Patricia trying to recover.

"That's what happens if you live long enough," Mary Helen said lightly. "You become a Senior Sister."

Her attempt at humor went right past Patricia. *Uh-oh,* Mary Helen thought, with good reason.

"To be candid," Patricia said, her tired eyes filling, "I worried all night about it. They must feel terribly trapped. And so do I. How am I going to solve it?" she asked, although Mary Helen knew she didn't want an answer.

"No one is trapped unless she lets herself be!" Mary Helen wanted to shout. "Old is not helpless!" She knew Patricia meant no harm. Despite this, she felt her blood pressure rising. Trapped indeed!

Suddenly her words seemed to have a life of their own. She leveled her eyes at Patricia.

"Don't give my solution another thought, Sister," she said crisply. "As of this minute"—she glanced up at the kitchen clock; it read five past six—"I quit! I was going to wait until office hours to tell you, but this seems to be an appropriate time."

Patricia's head shot up. Her mouth snapped open and shut. No sound came out.

Mary Helen ignored it. "I'll have my secretary type up my resignation as soon as possible. We have a file drawer full of résumés." She paused for breath. "Résumés from capable people who want my job. I'm sure you will have no trouble replacing me."

Finished, Mary Helen rose and put her cup and plate in the dishwasher. She wasn't sure who was more relieved, Patricia or herself. She'd wager it was a toss-up.

❧❦❧

By ten o'clock, Mary Helen had announced her resignation to Shirley. To her relief, her secretary seemed delighted.

"I've been wanting to quit myself," Shirley said, her dangling lapis earrings bringing out the blue in her eyes. "As you know, Don has been urging me to, now that he's retired. But I didn't want to let you down. Now it's no problem. We can both resign. Besides," she said with a wink, "I don't know that I'd work this hard for anyone else."

Mary Helen watched Shirley spring into action.

"I'll have these letters to Sister Patricia—is that the new one's name?—before noon!" she called over her shoulder. "And by the way, how are you going to tell Sister Eileen?"

31

"Airmail. It should get there in a few days."

Shirley looked surprised. "It's early evening Irish time," she said, motioning toward the phone. "The Development Office can afford it."

Sister Mary Helen shook her head. "I think I'll drop her a letter," she answered. There was no sense calling Eileen in Galway and having anyone pay the long-distance rates for the big silence that would undoubtedly follow her announcement. It should take Eileen at least a full two expensive minutes to find an "old saying from home" to fit this situation.

❧❧❧❧

"Good morning, the Refuge," Sister Anne answered the telephone on the third ring. She covered her other ear to keep out the din. "Hello," she repeated and was surprised to hear Sister Mary Helen's voice.

"I did it!" the old nun said, sounding uncharacteristically shaken. "I resigned. As of the day after Labor Day, I am all yours."

"All mine?"

"Yes, Anne," Mary Helen snapped, all at once sounding much more like her old self. "This morning, I resigned. I've called the Superior General. She was a bit nonplussed, at first."

I'll bet, Anne thought. She could see the Superior's face as she struggled to keep from blurting out, "You did what now?"

"I told her that you had invited me to volunteer at the Refuge. You did, didn't you?"

"Of course I did." Fortunately, Anne was able to keep her voice even. "I'll . . . I'll be delighted to have you."

She heard Mary Helen laugh. "I hope you will be able to say that in a month."

"I'm . . . I'm sure I will," Anne stammered, her fingers crossed.

"And I've just mailed a letter off to Sister Eileen. What is it that she always says? 'It's an ill wind turns none to good.' "

Mary Helen paused. Anne knew she should respond, but she wasn't sure just how. Although Mary Helen was a favorite of hers and she had invited her, she had never expected the old nun to take her up on it.

"Let's hear it for the wind," she said finally.

Fortunately, Mary Helen had already hung up.

Tuesday, September 8

❧❧❧❧

The Birthday of the Blessed Virgin Mary

S ister Mary Helen awoke with a vague feeling of apprehension. Her stomach churned as she slipped out of bed. This was to be her first day at the Refuge. What had she gotten herself into? She shivered as her bare feet searched the bedroom floor for her slippers.

"Our Blessed Mother's Birthday," her liturgical calendar read. *And a birthday of sorts for me, too.* Mary Helen almost laughed. *Born to a new ministry at my age! Who would have believed it?* she thought, examining her aging face in her medicine chest mirror. Carefully she brushed her teeth, then dressed quickly.

Despite the fog-free sky and the fact that the overly cheerful weatherman on the news last night had promised an Indian summer day, the morning was still chilly.

Anne had advised her to wear her most comfortable shoes and an old skirt and blouse. She took a heavy sweater from her dresser drawer. Although the weather in downtown San Francisco was usually warmer than at the college, one could never be sure. She stuffed the sweater into a canvas tote bag, similar to the one Sister Anne carried to work. It was fortunate that she had kept the bag from her pilgrimage to Spain, never dreaming where it would come in handy.

All at once, her stomach felt queasy again. No wonder, considering that this morning she was leaving Mount St. Francis College Development Office for the Refuge. The thought crept over her with the chill. She squared her shoulders. *A new venture makes any normal person a bit uneasy*, she reminded herself. *And, God knows, I'm as normal as the best of them.*

Determined not to give in to her uneasiness, she set out for the chapel. After morning Mass she would have a hearty breakfast. *Everything goes better when you've eaten a decent meal*, she thought, aware that this outlook accounted for several rolls around her middle.

The first fingers of morning were creeping over the college hill. As she made her way across the campus savoring its peace and beauty, she wondered once again about her choice. Too late now!

"I signed out a car for you, so take your time about coming down," Anne had said kindly last night. "Whenever you get there, we'll be glad to have you."

Let's hope she's as happy a month from now, Mary Helen thought, pulling open the chapel door. The familiar aromas of beeswax and incense greeted her. The dim red glow of the sanctuary lamp on the side altar shone like a beacon reminding her of what she already knew: that all her life God had traveled with her, going before her to meet her on the way. Why should now be any different?

About nine o'clock, after some maneuvering with the one-way streets in downtown San Francisco, Mary Helen arrived at the corner of Eighth and Howard. The Refuge was not difficult to spot. The newly renovated storefront was the best looking building on the block, not that it had much competition. She pulled into the adjacent parking lot, locked a Club on the steering wheel of the convent Nova, straightened her skirt, and strode to the front entrance.

Before she could open the door, a pale young woman stumbled through it. Struggling to keep on her feet, she cowered against the wall. Her painfully thin body trembled. Sister Mary Helen thought she caught a whiff of alcohol, but she could be wrong.

"Sorry," the girl mumbled, avoiding Mary Helen's eyes.

A brown stocking cap covered all but the straggly ends of the girl's blond hair. Her left eye was red and swollen. Before nightfall, Mary Helen was sure, it would be black.

"Are you all right?" she asked.

Blinking in the sunlight, the girl looked at her. "No," she said, "I'm not all right. I'm going to be killed." She wagged her head and began to sob. The sound was pitiful. "One of these days, Andy is going to kill me," she added, stumbling past Mary Helen.

Before she could gather her wits and shout, "Wait!" the tiny blonde had fled around the corner. This would never do!

"Someone is going to kill that girl!" she cried, spotting Sister Anne just inside the door.

"You must mean Melanie," Anne said sadly. "You're probably right. She has a very vicious 'boyfriend.' Most likely, she didn't deliver the money he expected from her night on the street."

"Shouldn't we call the police?" Mary Helen felt her blood

pressure rising. How could Anne be so matter-of-fact about an impending murder?

"We have," Anne said, "several times. But Melanie won't press charges. There is really nothing we can do until Melanie is ready to do something herself."

I can't believe that, Mary Helen thought, her heart still pounding. But she held her peace.

Sister Anne led her into a large main room. Although the sound of women's voices had reached a frightening pitch, the place had a friendly feel. Walls of square glass bricks let in the light but kept out the street. Prints of Van Gogh and Georgia O'Keeffe hung around the room. A bookshelf bulging with paperbacks was in one corner. The aroma of freshly brewed coffee and the sugary smell of doughnuts filled the air.

Women sat at small square tables covered with brightly colored cloths. Each table held a vase of perky yellow daisies. If Mary Helen hadn't known better, she'd think that she had mistakenly stumbled into some upscale south of Market café.

The sight of a middle-aged white woman, sitting alone sewing and talking brightly to imaginary table companions, brought her up short.

"This is Sister Mary Helen" Anne announced to the room in general.

"A new one or should I say an old one?" the woman asked the empty places, waiting for an answer.

Mary Helen had the distinct feeling that she was being discussed.

The woman winked coquettishly, tossed her long black hair over her shoulder, and giggled.

"That be Crazy Alice." A tall, thin woman with hair like buds of black broccoli sidled up to Mary Helen. She flashed a minus-one-front-tooth smile. "She don't mean no harm. . . .

Most of the time," she added, her dark eyes dancing. "They calls me Venus. 'The goddess of beauty,' my mama say." She pulled her black windbreaker around her.

"And I'm Peanuts." The deep voice startled Mary Helen. She had not even noticed the miniature woman on her left with skin the color of café au lait. The woman smiled wryly. "Don't you pay Venus no mind, Sister. Or Crazy Alice, neither. Uh, uh!" Peanuts grinned up at her with yellowed teeth. "You be just fine here with us."

Standing beside her, Anne beamed proudly like a mother whose backward child had found a friend. Actually, Sister Mary Helen was amazed at just how good Peanuts's words did make her feel.

"Do we call her Crazy Alice to her face?" Mary Helen asked. She didn't want to start off on the wrong foot. "Isn't she insulted?"

Venus shrugged. "She don't seem to be. That's what we all calls her. I think she like it."

Mary Helen tried not to stare, but she might not have succeeded except for the sudden appearance of a short, square volunteer rushing by pushing a cart laden with clean cups, pastries, and napkins.

"I had better help Betsy," Anne said, quickly introducing Mary Helen to the woman. Then she busied herself replenishing the snack table.

Betsy Dodd. Mary Helen was sure Anne had said that was the woman's name. It sounded familiar. It took Mary Helen a few minutes to realize why. Betsy Dodd often made the social pages of the *Chronicle*. Today even the most astute society writer would have trouble recognizing her in her bulky gray sweatshirt, baggy jeans, and scuffed tennis shoes. She wore no jewelry except for tiny gold loop earrings.

Watching Betsy set up the cups, Sister Mary Helen noticed her left ring finger had a strip of white skin showing where her wedding rings had been. Was it that dangerous to wear jewelry in this neighborhood or were her rings extraordinarily expensive and attractive? Mary Helen bet on the latter.

After all, Betsy was the wife of Richard Dodd, once a Cal Berkeley football star, now a prominent San Francisco attorney with Dodd, Roach, Crosby, and Chin. If Mary Helen remembered correctly, Richard Dodd was rumored to have some political aspirations. Some said he wanted to throw his old helmet into the ring for governor.

"I'm Miss Bobbie, Sister." An older woman came over to Mary Helen. Her graying hair was braided tight against her head. Her skin was the warm rich brown of good brandy and smooth except for the scar tissue circling her left eye.

"These young ones will get on your nerves if you let 'em, Sister," Miss Bobbie said. "Why don't you sit down and rest awhile before you start?"

"I just got here," Mary Helen protested. "I should help Sister Anne." She turned toward the kitchen.

"Suit yourself," she heard Miss Bobbie mumble. "It's your nerves."

The morning went quickly. Too quickly! Mary Helen scarcely had the opportunity to say, "How-do," to all the interesting women who dropped into the Refuge, let alone to get their names straight. Yet, all the while, she had the uncanny feeling that she was the one being studied and evaluated. Would she pass their unspoken test?

By the time she had rinsed cups, replenished the sugar and cream, handed out towels, soap, and shampoo to the bathers, and given away far too many aspirins, she was too tired to care. Furthermore, she was ready to take Miss Bobbie's advice. Mary Helen sank into the chair next to the older woman. She must have looked exhausted, because Sister Anne suggested that she go home after lunch and take a little nap.

"Didn't I tell you?" Miss Bobbie said, shaking her head. "Pace yourself, girlfriend, or you ain't going to last."

Girlfriend? Had she heard correctly? Had this woman called her girlfriend? For some unexplainable reason, Mary Helen was thrilled. Maybe she had made the right decision after all. Maybe, at this time of her life, here was where she belonged. No real pressure, no unrealistic expectations, no irate phone calls. At least not so far. Her uneasiness was all but gone. She had thoroughly enjoyed her first morning. She planned to enjoy tomorrow as well.

She should have known better. She should have remembered what some wise wag once said: "If you want to make God laugh, just tell Him your plans."

❦❦❦❦

Betsy Dodd checked the clock on the wall of the Refuge. Twelve-thirty! Ruth Gill, the afternoon volunteer, had arrived on time. Actually, Ruth was a little early. Fighting back her disappointment, Betsy greeted the woman warmly and hung up her own apron.

Some Tuesdays, Ruth was unavoidably detained. Sometimes she was unable to come at all. Although Betsy knew that Ruth was taking advantage of her whenever this happened, and it was becoming more frequent, Betsy was secretly delighted. It gave her a perfectly legitimate reason to call home and tell Rosa, the Dodds' housekeeper, that she would be late.

After saying good-bye to Sister Anne and the new nun—what was her name?—Sister Mary Helen, Betsy made her way to the parking lot and her silver Lexus. Two Refugees, an affectionate nickname the volunteers had for the women at the center, leaned against her car. One sat on the fender. All three were smoking cigarettes.

If only Rich could see them. Betsy savored the thought of her husband's discomfort. He was nearly fanatical about scratches and dents on his cars. *Would that he was as concerned about scratches and dents in his character*, she thought savagely.

"We just be dreaming," Sonia said with a wistful smile. "Dreaming, girl, your car be our car." She pushed herself off the fender.

Betsy laughed as she unlocked the passenger door. Little did these women know what else went with this dream.

The sun beat down on the silver steel as she slowly made her way through the slow snarl of downtown San Francisco, detouring around construction sites and repair crews. The sharp blast of a taxi horn startled her. Was the driver honking at her, the stalled Muni bus, or the bike messenger?

Before too long, she was on Sacramento Street driving west toward her home in Presidio Terrace. The terrace, a circle of upscale homes in the shadow of Temple Emanu-El, was off busy Arguello Boulevard. Driving through its gates reminded Betsy of entering an oasis of quiet in a maelstrom.

To the casual observer, the terrace seemed so peaceful with its green lawns, formal flower beds, and solemn-fronted mansions, curtains and drapes pulled just so. Even on a day as warm as today, the windows were rarely open and then only on the top floor where the children slept. Prominent and wealthy families occupied these picture-perfect homes and, to all appearances, led picture-perfect lives.

Betsy pulled her Lexus into the garage. Turning off the ignition, she sat in the coolness gearing up her courage before going inside. She ran her fingers through her curly black hair. The heat had made it damp and frizzy. If Rich were home, he'd tell her in that arrogant, lawyer voice he was beginning to use too frequently to "fix yourself up" before they went out tonight. As though she wouldn't.

Betsy wondered what awaited her inside. Recently Rich had taken to coming home unexpectedly for lunch, sometimes going into a sulk if he didn't find her there. It was almost as if he didn't trust her.

"A compliment," her sister Ginger had said when Betsy complained. "Or maybe he's a little jealous." But Betsy knew better.

Carefully she opened the side door into the kitchen. The relaxed expression on Rosa's face told her that the housekeeper was home alone.

"Hello, Missus!" Rosa called cheerfully. The kitchen smelled of cinnamon, lemon, and apples.

"What are you making?" Betsy asked, suddenly realizing how hungry she was. Though she shouldn't be. She'd had two cups of coffee and a large piece of coffee cake before she left the Refuge.

Depressed eating, her sister called her need for food. Maybe it was. Maybe her sister was right, Betsy conceded. Although she would rather die of hunger than tell Ginger why she was depressed.

Rosa dished up a bowl of hot applesauce. "Apples were wasting," she said.

Betsy put a heaping spoonful of the warm, golden sauce into her mouth. She savored the tartness.

Ginger always followed her declaration with, "For the life of me, I don't know what you have to be depressed about. You have a fine husband, money to burn, and more luxuries than you can ever use."

Almost true, Betsy thought. "Did Mr. Dodd call?" she asked Rosa.

"He called about an hour ago. He forgot it was one of your days at the Refuge." The housekeeper rolled her brown eyes. "He says to remind you, missus, that you're going to the Blacks' for cocktails before the symphony benefit."

As if I were too stupid to remember! Betsy felt the bile rising in her throat.

"He wants you to meet him at Stanford Arms. He'll get changed at the firm's apartment," Rosa said.

A sharp pain in Betsy's stomach made her gasp. She felt hot all over. It was starting again. As much as she tried to deny it, she'd felt it. The signs were all there.

"Are you all right, missus?" Rosa's large eyes clouded with concern.

Betsy nodded. Changing at the apartment. She felt dizzy and her head throbbed. *Who does he think he's kidding, the insufferable jerk?* She could tell by Rosa's expression that the housekeeper wasn't fooled, either. He would be furious that she wasn't home when he'd called and that he had been forced to give his message to Rosa. "She knows too much of our business already!" He would shout. Let him!

"Why don't you go home early today?" Betsy suggested when she finally caught her breath. "There's really nothing more for you to do here. I am going to take a short nap. I'll just turn on the answering machine."

Betsy felt a surge of satisfaction. She knew how much Rich hated it when she sent Rosa home before he got his "money's worth." Betsy knew he wanted his fancy friends to have their phone calls answered. Too bad about him! She'd make sure to let it slip at the Blacks' party that she'd sent the housekeeper home early.

And I'll simply "forget" to wear Rich's latest "sorry" gift, she thought maliciously. He'd love to have his buddies dazzled by the diamond-and-emerald bracelet he had given her. Show-off!

What would really dazzle them was the reason that the great man gave gifts, she thought bitterly. Or would it? Was she always the last to know?

What if there was hell to pay when they got home? His

shouting was easier to endure than the uncomfortable silence that developed between them when he started again. The grateful look on Rosa's face was an added bonus.

There was a time when Betsy would have done anything rather than provoke Rich's wrath. A time when his shouting hurt her feelings, even frightened her, although he'd never actually hit her.

But that was long ago now, before she was aware of the others. Before she had a rage to match his own. Even before she knew that bruises heal much quicker than many other kinds of hurts.

❧❧❧❧

Richard Dodd slammed down the telephone. "Damn," he said, glad that a thick wooden door separated him from his secretary. It would never do for the efficient, horse-faced Catherine to know how frustrated he was with his wife. He had worked too hard at creating the image of a happy marriage to blow it now.

He glared at their formal portrait in its leather frame that occupied one corner of his enormous desktop. Betsy smiled back at him. Just like her to be at that ridiculous shelter when he needed to get hold of her.

Rich put a red-hot Tic-tac into his mouth and sucked furiously. He'd been forced to leave the message with that nosy Rosa. He could tell from her cold, one-syllable answers that she didn't believe him.

Frustrated, he slammed down his fist on the desktop. What the hell did he care what some half-baked housekeeper thought of him? Goddamn it! He was paying her to clean, not to think!

The intercom on his desk buzzed. It was Catherine. "Is everything all right, Mr. Dodd?" she asked.

He could see her soulful brown eyes. "Fine, Catherine,

44

thank you. I just dropped my—my paperweight," he said with a forced laugh.

Why the hell was he making excuses to Catherine? He could throw the damn paperweight if he chose to. It was none of her business. Nosy bitch!

Rich felt the perspiration forming under his armpits. Swiveling his chair toward the picture window, he wished for the thousandth time that he had a better view of the Golden Gate Bridge. For the amount the law firm paid in rent, they should have a much better view. He'd bring that up at their next partners' meeting. They'd tell him, as they always did, that what they were paying for, and paying dearly, was a panoramic view that extended from the Bay Bridge, past the Transamerica Building, to the marina where the Palace of Fine Arts stood in the distance like a miniature.

That smart-ass Crosby would tell him again that not even the Top of the Mark Hopkins Hotel had as good a view, but Rich didn't care.

Rich mopped his forehead with a monogrammed handkerchief. This was all Betsy's fault. She and that nun! Was her name Anne? Nothing but a couple of do-gooders putting Band-Aids on insoluble problems. Acting as if they were all Mother Teresas. Pure nonsense, except for the fact that it would make good copy when he put in his bid for the governor's race.

Rich closed his eyes. He visualized himself at the victory party. Smiling, waving from the podium. Accepting the nomination with humility and gratitude, as though he hadn't worked his tail off to procure it.

Next to him would be Betsy. Plump, plain Betsy, looking like a middle-aged housewife despite the fortune he had spent on her clothes and jewelry. Why couldn't she look better? For godssake, didn't she care about his image?

45

The ring of the telephone startled him. His private line! This should be Amanda. At last! He really needed her today. He had to appear calm and in control tonight at the Blacks' party. He needed Black's backing, both politically and financially.

Amanda could do this for him. She could do things for him that Betsy never could do. Rich had met the lovely Amanda Cribbs at an office party after the firm had won an especially big case. Admittedly, they had both had a little too much champagne. They had ended the evening on his office sofa. Those things happen sometimes at office parties, but their time together had been so good! Rich had met her several more times at a small apartment the firm kept in the city for out-of-town clients and business associates.

He hadn't meant to get so involved. It was really bad timing, he knew, what with the governor's race in the offing. But Amanda was tall and slim—*statuesque* might be a better word. And she could do things for a man that poor Betsy had never dreamed of, things that made him feel young and virile and ready to take on the whole world, let alone the state.

"Hello," he answered in a businesslike tone, just in case it was his wife.

"Hello yourself, Dickie." The voice was low and sultry. No one had called him Dickie since he was a small boy. Somehow when Amanda said it, he felt young again—kiddish, really— and very loved.

"Amanda," he said softly. Catherine had keen ears. "It's you at last, my darling." He knew he sounded smitten, but he didn't care. He wanted to go right through the phone into her ready arms. "Can you get away by three?" he asked.

"I think the other girls are beginning to get suspicious," she said throatily. "What shall I use for an excuse?"

"You can tell them I want to meet with you. Make up a reason. No one in your department will dare question me."

Amanda giggled softly, then stopped and cleared her throat.

Someone must have come into the room. Rich's stomach knotted, not so much from fear as from excitement.

"Yes, sir," she said with great diffidence. "I can be at your office by three, if that's what you'd like."

Rich chuckled at her sudden change of manner. "Someone is listening, I take it."

"Yes, sir," she answered.

"Well, I hope they don't overhear that my office has moved to the firm's apartment," he said, "and, Amanda—"

"Yes, sir?"

"Start getting unbuttoned on your way up in the elevator!"

❀❀❀

Melanie cowered by the corner of the large upscale apartment building that stood amid luxury hotels on Powell and California Streets. Despite the warmth of the afternoon, her nose and eyes were running. In the glare of the sun, she felt her body begin to tremble. She would need a drink soon if she didn't want to be a mess.

In one hand, she held a torn piece of cardboard that she had found in a gutter. It already had a hand-printed message: "Will work for food."

What a joke! No one in this neighborhood would be remotely interested in hiring me for the kind of work I do, she thought sadly.

With her free hand she removed her woolen cap and tried to smooth down her straggly blond hair. As she ran her fingers through it, she could feel that she needed a haircut badly. Even a good shampoo would be helpful. Maybe she'd risk going to the Refuge tomorrow for a hot shower and to wash her hair.

All her instincts told her that this was not a good idea. She'd been frightened when she dropped in there this morn-

47

ing. Frightened and a little high maybe. She wondered what that old nun must have thought.

No. She was not going back. That's where Andy'd look for her. Fear ran through her frail body like a sharp pain. She never wanted to see him again. Never wanted to hear his cruel laugh as he twisted her arm or dragged her by her hair. Last night had been the end. She had only spent a little money on a couple of beers. She'd needed them and he'd been furious.

After every beating, the Vice cops had warned her to stay out of the neighborhood where Andy could find her. As much for their sakes as for hers, she suspected. Melanie leaned against the warm stone side of the building. The Vice cops really were nice guys. Most of them were a lot nicer to the girls than their pimps were. She felt her eye. It was still sore to the touch. She was finished with hooking.

And she'd gotten out of the neighborhood like the cops said. This time for sure. In fact, she'd been coming to this corner to beg for a couple of weeks now, on and off. Yes, she was beginning to feel like this was her corner. She'd always made enough money on the street to satisfy Andy. While he was off spending it, she'd picked up a little extra for herself by begging. Last night had been a fluke. Her corner had let her down.

Thank God she hadn't told him where she'd been hanging. She sniffed. Why did she even go near him? Because she'd been scared of being alone. How silly!

So far, she hadn't had to fight anyone for the corner. Although she had seen Jungle Jumbo eyeing her. At first, Melanie was nervous. Jumbo had earned his nickname because you never were sure when he was going to go wild and roar.

"Slim pickings," she had told him frankly when he approached her. Jumbo seemed satisfied to find another, more profitable spot. At first, she was afraid he might tell Andy. But he hadn't. Probably Jumbo didn't like Andy any better than she did.

God, how she needed a drink. Would anyone ever walk by and look at her? Once she caught someone's eye, he or she would most likely feel too guilty not to give her something. Even a few cents in change was fine. It didn't take much to buy a couple of cans of malt liquor.

She felt deep in her pocket for the can she'd been nursing all day. It was warm, and she only had a few ounces left. She couldn't finish it before she knew where her next can was coming from.

Catching someone's eye was the most difficult part of panhandling, she'd discovered. Not like hooking, where they came to look at you. She shivered at the memory of all those lustful, leering eyes. When she begged for money, most people walking by either shifted their eyes to avoid any contact with her or looked through her as though she were invisible. Sometimes she wanted to scream, "See me! I'm a person!"

But this was not a neighborhood where you could raise a fuss. These people were rich, and they would have you arrested without a second thought. Melanie didn't want to go to jail. Andy would find out if she did. Her throat went dry. No! She couldn't let that happen.

Without warning, Melanie's legs felt wobbly. She slid down the stone wall and sat on the pavement, leaning her back against the building. Crossing her legs, yoga fashion, she rested the cardboard sign against her knees. She turned the palms of her hands up, in case any passersby wanted to drop some money into them.

With the sun's warmth on her legs and shoulders and the back of her neck, Melanie let herself dream of a time when she was clean and had a good job and her own apartment, and a family that was happy to see her. But that was before it all went sour and beer became her best friend. If she'd only known where it all would lead, would she, could she, have stopped?

A tear slid down her cheek. She wiped it away with the sleeve of her jacket and studied the cars parked along the curb on California Street. She noticed that only one was fancy. The rest were old and beat-up. Probably belonged to employees of the Fairmont Hotel. No handouts there.

Melanie was wondering if she should move closer to the entrance of the building when she heard the click of high heels. Her heart quickened. That distinguished looking man was approaching. And he was with the same striking blonde, the one who owned the high heels. *The blond must be half his age*, Melanie thought, sure that they were having an affair.

How must his wife feel? Melanie wondered, although she'd never had such thoughts when she was the young, attractive office worker having affairs with other women's husbands.

She'd heard the woman call him Dick, sometimes Dickie, in baby talk. He'd seemed to like it, although, in Melanie's opinion, he had a cold look in his eye. It's amazing how much you can notice about people when they treat you as if you weren't even there.

She'd asked him for change once when he was alone. He'd been leaving the apartment then. He'd given her a cruel, hard stare and said, "Drop dead!" as if he really meant it.

Maybe she'd tell Andy what this guy said. Maybe Andy'd get all protective and punch the guy for her. Maybe he'd punch her, too, for being here without asking him. Melanie grew cold. *Better to be without him,* she thought, taking the can from her pocket and sneaking a little sip.

As the couple passed her, Melanie struggled to her feet. "Work for food!" she called out, jiggling her sign. She'd force them to notice her, to give her something. She needed a drink.

Melanie watched the young woman recoil in fear. "I won't hurt you, miss," she said. "I'm just hungry."

"Please, give her something, Dick," the young woman said.

The look of disgust on the man's face cut into Melanie's heart like a scalpel. She felt her cheeks redden.

"If you insist, Amanda," he snapped angrily. The veins in his neck stood out like thick cords. Without ever meeting Melanie's eyes, he fished into the breast pocket of his jacket for his wallet. Pulling it out, he flipped it open.

Fascinated by all the currency he carried, Melanie watched him thumb through the bills. Carefully he extracted one crisp new dollar bill. He handed it to her. Then something else caught her eye.

"What are you staring at?" he demanded, shoving the bill at her. "You were expecting more, I suppose."

Melanie shook her head.

"Then what the hell are you staring at?" he shouted.

"Betsy," Melanie whispered, pointing at the picture in his wallet.

Eyes blazing, the man looked at her for the first time. "Did you say, 'Betsy'?"

Hurrying away, Melanie wished she hadn't. She didn't want anyone at the Refuge to know where she was. Someone might slip and tell Andy.

"You left your sign!" the woman called after her.

Melanie didn't care. She had no time for signs. She needed to get down Powell Street to the liquor store. She needed a beer.

❦❧❦❧

Officers Mark Wong and Brian Dineen were just beginning their shift when Wong spotted Melanie. At first, he wasn't sure it was she. The girl was definitely in the wrong neighborhood. But then, so was he.

Some hotshot lawyer had called a complaint into the Vice Crime Section about loitering and solicitation up on Nob Hill—"Snob Hill" to the natives—and the duty sergeant had sent Mark and his partner to check it out.

"If I didn't know better, I'd say that was our friend Melanie," Mark said to Brian.

Dineen, an enormous redhead, shifted in his seat. The other guys in the Vice Detail referred to the pair as "the long and the short of it." What Mark at five-foot-seven lacked in height he made up for in temper. Or so his partner claimed. Mark suspected that Brian might be on to something. Rarely, however, had he been put to the test. Having the big guy for a partner helped avoid a number of conflicts.

"That's her, all right," Brian Dineen growled watching the cowering figure rush down the hill. "I'd recognize that brown stocking cap anywhere. What's she doing up here?"

"Maybe trying to upscale her business," Wong joked, quickly pulling the police car to the curb.

At the suddenness of his move Melanie let out a yelp like a wounded kitten. Apparently she hadn't seen them coming.

"What are you up to, Melanie, my love?" Wong asked in a pleasant voice.

"Nothing." Melanie ducked her head as though she was afraid to look at them.

Uh-oh, Wong thought. "What's wrong with your face?" he asked.

By now, both Wong and Dineen were out of the car. Their bodies made a cocoon around the trembling woman.

"It's nothing," she said, avoiding Wong's steady gaze. Her breath was heavy with the smell of beer.

Gently he lifted her chin. Her face showed signs of bruising, and her left eye was nearly swollen shut.

Mark Wong could feel the rage swirling within him. "Who

did this to you?" he demanded, knowing full well it was Andy, her pimp.

Wong clenched his fists, grabbing for control. He'd like to smash the bastard. Nothing would make him happier than to kick down the door of Andy's comfortable apartment on the Avenues and beat him senseless.

Wong shut his eyes and ran his fingers through his short-cropped hair. Breathing deeply, he struggled with an ancient voice from his childhood: By nature men are nearly alike; by practice they get to be wide apart.

Forcing himself to look at her, Wong asked, "Why do you let him do this to you?" With effort he kept his voice even, reasonable.

Melanie's blue eyes flooded with tears. "Don't be mad at me, Wong," she pleaded. "I tried to get away from him."

"Why don't you file a complaint?" He studied her battered face. "We can protect you," he added, although he knew that Melanie would never believe him. He was not so sure he believed himself.

Suddenly Melanie was angry. The beer had made her brave and a little careless. "How can you protect me? You're not even so good at keeping this snooty neighborhood safe."

"What does that mean?" Dineen loomed over her, but Melanie was not afraid.

"There's hookers up here, too, fellows, just like in the Tenderloin. Only dressed better." Melanie's chin rose in defiance.

Brian Dineen snickered. "Now, Miss Melanie, how do you know that?"

"I saw one. I even know her name!" Her words were beginning to slur.

"What's her name?" Dineen asked.

"Amanda," Melanie said smugly. "And his name is Dick! He knows Betsy, the volunteer at the Refuge."

Clearly she's feeling her beer, Wong thought and wondered whether or not to run her in. He checked his wristwatch. By the time their shift was over, she'd be back on the streets. Besides, they should head for the Tenderloin, where the real action was.

The Tenderloin—odd name for a neighborhood. One night on a stake out, Dineen had told him that the name came from a tradition of paying more to policemen who work in high-crime areas. Thus they were able to buy expensive cuts of meat.

It sounded like pure baloney to Wong, but then Dineen had told him lots of things that sounded as if he'd made them up. You have to talk about something when you're sitting still for hours.

"Where are you going now, Melanie?" Wong asked.

As she contemplated his question, Wong watched her deflate like a runaway balloon.

"To a shelter, I guess," she whispered.

"Hop in. We'll give you a lift," Dineen offered, pointing to the backseat of the police car.

"Am I under arrest?" Melanie was blubbering now.

Wong glanced at his partner. "No," he said, "not this time. Let us take you to a shelter."

"How would that look?" Melanie was suddenly worried about appearances. "Like I'm a snitch, that's how! No, thank you, Officers." She pulled herself up to her full five feet. "I'll take myself."

"It's up to you, my love," Dineen said, folding his huge frame back into the police car. "But we don't want to see you again tonight."

Mark Wong settled behind the wheel. Tires squealing, he pulled away from the curb. His eyes focused on the rearview mirror, where he watched the tiny woman stumble down the hill. They probably would see her again tonight turning a trick on Ellis Street. He gunned the motor.

"Take it easy, tiger," Dineen commented as they sped down Mason Street. "What's eating you?"

"Nothing," Wong lied. "I just hate wasting time."

"You just hate wasting time with Melanie. Admit it."

"You're nuts, big guy," Wong said, but he knew his partner had hit the nerve of truth. Wong did care for frail Melanie, who he had known for several years and had arrested a dozen or more times. Though he'd never admit it, where once he had felt sympathy for her, he now felt anger that she allowed herself to be victimized.

"She's caught in the web." Brian was always philosophical.

Mark knew he was right, but when he saw a sweet, attractive young woman like Melanie, well educated and probably loved and missed by her family, allowing herself to be abused, it was all that Mark could do not to grab her and shake her himself.

❦❦❦❦

Geraldine Jackson sat down to rest on the bus stop bench next to another black woman who looked as if she was just resting, too. They were the only two people on the bench. No matter what they said about Muni buses, they did have good benches.

"How do?" Geraldine said, but the other woman looked away. *Must not feel like talking,* Geraldine thought. *Suits me just fine. Too much noise in the world anyway.*

Taking a deep breath, she settled in. Her arm ached from carrying the sack of groceries. It must be the two apples that she had bought herself. She should have asked the A-rab to put the food into two plastic bags instead of one. Although she hated to hear all his complaining while he did it.

You'd think his bags were made of gold. If you asked her, the

55

apples were the gold. Golden apples—Geraldine laughed at her little play on words. They were golden—Golden Delicious.

She closed her eyes. The afternoon sun felt warm on her shoulders. If she sat here long enough, she'd drift off to sleep, which would never do.

She clutched her grocery bag to her chest. No telling who'd come along and snatch it. *Damn druggies!* she thought. Quickly opening her eyes, she looked around. The other woman had gone. Geraldine had the bench all to herself.

A beat-up black Ford slowed down as it passed her. She felt rather than saw herself being ogled. Some man looking for a trick.

Must have seen my gray hair, Geraldine thought, watching the car move on. *My legs are still good,* she thought, examining her slim ankles. *Or maybe he noticed I didn't have my teeth in.*

Actually, Geraldine had not worn her ill-fitting false teeth since she retired. *Praise the Lord,* she thought and wearily pushed herself up from the bench.

It was early yet, but she was tired. Time to get to her little apartment and fix herself some supper and go to bed. As she walked along crowded O'Farrell Street, she mentally reviewed the television scheduled for tonight.

Since her retirement, Geraldine had enjoyed going to bed early and watching her favorite television programs. After all those years on the street, it was a real treat to go to bed alone.

Several young women passed her on their way to work—young, hard-faced girls dressed in short skirts and tight tops. Thank goodness, for their sakes, it was going to stay warm tonight.

Some nights when Geraldine was working, the cold and fog used to cut right through her bare arms and legs and raise goose bumps all over her body. She shivered at the memory.

"Hi, Genie," a skinny platinum blonde said as she passed.

Geraldine was startled to hear someone call her by her street name. Looking over, she recognized the heavily made-up face. Olivia! When they were young she used to call herself Candy. No amount of makeup was going to make poor Olivia look like the young Candy again, Geraldine thought, forcing a friendly smile.

"Well, of all people! How you doing?"

"Fine, thanks," Olivia answered.

Geraldine knew better. The woman would be up all night trying to make enough money to get herself a meal and the night's rent.

For an instant Geraldine was tempted to ask Olivia in for supper and to spend the night. But she knew better. You couldn't be too nice to Olivia. She was too far gone to count on. No telling what she might up and do.

What was worse, Olivia had a mean streak. To tell the truth, she could be downright cruel. Several of the other girls had scars to prove it.

Best Geraldine could do was slip Olivia a couple of dollars. She sighed and forced the paper money into Olivia's clenched fist. Pinching the bills with her long red fingernails, Olivia slipped them into the pocket of her tight skirt.

"Thanks, Genie," she whispered, and Geraldine thought she sounded sincere.

Bless the Lord, Geraldine thought, watching Olivia approach a surly looking white man on the corner. He was covered with tattoos. She slipped her arm into his.

Geraldine could be in that same boat herself if she hadn't run into Lou, God bless him. Lou was a regular customer for years. In their own peculiar way she guessed they loved each other. Many nights all he wanted to do was talk. She had listened.

To her surprise and relief, when Lou passed away in his will he left her a nest egg.

"It's for your retirement," Lou's attorney had told her. "Lou knew you have no retirement plan."

Much to the lawyer's confusion, Geraldine had laughed uproariously, then retired as soon as the money was hers.

That kind of thing would never happen today, she thought, and felt sorry for the young prostitutes who had their whole lives ahead of them. These poor girls had to put up with drug addicts, abusers, brutal pimps, and constant worry about getting AIDS.

She ran into a number of them at the Refuge, a women's drop-in she liked because it was run by nuns. Geraldine liked nuns. When her mama died, she had been sent to a Catholic orphanage near New Orleans. The nuns had been kind to the little Negro girls.

Besides, she liked the company. It was nice to be retired, but it could get lonely.

Still deep in thought, Geraldine turned into the entryway of her apartment building. She nearly stumbled on a figure crouched in the corner under the row of mailboxes. Fear shot through Geraldine's whole body. Her heart thudded.

"Hi," a small, unsteady voice said. A thin white face stared up at her.

Geraldine's legs felt like pudding. She steadied herself against the wall. "Melanie, girl, what are you doing here?" Geraldine finally managed to keep her voice steady enough to speak.

"I'm scared, Genie," Melanie whined.

And a little drunk and tore up, Geraldine thought, studying the pale, bruised face and the blackened eye.

"Come in for a cup of tea, why don't you?" Geraldine asked. She'd listen, feed the child, then send her on her way.

Melanie shook her head vehemently. She looked distraught. "No," she slurred. The stench of beer and human fear filled the small entryway. "I can't." Melanie's voice was low.

"Why not?" Geraldine bent over, hoping to catch what the girl was saying.

The words and phrases ran together, making no sense that Geraldine could figure out. "Andy is looking for me . . . I need his money . . . I tried . . . oh," she groaned. "Dickie knows Betsy from the Refuge . . . Amanda with the high heels . . . Wong will kill me . . . and mean old Olivia might tell." All the while, Melanie's blue eyes darted about as if she were being possessed by the devil himself.

"Come in, child. You'll be safe with me," Geraldine coaxed.

"No!" Melanie was near hysteria. "Let me think!" Keening, she pressed her temples with the palms of her hands. And then, as though she'd suddenly been exorcised, she scrambled to her feet. "I know where I can get it," she said with a canny smirk. "I know exactly where."

What in the world's got into her? Geraldine wondered as she watched the tiny figure disappear into the growing crowd along the sidewalk. *What in the world can it be?*

❀❀❀

I can't remember the last time I took a nap in the afternoon, Sister Mary Helen thought, turning down her bedspread. The weatherman on last night's news had proven correct. It was an Indian summer day. The sun made her bedroom warm and cozy.

It also seemed to drain her of most of her pep. Of course, she had enough left to read the airmail letter from Sister Eileen that she'd found in her mail slot when she came home. *That was a quick response,* she thought, ripping open the flimsy blue paper. She skimmed the familiar spidery penmanship.

Molly was as well as could be, under the circumstances.

Eileen missed them all. As Mary Helen expected, her friend was surprised but very pleased at her decision to leave the college Development Office and volunteer at the Refuge.

"Be careful," Eileen had warned, and, underlined it. "As they say here at home, 'A lion is not a safe companion for all persons.'"

Whatever that means, Mary Helen thought, putting her letter on the bed stand. She wished she could run down the hall and reassure Eileen that today she'd met only lambs.

The moment Sister Mary Helen put her head on her pillow she fell into a deep dreamless sleep. She was surprised when she awoke and realized it was suppertime. Still groggy, she made her way to the Sisters' dining room.

"I was just beginning to worry about you," Anne said when she spotted Mary Helen in the doorway. "Are you all right?"

"Of course I'm all right," Mary Helen hissed, avoiding the curious glances of the other nuns. *Good night, nurse. All I need at my age is a caretaker,* she thought, taking her place behind Donata in the food line.

"How was your first day?" Donata asked loudly, without taking her eyes off the server dishing up her meal. "A little more gravy on my spuds, please." She smiled. "They're as dry as sawdust without it," she said to Mary Helen in a stage whisper. When she was satisfied with the ratio of gravy to potatoes, she caught Mary Helen with her full gaze. "Come sit down with me," she ordered. "I want to hear all about the Retreat of Anne's."

"Not the Retreat," Mary Helen corrected, "the Refuge." But her correction literally fell on deaf ears.

Before she knew it, the group of retired Sisters had gathered around Donata and her. Mary Helen quickly became the center of attention. Through dessert, she regaled them with her half-day's adventures, such as they were, and her first favorable impressions of meeting the women who took shelter at the Refuge.

The nuns listened sympathetically while she told them of Venus and Peanuts, of Crazy Alice and Miss Bobbie, of Sonia and poor, frail Melanie with the cruel pimp and the black eye.

Donata clucked her tongue. "Someone should do something about that pimp boy," she said.

Sister Mary Helen agreed with her. "What would you suggest?"

"Don't you know Kate Murphy quite well?" Donata asked, her eyes needle-sharp.

Mary Helen's stomach knotted. Donata's mention of Inspector Kate Murphy of the San Francisco Police Department was as unexpected as a hiccup. It brought back to everyone's mind several unfortunate situations in which Mary Helen had been involved over the years, situations that were best forgotten. A tense silence settled on the small group.

"She is from Homicide," Therese broke it with a sniff. "Please God, this convent will not be connected with another murder." She shot an accusatory glance in Mary Helen's direction.

"I was not the murderer!" Mary Helen wanted to shout, but knew it would do no good. "We all hope that," she said crisply. She continued her story, telling the others about meeting the socialite Betsy Dodd.

"Some people can make a trip to Paris sound like a trip to the five-and-dime," old Agnes said in awe, "while you, Mary Helen, make a trip to the five-and-dime sound like a trip to Paris."

Even Mary Helen had to laugh.

Before leaving the dining room, Sister Patricia dropped by the table. "How was your first day?" she inquired.

Sister Mary Helen thought that the new president was visibly relieved when she said that it was delightful.

"We missed *Jeopardy*," Ursula lamented when she looked up at the clock.

"This was better than *Jeopardy*," Donata snapped. "But if we hurry, we can just make *Wheel of Fortune*."

Several minutes later, most of the group had gathered in the community room to watch the game show. Donata muted the commercial. "On my way across the campus, I had a brainstorm," she announced. Although not everyone agreed, Donata considered most of her ideas "brainstorms." Mary Helen braced herself, hoping she hadn't painted too rosy a picture. How would Anne take to four or five Senior Sisters volunteering at her shelter?

"I'm bored to tears knitting these ridiculous bed booties for people who never use them," Donata grumbled. "Sister Cecilia excepted. What if I organize a campaign to knit woolen caps for Anne's Retreatants? We have boxes of leftover yarn and, I'm sure, dozens of willing hands."

"Refugees," Mary Helen corrected, relieved. "I think that would be a splendid idea," she said, thinking of the worn cap that had covered Melanie's straggly hair. Thin, trembling Melanie with the blackened eye—she wondered what exactly would happen to Melanie.

Unfortunately, she didn't have to wait long to find out.

Wednesday, September 9

❧❧❧

Feast of Saint Peter Claver, Priest

Sister Mary Helen woke before her alarm clock went off. She was full of the energy that comes from a new challenge. At least, that's what she thought it was. Although, if she was perfectly honest, the fact that yesterday she'd had both an afternoon nap plus eight hours' sleep might have accounted for some of her surge of pep.

She pulled open her drapes. A trapezoid of sun fell across her bedroom floor signaling another glorious day. After a quick shower, she left her room to see what it would bring.

"Meet you at the Refuge," Sister Anne whispered as she left the chapel at the end of Mass.

"Where are you going so fast?" Mary Helen asked, wondering if she should offer to go along.

"I'll ride the Muni down and go by Starbuck's to pick up a donation of coffee before I go in," Anne explained. "You have breakfast, then take the car and come down. Take your time.

We'll be there when you get there. I can assure you we are not going anywhere."

True but sad, Mary Helen thought, lingering in her pew a few moments to pray.

Today was the Feast of Saint Peter Claver, a seventeenth-century priest who spent his adult life ministering to African slaves. He did everything in his power to alleviate their suffering and to bring dignity to their lives.

This morning, alone in the dim, silent chapel, Mary Helen invoked his intercession for the African-American women she had met recently at the Refuge. Some of them, she feared, were just as enslaved as their ancestors had been by the cruel masters of addiction and mental illnesses and lack of education. They needed people to minister to them in their suffering, to bring a sense of dignity to their lives.

The Refuge is a small step in the right direction, Mary Helen thought, feeling a sudden rush of gratitude that she could be a part.

❧❧❧

By nine o'clock, Sister Mary Helen was pulling into the parking lot of the Refuge. A few women lingered just outside the entrance savoring the last puffs of their cigarettes. Anne had a "no smoking" rule indoors.

Fascinated, Mary Helen watched them flick off the lighted ends, then stash the tiny butts in their pockets. To her these butts didn't look long enough to light without burning your nose.

"Good for later," Sonia said, noticing Mary Helen's interest.

"How are you today, Sonia?" Mary Helen asked, slightly embarrassed by her own curiosity.

"I be blessed," Sonia said, leaving Mary Helen pondering her own blessings and her lack of awareness.

"Morning, Sister." A black woman she hadn't met yesterday held the door open for her.

"How do you know that I am a Sister?" Mary Helen asked in amazement.

The woman shrugged. "You be white and old and clean, and you got a cross around your neck. Who else you gonna be? Besides." The woman gave a wide, toothless grin. "The word's out on the street that yesterday we got a new one. That gotta be you. Right?"

"Right," Mary Helen agreed and entered the crowded room.

"I be Geraldine!" the woman called after her.

The shrill ring of Crazy Alice's laughter rose above the noise. A long line had formed by the supply room. Red-faced, Betsy was trying to fill the requests as quickly as possible. Mary Helen was surprised to see her. She thought Betsy's volunteer day was Tuesday. Maybe she was substituting. In the distance, the sound of the water from the showers hit against the tile and a pair of tennis shoes bumped around in the dryer.

Peanuts, who was on the telephone, waved when she saw Mary Helen. Venus sidled up to her. "It be crazy in here today. Sister Anne running her legs off. She gonna be real glad to see you."

"Doughnuts. More doughnuts," Anne said, passing her with two pots of water for the coffeemaker. "Use the cart."

Quickly Mary Helen made her way to the kitchen and a large box of day-old pastries. She had just started to pull apart the sticky chocolate-frosted doughnuts from the apple turn-overs when she realized how stuffy the kitchen was. The room had no windows. *Should I open the side delivery door?* she wondered, surreptitiously licking the chocolate from her fingers. *At least, that will let some fresh air in here.*

She looked around for Anne to ask if there was any reason she shouldn't open it, but Anne was in the front looking as though she was settling a dispute. *No sense disturbing her with this*, Mary Helen reasoned, moving toward the side door.

She pushed down on the metal release bar and shoved out. The door moved, but only a few inches. It hit against something solid. Had someone left a box by the back door?

Gathering her strength, Mary Helen put her full weight against the door. With a scraping sound, it opened far enough for her to peek out. Overnight someone had left what looked like a pile of old clothes—a black padded jacket, faded jeans, worn tennis shoes. A stale, sickening odor rose from the pile.

Hoping whoever said that the olfactory nerves go numb in about three minutes was correct, Mary Helen pushed open the door a little farther. The bundle shifted. A brown stocking cap jutted out of the pile. Next to it was a small head with its skull savagely smashed. Dried blood had spattered the face and had coated the straggly blond hair, turning much of it brown. Open blue eyes bulged up at her from the dead face of Melanie—Melanie—

Sadly Mary Helen realized that she didn't even know the poor girl's last name.

❧❧❧

Inspector Kate Murphy picked up the telephone on the second ring. "Homicide," she said, swallowing her last mouthful of coffee.

"Kate?" a familiar voice asked. "I'm so glad you're in this morning. This is Sister Mary Helen. You'll never believe what happened."

"Try me," Kate said, deliberately omitting the word *Sister*. There was no sense sending her partner into a rage before it was absolutely necessary.

When she looked up, Inspector Dennis Gallagher's watery eyes were studying her suspiciously.

What am I doing to give this away? Kate wondered and turned her back to Gallagher. She was so distracted by what her partner's reaction would be that she nearly missed the nun's message.

"Say that again, slowly, please," she asked.

"I was putting some doughnuts on the tray to feed the crowd when I realized how stuffy it was and so I opened the back door."

"The back door?" Kate couldn't imagine exactly which door Mary Helen meant.

"Well, it's really more on the side," she dithered, "if you are going to get technical. But that's not really the point, now is it, dear? The point is that the dead body of the sad young woman has been dumped like garbage in our doorway."

"Where are you exactly?" Kate asked. As she remembered it, the college had numerous side and back doors in each of its many buildings.

"At the Refuge," Mary Helen answered.

It took Kate a few seconds to adjust her thinking. The Refuge was the name of the new drop-in center Sister Anne had founded for homeless women, wasn't it? If she remembered correctly, the young nun had renovated an old storefront south of Market. What in the world was Sister Mary Helen doing there?

"So, you're not at the college?" Kate tried to swallow the final word, but Gallagher heard it all the same.

"College!" He said the word as if it had a sour taste. "Did you say 'college'? Don't tell me it's the same college I think it is."

Kate covered her ear with her hand, but it didn't blot out his words.

"I thought you sounded funny on the phone. Like you were trying to put one over on me," Gallagher grumbled, chewing on the end of his unlit cigar. "The minute you heard her voice, Katie-girl, you should have passed the receiver off like a hot potato to O'Connor there." He pointed to the next desk.

"O'Connor needs to do penance for his sins. We've more than made up for ours."

O'Connor grinned. "Some guys just have all the luck," he said and went back to the coffee room for a refill.

"One moment please, Sister," Kate said politely. "Can you hang on for just one minute?" She pressed the hold button and glared at her partner. "Will you kindly keep still?" she hissed. "I can't hear a thing the poor woman is saying."

"Poor woman, my ass!" Gallagher shot back. "Unless I've got it all wrong, it's that nun friend of yours again with, God help us, another homicide. If you ask me, Kate, I think it's a first-class miracle that any parents in their right minds send their kids to that college of theirs. With that nun running around, no one is safe."

"For heaven's sake, Denny, you'd think she'd committed the murders. She just happens to stumble on the bodies. Besides, this homicide is not at the college."

"Now she's spreading them around!" he exploded. "Now she's the goddamn Typhoid Mary of murder cases!" Gallagher's face was dangerously red, and he loosened the knot in his tie. "Why isn't she at the college where she belongs? Better yet, why isn't she retired? I thought she'd be retired by now. Living in an old nuns' home. There must be one, preferably in another city." He stopped for breath.

"She is at that new homeless shelter south of Market," Kate said.

"As if those poor devils didn't have enough trouble," Gallagher mumbled. "What's she doing there?"

"If you'll be quiet for a minute, I'll find out. Why don't you go have a cup of coffee with O'Connor?" Without waiting for an answer, Kate pushed the phone button. "Sister, thanks for waiting," she said, hoping Gallagher would walk away.

Instead he sat heavily in his desk chair and swiveled toward the window where the new jail partially blocked the view of the James Lick Freeway. Obviously, he would be quiet, but he definitely would not be gone.

"Where exactly are you?" Kate asked, then wrote down the address of the Refuge. "And you're there because . . . ?"

She listened while Sister Mary Helen succinctly and, Kate guessed, as charitably as she could explained why she'd left her position at Mount St. Francis College. Mary Helen was not one for hanging out the dirty convent linen.

"Where's the other one?" Gallagher asked in a stage whisper.

Kate shrugged at her partner. "Is Sister Eileen there with you?" she asked.

"Sister Eileen is in Ireland for the year," the old nun said. "Her sister, Molly, has terminal cancer, and the family needed Eileen's help."

"Well?" Gallagher demanded, staring at her over his horn-rimmed glasses.

"One moment, Sister." Kate covered the mouthpiece of the receiver. "Will you please be still, Denny!" she demanded. "I'll bring you up-to-speed as soon as I get off the line."

With Gallagher sulking in his chair, Kate quickly instructed Mary Helen to call 911. "Don't touch anything, Sister," she cautioned. "Keep everyone else away from the scene. And as much as possible, try not to let anyone leave."

"Unfortunately, I know all too well what to do," Mary Helen said softly.

"Denny and I will be there within minutes," Kate assured her.

"Inspector Gallagher will be with you?" Mary Helen sounded pleased. "Frankly, I thought he'd be retired by now."

"And that's exactly what he thought about you," Kate wanted to say, but decided against it.

❧❧❧

69

As soon as Sister Mary Helen hung up the telephone, her hands began to tremble. Without warning her knees felt as if they were melting. *Steady, girl!* She took a deep breath and made her way to the kitchen sink.

Thank God there was an extension line in here, she thought, splashing her face with the icy water. Before she had to face Anne and the others with her discovery, she had been able to call Kate Murphy and 911. They'd both be here any minute. She'd best break the news before the police broke it for her.

Wiping her face and squaring her shoulders, Sister Mary Helen walked down the hall and into the large gathering room. Anne was at the far end pouring water through the coffeemaker for yet another pot. Quickly Mary Helen crossed the room.

"Anne," she whispered, gently touching the young nun's arm.

Anne turned with a smile. Something in Mary Helen's manner or perhaps the look on her face must have given her away. She watched as Anne's smile melted like a popsicle in the sun.

"What is it?" Anne asked anxiously. Her hazel eyes stared sharply as if they were trying to pierce their way into Mary Helen's mind. "What happened?" she asked through lips stretched as thin and tight as rubber bands.

In the distance, Mary Helen heard the wail of the police siren. She knew she didn't have much time for details. "Melanie is at the side delivery door," she whispered.

Anne looked puzzled.

"Dead," Mary Helen added.

All at once, the color left Anne's face. She gulped in short breaths.

As if someone had rung a bell, the noisy room fell silent. Tension crowded in like a deadly chill. All eyes were on the two nuns.

Only Crazy Alice's giggle rose on the air.

"Three blind cops,
Three blind cops,
See how they run,"

she sang out.

She laughed uproariously.

"What's a matter?" Geraldine asked. You could hear the uneasiness in her voice. "Is something a matter?"

The *whoop, whoop* of the siren grew almost deafening, then died.

"I'm outta here!" Miss Bobbie yelled, her chair crashing backward.

"No, please!" Mary Helen called. "Please just stay."

But the place had turned to bedlam, with everyone shouting and rushing to leave. "Some of them got warrants," Peanuts explained, grabbing her own plastic sacks and making for the side door.

"Not that way!" Mary Helen shouted. "You can't go that way."

"That's what you say," Peanuts challenged. "You just watch me."

"But that's where the body is—" As soon as the words left her mouth, Mary Helen regretted them. The situation was frenzied enough already. Peanuts turned a sick shade of gray.

"The body!" Venus shouted above the clamor. "There's a body? A dead body?"

Mary Helen could almost see the panic spreading through the room. The noise was deafening. Women pushed, grabbed, shouted, frantic to escape, bumping one another in an effort to get out.

"Quiet, ladies, please just sit down." She tried to make herself heard above the din, but it was useless. Afraid that she would be knocked over herself, Mary Helen sat in the nearest chair. *Please, God, don't let anyone get hurt*, she prayed, and was very relieved when four broad policemen appeared in the front doorway.

❧❦❧

By the time Inspectors Kate Murphy and Dennis Gallagher arrived at the Refuge, things were pretty much under control. Anne had seen to it that most of the women were settled at the tables in the large gathering room. The sight of the police officers had subdued the majority. Others had taken a little more persuasion. Nine or ten had managed to slip away, but their names were on the daily sign-in sheet.

The color had returned to Anne's face. In fact, she looked flushed as she replenished the snack table with fresh muffins and ice-cold milk. "All our nerves are bad enough," she said when one of the women asked for more coffee.

As Mary Helen expected, after Kate Murphy had viewed the body she asked to speak with her. Following Kate toward the back of the building, the old nun quickly explained that she had actually seen nothing, only opened the door to get some air. "As I told you on the phone," Mary Helen said, "the kitchen was stuffy."

"And when you opened the door?" Kate asked hopefully.

"I was so busy trying to see what was keeping it from opening that I never even thought to look around."

Steeling herself, she followed Kate out the side delivery door. Inspector Gallagher was already there calling the medical examiner, the coroner, Forensics—all those people who need to come to the scene of a crime.

This time there will be no media interest, Mary Helen thought inanely. This body was a nobody who had been dumped like a pile of discarded clothes. Jacket, jeans, tennis shoes, a brown stocking cap, all that was left of Melanie lay crumpled in a side

72

doorway. Her blue eyes, milky now, seemed to be staring right through Sister Mary Helen. Her jaw hung open as if she were ready to scream.

Covering his mouth with his handkerchief, Gallagher leaned over the body. "Looks like the right side of her cranium was crushed," he said, pointing to a gaping wound.

Forcing herself to examine Melanie's skull, Mary Helen saw that it looked as if someone had given her several horrific blows. Instinctively she reached out to push a stray piece of hair off the girl's blood-spattered cheek.

"Just look; don't touch!" Gallagher shouted before her hand was fully open.

"I know," she said. Tears flooded her eyes.

"What's the matter? Did you know her?" he asked.

"No. Yesterday was the first time I ever saw her. She was frightened of her boyfriend." Mary Helen fumbled in her pocket for a tissue.

Gallagher nodded. "Probably her pimp. I'll check with Vice. See if they can ID him." He straightened up and ran his hand over his bald crown. "Jeez, it's hot out here," he said. "Let's get inside." He motioned Mary Helen back into the Refuge. "After you, Sister," he said. Kate followed her.

"What now?" Mary Helen asked.

Kate Murphy checked her wristwatch. "Should take a couple of hours to question the ladies. If you can, I'd like you and Sister Anne to stay."

Mary Helen knew from experience that this was more than a request. "We'd be happy to," she said. "Do you think one of the women could have done this?"

"Could have," Gallagher said, "but in most cases the pimp is at the bottom of it. She did something to get on his nerves."

"Like what?" Mary Helen asked.

"Like not turning enough tricks, or holding out some

money, or . . ." Gallagher's face began to redden. "Or—you don't want to know, Sister."

Mary Helen felt her own cheeks warm. Did he think she was too sheltered to be told, too delicate? Certainly he couldn't think she was too young.

"All you need to know is that, if you ask me, this will be a slam dunk, a piece of cake. Find the guy and we'll have the perp." He nodded his head, agreeing with himself.

"What happens to her body?" Sister Mary Helen asked, suddenly aware of how impersonal the death of a homeless woman can be.

"Unless someone claims it, the city will take care of it," Gallagher said, fumbling in his jacket pocket for his notepad and pencil.

Mary Helen felt gooseflesh raise on her arms. Numbly she sank into the nearest chair. A slam dunk, a piece of cake for the Homicide detectives, barely a statistic . . . a nobody of interest to the media. All true, yet once upon a time this young woman had been precious to someone. Precious to her parents, her sisters and brothers, to someone. *Above all, she was—still is—precious to God*, Mary Helen thought. *Her death should not go unnoticed.*

❦❦❦❦

"Here she come," Peanuts said when Mary Helen walked into the large front room. All eyes were on her.

"What's happening?" Miss Bobbie asked.

Mary Helen could tell that every woman in the place was waiting for the answer. Even with most of the small tables filled, the room was so quiet that she could hear the thunk of the electric clock counting off the seconds.

Was it her place to tell them? She didn't think so. She was

the "new kid on the block," to stretch a metaphor. Surely Anne should make the announcement, if anyone should.

"What's going down?" Venus asked, an anxious edge on her voice. "Won't someone tell us? We got things to do." Her dark eyes darted around the room.

One police officer stood blocking the hallway, while another was standing guard at the front door. No one was getting in or out without their knowing it.

"It's the KGB. I tell you, honey. The regular old KGB!" Crazy Alice was squealing, and Mary Helen felt the tension tightening.

Someone should tell them what is going on. It's only fair, Mary Helen thought. She tried to make eye contact with Sister Anne, who seemed to be studying something on the far wall.

"I asks what's happening." Miss Bobbie's tone was sharper, more demanding.

The room seemed to become even quieter, if that was possible. Mary Helen felt the hairs on the back of her neck prickle. She might have given in to the temptation to answer Miss Bobbie's question if she hadn't heard Kate Murphy's voice coming down the hall.

"Ladies, I'm sorry to detain you," Kate began, "but a woman has been murdered, and we need to ask some questions."

For the second time that morning, the room exploded. Women shouted about having appointments, taking care of their business, picking up their kids, while Crazy Alice giggled hysterically.

Much to Mary Helen's surprise, Kate seemed able to make herself heard over the hubbub. With authority, she explained that she'd set up an office in a small sleep space off the main room. She promised that she'd only ask them a few questions and, for the most part, she'd simply take their names and contact them again at the shelter.

Wisely Kate started her investigation with Venus, whose dark eyes were beginning to burn like fire under a pot. The group watched silently as Venus and Kate left the room.

"That lady be smart to get old Venus outta here," Peanuts said, "or they be a second murder going on."

The whole crowd laughed. "You be right about that, girlfriend!" Miss Bobbie spoke for them all, and for the time being the tension seemed to be burning off like morning fog.

While several of the group helped themselves to muffins and milk, Sister Mary Helen made her way across the room to a small table where a red-faced Sister Anne was sitting with Betsy Dodd, the volunteer.

Betsy's face, unlike Anne's, was the color of her white T-shirt. Her thick dark hair, usually so carefully styled, looked as if birds had been flying through it.

Sister Mary Helen noticed that the woman she'd met at the door—was her name Geraldine?—occupied the fourth chair.

"Who dead?" Geraldine asked as soon as Mary Helen was seated.

Surely she'll know in a few minutes, Mary Helen thought. *What could be the harm?* "Melanie," she said.

Geraldine stiffened. Small beads of perspiration broke out on her upper lip. "Not little blond Melanie?" she asked at last. A tear ran down her dark cheek.

"Was she a good friend?" Mary Helen asked.

"No, not really." Geraldine fumbled in her jacket pocket and pulled out a wad of toilet paper. Anne quickly substituted a tissue from her own pocket. They waited for Geraldine to compose herself.

"But I be knowing her for a long time," Geraldine said sadly. "Matter of fact, I seen her around suppertime last night." She shook her head. "I should have made her come in with me and eat something. I just should have."

"You can't blame yourself." Sister Anne patted Geraldine's hand reassuringly.

"I shoulda known," Geraldine said, her voice choked. "I shoulda. Poor kid was all tore up."

Mary Helen wasn't sure exactly what Geraldine meant, but she knew if she listened long enough, she'd find out.

Betsy Dodd leaned forward, her hazel eyes studying Geraldine's face. "In what way?" Betsy asked.

Geraldine blinked at the question. "What you mean?"

"How was she 'tore up'?"

"Just tore up." Geraldine was beginning to sound impatient. "You know—drinking, scared like, talking crazy, talking about Andy. That's her pimp. And Olivia. She's a mean one. And somebody named Amanda. I think I heard her right. My hearing's not all that good anymore. Amanda and a man she called Dickie."

A sudden shrewd light flashed deep in Geraldine's eyes. "You know, Miss Betsy, ma'am, Melanie says this Dickie knows you."

Betsy's jaw muscles tightened. Her eyes shifted ever so slightly.

Geraldine studied her. "I tell you, ma'am, she was talking real crazy. Out of her mind with the drink. Like I say, Miss Betsy, Melanie be all tore up." She wiped her eyes, again.

One look at Betsy Dodd's face and Mary Helen wondered if "all tore up" wasn't the perfect way to describe her, too.

✿❧❦✿

Betsy Dodd's stomach plummeted like a runaway elevator. She was light-headed, and the Refugees at the tables around the room seemed to sway with her. When Miss Bobbie's substantial frame began to oscillate, Betsy closed her eyes.

Steady now! Calm down! she cautioned herself, willing her heart to stop thudding as Geraldine's damning words pulsed through her mind: *"Amanda and a man she called Dickie. . . . This Dickie knows you!"*

How long would it take the police to make the connection? They were probably doing so right now. Of course, she could claim it was just a coincidence. There must be thousands of men in this city called Dick. Besides no one had called Richard "Dick" in years. If anyone used a nickname at all, it was Rich.

Her heart pounded. *And lots of people know me,* she reasoned. *I go to dozens of social events where it's not uncommon to meet five or six other fellows with the same first name as my husband. It's not as if his name were Horatio or Norton or Guido—anything unique like that. Why, I can think of at least ten other Dicks I know . . . like Dick Humphrey and Dick Long,* she began. Then realized that, as a matter of fact, she couldn't. She was stuck with three.

Betsy felt the perspiration gathering around her neck. *Get a grip on yourself before you make a scene,* she thought. She took a deep breath and opened her eyes to find the three other women at the table studying her with concern.

"Are you all right?" Sister Anne asked. "You were so white there for a minute I thought you might faint on us."

"I'm fine," Betsy said, hoping she sounded convincing. "It's nothing, honestly," she said. "I didn't eat anything before I left the house this morning and with all the excitement I think I'm just hungry."

That much was true. She was hungry. Lately she was always hungry. Depression eating, as her sister Ginger called it. Betsy fiddled with one of her gold loop earrings.

"Besides," Sister Mary Helen's voice broke into her thoughts, "even if you've had breakfast, it's coffee break time."

"Mary Helen is extremely religious in the observance of her coffee break," Anne joked, "even when there is no coffee."

"Are you sure you're all right?" Anne asked again.

"Just hungry," Betsy repeated.

"Well, that's easy to fix!" Sounding relieved, the young nun walked over to the refreshments table and quickly returned with a plate of muffins. Peanuts followed, balancing two glasses of milk, and Sonia brought up the rear with two more.

Grateful to find a perfectly legitimate way out of having to carry on a conversation, Betsy bit into a large banana nut muffin. Surely no one expected her to speak with her mouth full. Morsels of toasted walnuts from its top hit like hail on the front of her T-shirt. Carefully she picked up each tiny piece and popped it into her mouth.

Who was this Amanda? she wondered as she chewed. She suspected that was the name of Rich's latest fling. And if the police connected this Amanda to him, what would they think? It struck her like a smart bomb. She couldn't have planned it any better if she tried! Naturally they would suspect that he was involved with Melanie and maybe with her murder! Betsy wanted to laugh aloud. *Serves him right!* she thought. *And, in a way, he is a murderer. He has killed every bit of love in me.*

Her muffin tasted especially sweet when she decided that she wouldn't make the slightest move to help him. *I'll simply tell the police the truth, that I was a little late meeting him at the firm's apartment and when I got there he had seemed unusually nervous. Let Mr. Big Shot explain, if he will, that he had every right to be nervous,* Betsy thought, *because he didn't want me to discover his latest affair and confront him with it just before we were scheduled to perform our "perfect couple" act. Then, when he felt almost sure that I wasn't aware of it, the old lecher turned back into his charming self. By the time the cocktail party at the Blacks' was in full swing, he was "schmoozing" with the crowd as usual.* Suddenly she was hot all over and her heart was hammering. *We'll see how far his charm will take him when he's dealing with Homicide inspectors.*

Betsy Dodd made an elaborate show of checking her wristwatch. "I had better call home," she announced dutifully. "I have a feeling I'll be late."

"Help yourself to the phone in my office," Anne offered. "You'll have some privacy."

"Thanks." Betsy wanted to kiss her. She had been wondering how to prevent herself from being overheard without tipping her hand. Anne had solved the problem.

When she was satisfied that the office door was securely locked, Betsy dialed.

"Dodd, Roach, Crosby, and Chin," a perky voice answered.

"Could you please tell me if anyone named Amanda works there?" Betsy asked.

"May I ask who's calling?" The perky voice was also well trained not to divulge any information.

"This is Mrs. Dodd." Betsy couldn't think of a quick lie.

"One moment please, Mrs. Dodd," Perky Voice said, and before Betsy could protest, the line was picked up.

"Mrs. Dodd, this is Catherine."

Betsy recognized the efficient voice of her husband's secretary. Her palms went wet.

"At the moment, Mr. Dodd is meeting with a client," Catherine said. "He should be finished in a few minutes. Shall I have him return your call, or is there something I can do for you?"

What the heck! Betsy thought. *Either way Rich will find out I called. I might as well relieve my mind quickly.* "Maybe you can help, Catherine," she said. "Does the firm employ a woman named Amanda?"

The telephone wires crackled. Betsy imagined Catherine's long, thin face contorting as she tried to figure out exactly what to say.

"I believe that there is an Amanda who works as a paralegal." She sounded as if the woman were a virus infecting the department. "Would you like to speak with her?"

Suddenly Sister Anne's office became unbearably hot. Betsy's throat felt as if it were closing. The woman was right in the firm! The nerve of him! Too lazy to even hunt! If she had found Amanda so easily, surely the police would be on to her in a heartbeat. She almost felt sorry for Rich. Almost!

"No, thank you, Catherine," Betsy said, hoping she did not sound as frenzied as she felt. "That's all I really wanted to know."

Her hand trembling, she replaced the receiver. Blinking, she steadied herself against the corner of Anne's desk. The bile rose in her throat, and for a few desperate seconds she thought she might be sick. When it finally passed, Betsy Dodd dialed the phone again.

❧☙❧

Puzzled, Sister Mary Helen watched Betsy Dodd hurry across the large gathering room toward Sister Anne's office. Her tennis shoes moved so quickly that she might have been power walking.

Crossing the room, she seemed unaware of anything or anyone around her. She didn't even react when Peanuts called out, "Where you going, Betsy? You look like you got the devil on your tail."

> "Tail, tale,
> Tell tale tit,
> Your tongue shall be slit,

81

And all the dogs in our town,
Shall have a little bit,"

Crazy Alice chanted.

She would have kept it up, too, except that Miss Bobbie shouted, "Put a sock in it, girlfriend!" For a moment, Mary Helen was afraid she might.

Watching Betsy, Mary Helen wondered what in the world had gotten into the woman. Something Geraldine said, no doubt, had triggered her. It was right after Geraldine spoke that she'd become deathly white   not that she'd had much color before that.

Pensively Mary Helen cut her poppyseed muffin in fourths. Somehow, cutting the thing in quarters and eating them one at a time seemed less fattening than eating the muffin whole. She knew a number of other people who shared the same opinion, including her friend Eileen. Oh, how she missed Eileen at a time like this! She'd know exactly what set Betsy off.

Mary Helen was about to reach for the second quarter when it struck her. Of course it was something Geraldine had said: "Dickie knows you." Dick, Richard! Wasn't Betsy Dodd's husband named Richard? Indeed he was—Richard Dodd, the attorney.

Why had it taken her so long? Was she losing her touch? More than likely it was because, to her way of thinking, no one would even be tempted to call that imposing figure of a man Dickie.

How in heaven's name would he have known Melanie? Surely she couldn't be a client of his prestigious firm.

The sleep area door swung open, and Venus leaped from the room like a flounder from a frying pan. "I'm outta here," she announced and straightaway made her exit, but not before snagging a muffin for the road.

"You go, girl!" Peanuts called after her.

Inspector Kate Murphy stepped out into the gathering room. A beam of morning sun gave a backglow to her short auburn hair. Calm as always, she referred to her notebook.

"Geraldine!" she called. "Is there a woman named Geraldine in the room? Her street name might be Genie."

Her street name—this was a new concept for Sister Mary Helen. She wondered if all the women had "street names."

Watching closely, she noticed that Geraldine swallowed hard, but she did not move. Why should she? It was obvious that the Homicide detective had no idea who she was. Or maybe her street name wasn't Genie. She might never have stood if it hadn't been for Crazy Alice.

"Geraldine, honey," she sang out so loudly that no one missed it, "the lady cop is calling you. *'It's you, it's you. You're in a rabbit stew.'* "

❧❧❧❧

If looks could kill, Crazy Alice would have been the next corpse. "I'm Geraldine," she said finally. Shaking her head, she reluctantly rose from her chair. "But I don't know nothing, ma'am."

"If we could see you for a few minutes, please. We just have a couple of questions," Kate stated politely, but no one was fooled. They all knew there was no choice.

With her shoulders slightly stooped, Geraldine left the table and followed Kate Murphy into the room.

Sister Mary Helen and Sister Anne were left alone. *Perfect,* Mary Helen thought. Anne certainly wouldn't care if she didn't talk for a few minutes. She needed to write down what Geraldine had said before it slipped her mind. She fumbled in her pocket for a pen and wrote the names on her napkin—Andy, the pimp, Olivia, Amanda, and Dickie and, of course,

83

Betsy. This short list might at least provide a place for Kate Murphy to begin her investigation.

When she had finished, Mary Helen looked up. "How are you doing, Anne?" she asked. The young nun's face was still flushed, and it appeared as if it wouldn't take very much to make her cry.

"I think I'm in shock," Anne said. "I just can't believe this has happened. This is not the kind of thing that happens to me. This is the kind of thing that happens to you." She pointed at Mary Helen.

The old nun was taken aback. Was Anne blaming her for what had happened? Hadn't she tried to warn Anne the very first time she'd seen Melanie? Hadn't she said that something should be done? In her opinion, if the fault belonged anywhere, it seemed to be leaning toward the young nun.

Mary Helen felt her blood pressure rising. Anne's accusing finger was still out. *The kind of thing that happens to me, indeed! Actually, this murder thing did not "happen" to either one of us. It happened to Melanie, who deserved better.*

She was just about to say so when Crazy Alice sang out, "Don't point that thing, honey! It's got a nail on the end."

The room, honeycombed with tension, exploded into laughter. Even the two patrolmen standing guard laughed. Crazy Alice, pleased at the response, giggled wildly.

The sleep room door swung open. Geraldine, her brown eyes enormous, gave a grunt of surprise. "What's so funny?" she grumbled.

No one answered.

"You think it's so funny? It's your turn, Sister." She dipped her head toward Mary Helen.

Sister Mary Helen's stomach knotted as she hauled herself up from her chair. *Here we go again,* she thought, clutching the wrinkled napkin with its list of names in her hand.

Kate Murphy would be glad of a little help, she knew. As always, she was unsure of Inspector Dennis Gallagher's reaction.

❧❦❧❦

As soon as Sister Mary Helen stepped inside the small, dark sleep room, she felt claustrophobic. At least, she thought she did. She'd never been claustrophobic before, but the hot, sticky, not-enough-air sensation she experienced when Kate Murphy shut the door behind her convinced her that she was now.

Instinctively Mary Helen scanned the walls for a window, but there was none. Only two rather poor prints of "Blue Boy" and "Pinkie" in ornate gold frames hung on the wall. *They must have been donated,* Mary Helen thought pointlessly. *No one with any taste would buy them on purpose.*

The room's only light was a single lamp set on a tiny, round vanity table, which had been pulled out from the corner. Three chairs flanked the table, giving the area a "Gestapo" feel.

With a grunt, Inspector Dennis Gallagher rose from his chair. "S'ter," he said and sat back down.

In contrast, Kate Murphy gave her a friendly hug. "How nice to see you, Sister. Please, sit down," she said.

Hugging Kate in turn, Mary Helen hoped the young woman hadn't felt her tremble. "You look wonderful," she said, and Kate did.

Although the two women had not seen each other in several months, they had kept in touch by phone. Their paths had first crossed when a history professor at Mount St. Francis College was found murdered. Over the years and in the course of several homicide cases, their mutual respect and genuine affection had developed into a solid friendship. In fact, Sister Mary Helen had been a member of the wedding party when Kate

85

married Jack Bassetti and she was godparent to their four-year-old son, John—an honor she shared with Inspector Gallagher.

"Motherhood seems to be agreeing with you," Mary Helen said. Even in the dim room, she noticed that there was no visible gray in Kate's short auburn hair. The few wrinkles on her freckled face were in the laugh lines at the corners of her blue eyes.

Kate beamed. "Little John is a joy," she began and picked up her purse.

Mary Helen was sure that Kate was about to produce her latest baby pictures when Gallagher cleared his throat. "Ladies," he said in his usual grumpy way, "if I remember correctly, this is not the annual Mount Alumnae Tea Party. This is a homicide investigation!"

For the first time Mary Helen actually looked at Inspector Gallagher, and she was genuinely taken aback. The poor man looked as though he could be ill. His skin, usually ruddy, was pasty. And his horn-rimmed glasses did little to hide the miniature blimps of flesh that had formed under his eyes. First chance she had, she'd ask Kate about him. She knew better than to bring it up to Gallagher himself.

Sister Mary Helen smiled sweetly at the detective. "Of course, you're right, Inspector. This is, indeed, a homicide investigation. I'll be more than happy to tell you anything I know, which, to be perfectly honest, is precious little." She was just about to mention the names on the napkin when a fierce look from Gallagher cut her off.

"First of all, Sister," he said, straining the words, "what in God's name are you doing here? Don't you still live at Mount St. Francis College?"

"Of course I still live at Mount St. Francis, but—," she began.

"Then why aren't you up there where you belong calling

alums, raising money, doing whatever it is you do? What in the name of all that is good and holy are you doing down here in this neighborhood?"

Mary Helen had no intention of telling him about Sister Patricia and her "clean sweep" policy, nor that she'd quit before she surely would have been fired. Neither one was any of his business, and surely none of it was pertinent to the murder of the poor little prostitute.

"So?" he prodded impatiently.

Sister Mary Helen felt her face flush. "Well, not that it's really any of your business," she began crisply, "but I just felt drawn—in the name of God, as you put it—to spend a few of my remaining years serving the poor." She was hoping she sounded pious. It was true in a sense, although she really had been more pushed than drawn. What difference did it make? The results were the same.

"And the other one?" Gallagher asked. "Where's the other one?"

"You mean Sister Eileen?"

Gallagher nodded.

"She's gone to Ireland for the year. Her sister is dying of cancer, and the family needs her."

Gallagher's face seemed to soften, or at least it was no longer pure Mount Rushmore. "Sorry," he mumbled. "At least, the trouble is halved."

Surely Kate had told him all this. Was he just trying to be unpleasant? Well, she wasn't biting. Instead Mary Helen chose not to dignify the inspector's remarks with any replies. Chin high, she sat tall in her chair, at least as tall as she could manage, pulled her blue suit skirt over her knees, then smoothed out her napkin. "I believe what you want to ask, Inspector, is have I any idea who killed little Melanie."

Gallagher's face reddened. It looked to Mary Helen as if he

was about to say something unpleasant. She was glad when Kate Murphy's glare stopped him. She was beginning to feel weary.

"Please, Sister," Kate said, "if you have any ideas we'll be glad to hear them."

"How long exactly have you been down here serving the poor, Sister?" Gallagher grumbled.

This question Mary Helen ignored, too. Selective hearing was one of the benefits of aging. She might as well take advantage of it. Otherwise, what was the point of getting old?

She turned halfway in her chair and faced Kate. "I was talking to Geraldine before you called her in—"

"So, you know old Genie?" Gallagher chuckled.

"Yes," Mary Helen said. This was going to get complicated, she thought, what with indoor names and street names. She wondered if there was another kind of name she had missed.

Right now all she wanted to do was give the two inspectors the names she had written down on her napkin. The Refugees waiting outside were already getting restless. No sense waiting until they were ready to explode before sending them on their way.

When Mary Helen saw Kate raise her pencil she began. "Geraldine mentioned Andy, Melanie's pimp, I presume, and Olivia, who is a street person, I believe, and a woman named Amanda, and a man called Dickie who apparently knows one of our volunteers, Betsy Dodd.

"I hope that helps," she said, wondering how in the city of somewhere around eight hundred thousand people four names could be important. Oh well, it was a start. She crumpled the napkin. The sleep room didn't seem to have a wastepaper basket, so she stuck the napkin in her pocket.

"By the way, I did overhear Melanie when she was leaving the Refuge yesterday say that she was afraid Andy was going to kill her. At least, that's what I thought I heard her say! 'One of these days, Andy is going to kill me.' She sounded frightened."

Hitching his pants, Gallagher sighed. "The smart money is on Andy, Sister," he said with a satisfied smile. "If he didn't kill her himself, he had her killed. Like I told you before, this one is going to be a slam dunk!"

❧❦❧❦

Richard Dodd couldn't believe it when his secretary, Catherine, told him. At first he thought she was joking. But earnest, straight-arrow Catherine never joked. He could count on the fingers of one hand the times he had heard her laugh.

The moment his client left, Catherine had slipped into his office, her brown eyes enormous. "Mr. Dodd," she said, "while you were at your meeting your wife called with a rather odd question." She hesitated.

"What was that?" he'd asked impatiently. Betsy was full of odd questions, if you asked him. What was she up to now?

"She wanted to know if we have an employee named Amanda," Catherine said.

Rich felt his stomach lurch. He steadied himself. Nothing must show on his face. Deliberately he began to sort through the stack of papers he had left on his desk.

"And?"

"The only Amanda I could think of was the new girl in the paralegal department." Catherine nibbled on her lower lip. "Do you want me to check with Personnel?"

"No, no, thank you," Rich said quickly. Too quickly. "I'll give Mrs. Dodd a call. See what this is all about."

"Shall I try to get her for you?" Catherine asked.

Rich shook his head. "I'll use my private line," he said, lifting the receiver and making an exaggerated pretense of dialing.

On this line no one, not even you, Catherine, can pick up and

89

listen in "by mistake," he thought, conscious of the empty ring, then the words: "At the tone, the time will be twelve-o-one exactly."

"Thanks, Catherine," Dodd said, dismissing her with the nod.

He stayed on the line until the operator announced, "Twelve-o-four exactly." Then he replaced the receiver. The light would go off on Catherine's desk. She'd notice that he had spent several minutes chatting with his wife, satisfying her curiosity. That should do it until he had time to figure out what Betsy was up to.

Rich felt the perspiration roll down his ribs. Why had Betsy called asking about Amanda? How in hell had she found out? He'd been so careful. Nothing had happened at the Blacks' cocktail party to arouse her suspicions, had it? No one there had the slightest connection with Amanda. No one could have said anything to Betsy. Betsy had seemed to be enjoying herself.

It had to be that crazy homeless girl they had seen on Nob Hill. How had she managed to get to Betsy? At the shelter—that was the only logical explanation. But that couldn't be right. As far as he knew, his wife wasn't there today. He was safe for the time being. Or was he?

His private line rang, startling him. *What now?* he thought, snatching up the receiver. "Yes," he said, all business.

"So, you're out of your meeting."

Rich recognized his wife's voice. "Just this minute." He tried to keep his tone upbeat, as if he were happy to hear from her. "What can I do for you, Mrs. Dodd?"

"You sound chipper. It must have been a very good meeting."

"Good enough," he said, waiting, wondering how much she knew. "Where are you now?" he asked.

"At the Refuge," Betsy said.

Rich loosened his tie. It was as hot as hell in here. Was the air conditioner broken? he wondered.

"Just after you left this morning, they called me to substitute," his wife said. "The Wednesday volunteer phoned in with the flu."

Rich felt his stomach knot. Where was this going? "That's too bad," he said inanely.

"What's too bad?" Her tone was sharp.

"That the other volunteer has the flu. I hope you don't catch it."

Betsy gave a cold laugh. "That's the least of my troubles," she said.

This cat-and-mouse game was beginning to get on his nerves. "What can I do for you?" Rich asked again.

"Nothing, really. I just called to tell you, before someone hears it on the news, that this morning we found one of our ladies by the back door—dead."

"Doesn't surprise me," Rich said.

Betsy cut him off. "It was a thin blond woman. Her name was Melanie," she said and waited.

Trying to quell the panic rising in his throat, Rich stared out his office window at the pointed tower of the Transamerica Building. In the distance he watched cars, like children's toys, roll across the Bay Bridge. How should you respond? How much did Betsy know? How was she going to use the information?

His grip tightened on the receiver, and his mouth felt dry. "Did you know her well?" Rich asked, slipping a red Tic-tac into his mouth. It seemed like a safe question. The phone line crackled. He could hear his wife breathing.

"Betsy?" he said. His impatience was getting the best of him. He heard her inhale sharply.

"I think the real question is, Rich, how well did *you* know her?"

"What the hell does that mean?" he demanded, but the line was dead.

Still using his private phone, Rich punched in Amanda's extension. He didn't wait for more than a "Hello."

"Come to my office immediately," he ordered and slammed down the receiver.

Less than five minutes later, he heard a timid knock on his office door. "Come in!" he shouted.

"What is it, Dickie?" A pale Amanda stood before his enormous desk. Her voice, usually low and sultry, sounded frightened. "What is the matter?" she whispered. Her large blue eyes searched his face for an explanation.

"Sit down," he said civilly, motioning her to the client's chair.

Amanda sat on the edge of the leather seat. Her clenched hands rested on her knee.

Even in his current state of mind, Rich couldn't help noticing her shapely legs and the way her firm breasts heaved up and down with each breath.

He pushed himself up from his chair and, coming around the desk, perched himself on the corner. He was close enough to smell the sweet, intoxicating fragrance of her perfume.

"We have a problem," he said, reaching over to touch a lock of her blond hair. He felt rather than saw Amanda stiffen.

"What's that?" she asked softly.

"That young woman we saw on Nob Hill last night—"

"You mean the homeless blonde with the sign?"

Rich nodded. "My wife just called. They found a woman dead this morning at the shelter where my wife works. From the description, I'm sure it's the same one."

Amanda's eyes shifted. "What happened?" she whispered.

"What makes you think I know?" Rich snapped. Amanda seemed to recoil.

This will never do, Rich thought. Reaching over, he covered her clenched hands with one of his. "Sorry, Amanda baby. I'm just jumpy, I guess." He tailored his tone. "To answer your question, I don't know what happened. All I know is, if anyone asks us, the last time we saw her she was alive."

Amanda nodded.

"And"—he paused like any good lawyer hoping to drive home the importance of his next point—"we were on Nob Hill for a confidential business meeting. Right?" He winked and studied Amanda's face.

She was smiling now—a big, knowing smile. "Right," she said. But Rich noticed that somehow this same smile didn't quite cover the cunning lurking in her large blue eyes.

❧❧❧

Officer Mark Wong was not surprised when he received a pager call from Inspector Dennis Gallagher of Homicide. Actually he had expected someone to contact him. It was common practice for Homicide to contact Vice if they were looking for a pimp or a prostitute they thought might be involved in one of their cases. It saved lots of time, since the Vice guys knew almost everyone on the street by sight. If Gallagher hadn't called, Wong would have contacted the Homicide Detail to find out who was on the case.

Wong had heard the word from his partner, Brian Dineen. Dineen kept a police scanner at home—Wong couldn't imagine why—and the call had come in that a prostitute known as Melanie had turned up dead at the back door of the Refuge, the women's drop-in center south of Market. She'd been bludgeoned to death with a heavy blunt object.

At first, Wong could not believe his ears; then he felt a little sick. What a waste! Last night his partner and he had seen

Melanie alive and well, if a little bruised. Both of them liked her. She was a sweet, sad kid. An ache crept into his chest. He had hoped for something better for her.

When they'd left Melanie on Nob Hill, Wong was angry. He and Brian had hunted for Andy, the pimp, and actually found him coming out of a comfortable apartment on Fulton Street. Citing him as a public nuisance, they had hauled Andy off to jail.

After Gallagher and Wong had exchanged a few pleasantries, Gallagher got right down to business. Andy and his whereabouts turned out to be the main purpose of Gallagher's call.

"So what you're telling me, Mark, is that our Andy couldn't have killed her himself. He's in custody." Gallagher sounded disappointed.

"Not at all," Wong answered cynically. "My man could have been in and out before our shift was over." Even as he said the words, his cop's mind fought down his anger and frustration. "It happens."

"Will you check it out for me?" Gallagher asked. "I'm down here at the Refuge now with a room full of very upset women." He lowered his voice: "Including two nuns and a prominent socialite."

"Talk about the luck of the Irish!" Wong ran his fingers through his short-cropped hair. "The nuns have to be those two friends of yours from the Mount."

"Half-right." Gallagher sounded frustrated. "One of them is, but the second one is new—a young one, a very young one— in case I was hoping that the two of them would finally retire and get out of my hair. And don't you even think about saying, 'What hair?' "

Mark chuckled. "Who is the socialite?" he asked.

"Betsy Dodd," Gallagher said. His voice was still low, so he must have been where he could be overheard. "She is the wife of that big muckety-muck mouthpiece Richard Dodd, who, if the Chronicle is to be believed, is not exactly a pal of the police. From what I hear at the Hall, the guy's thinking of giving the governor's race a shot."

The moment Gallagher said the name "Betsy," Wong heard a tiny warning bell, like an old typewriter before you reached the right margin.

"Betsy Dodd?" Mark asked, just to be sure. Last night when they'd stopped her, hadn't Melanie talked about a man named Dick who knew a girl called Amanda and knew Betsy, the volunteer at the Refuge? His mind whirled like a slot machine and came up with three cherries—Betsy, Dick/Richard, Amanda. Was it a jackpot!?

At the time Wong hadn't given the names much thought. He had scuffed them off as the beer talking. Now it seemed too much of a coincidence to let it go. Could this be more than a street murder? he wondered. Was Melanie on to something? Something that could have gotten her killed?

"Hold on a minute, Denny," Wong said. He'd put it in Gallagher's lap where it belonged. "Last night, before we collared Andy, Brian and I stopped Melanie. She was in her cups, so we didn't pay too much attention."

Succinctly Wong related the incident to Gallagher. "Coincidence or no?" he said finally. "It's your call." He stopped, hoping Gallagher would pick up the ball. If this big shot lawyer was involved, Wong would like to see him nailed, for Melanie's sake.

"Are you there?" Mark asked when Gallagher didn't respond.

Dennis Gallagher let out a long, tired sigh. "Yeah, I'm here," he grumbled. "I just can't believe my ears. That's all. Can't believe my own ears. This whole thing looked like such a shoo-in. Hooker dead. Pimp for the perp. Now we're pulling in the wife of a big shot lawyer—a governor wannabe who hates cops, for crissake!"

Wong was sure that Gallagher's face was getting redder by the second. "Maybe there's nothing to it," he said, but Gallagher wasn't listening.

"Do you know how close I am to retirement? Do you know what this kind of case can do to a man's heart? To his soul, for godssake? I came down here on a routine homeless homicide. No big deal! Now I can see the beginnings of our own goddamn whatever-gate!"

"Whatever-gate?"

"Everything's a gate nowadays."

"Whoa," Wong said. "Who's on the case with you?"

"Kate Murphy," Gallagher said. "Here, let her talk to you for a while. I need a cup of strong black coffee."

Wong could hear the phone being passed.

"Hi, Mark," Kate said. "What did you say to my partner that put him into orbit? If he doesn't come down soon, NASA will be tracking him."

When Wong had finished telling her, Kate sighed. "Sister Mary Helen, one of the nuns who volunteers here, gave us the same names. Now I can see what's gotten to Gallagher. It has to be more than a coincidence."

Mark Wong heard Gallagher groan in the background. "Check on Andy!" he shouted. "With any luck at all, it's Andy."

Mark didn't think this was the right time to remind Gallagher that Andy, like most pimps, probably wouldn't do the real dirty work himself—too dangerous. Sure, he'd knock the girls around to show them who was the boss, but when it came to murder, he'd have someone else do the job.

"I'll get back to you," Mark said before Kate asked and

quickly wrote down their number. Within minutes he was back on-line.

Gallagher answered. He seemed to have calmed down somewhat. At least he was resigned. "What have you got?" he asked.

"You'll be happy to hear that Andy was out before our shift was over," Wong said.

"There is a God," Gallagher said, then added, "Sorry, Mark, that's got to be maddening."

"*Maddening* ain't the word for it." Wong felt all his muscles tighten.

"Must make you want to turn into a goddamn vigilante," Gallagher said.

"Damn right," Wong answered and pulled himself up to his full five feet, seven and a half inches. "A vigilante might be just what the department needs."

🐝🐝🐝🐝

"I got to go," Geraldine said as soon as she sat down at the table with Peanuts and Miss Bobbie. It was always good to make it clear when you took a chair that you were in a hurry. That way, if something came up that you didn't want to get into, you could leave without hurting anyone's feelings.

"Where you going?" Peanuts asked, her dark eyes twinkling.

"I got business," Geraldine said. She knew that even Peanuts was too well raised to ask, "What business?"

"It ain't none of yours!" Miss Bobbie joked. Miss Bobbie could get away with that kind of talk. She'd been something in her day, Geraldine remembered, with her tight curly hair dyed henna red and her high heels. She'd had jewels and fine hats and a nice apartment until she got hooked on the gin. She'd finally kicked the drink, but years of heavy use had taken their toll on her. To look at her now, Geraldine thought sadly, Miss

97

Bobbie might have been nothing but some rich white lady's housekeeper or cook.

"Tell us, girlfriend." Miss Bobbie looked directly at Geraldine. "What you tell them police?"

"I told them nothing but the truth, and I don't know much a'that," Geraldine said and stubbornly stuck out her chin.

"I thought I heard you telling the Sisters about seeing Melanie last night." The scar around Miss Bobbie's right eye twitched.

Geraldine studied Miss Bobbie's face and felt a wash of relief. She wasn't out to make trouble. She just wanted to hear the gossip. All right, if that's what she wanted, Geraldine would make it good!

"I did see Melanie last night," she admitted in a whisper. When you whispered something, it always made it sound more important. "She was in my doorway when I came home. Scared me half to death, I tell you, the way she rose up from the ground, all crying and scared. 'Geraldine!' she calls out to me. 'Genie.' "

"What did she want?" Peanuts interrupted, knowing Geraldine would embellish the story.

Miss Bobbie turned mean eyes on her. "Hold on, girl. You about to get on my nerves. Let Genie tell it her own way."

Peanuts sank back in her chair and took a bite of her muffin. Her dark eyes sparked, but she knew better than to sass Miss Bobbie.

Geraldine waited until she had both the women's full attention. No sense having to tell it another time. "I asked her to come in, have a cup of tea. I'd have fixed her a good hot meal. Poor Melanie! Her eye all black and swollen. She was shivering like a motherless child."

"It be that Andy," Miss Bobbie said in disgust.

Geraldine shrugged. "Could be, but she say something about Olivia, too."

"Olivia? You mean Olivia with the street name of—what is it?" Miss Bobbie hesitated, blinking her eyes, as if all that blinking would help.

She must be getting old, like the rest of us, Geraldine thought, sneaking a sideward glance at her friend. *It's not like Miss Bobbie not to remember a name.*

"Like some kind of eats."

She was getting warm. "Candy," Geraldine prompted.

"That's it. Candy. Milk Chocolate Candy. I don't know why they call her that," Miss Bobbie mused. "Far as I can remember, she weren't very sweet. And she's a white girl, so it can't have nothing to with her color. If it was for her skin, they'd likely have called her Cottage Cheese."

"You're right about that," Geraldine said, and they all laughed.

"So, who was she scared of?" Peanuts couldn't help herself. Miss Bobbie glared, but Peanuts didn't seem to notice. "Was it Andy or was it Olivia?"

"I didn't say she was afraid of either one." Geraldine was annoyed. This was her story, and she'd be switched if she'd let Peanuts take it over. "Far as I know, it could have been one of them others she mentioned." Geraldine could tell by the two sets of eyes fastened on her face that she was back in control. "Yes, ma'am. She talked about a woman named Amanda."

Miss Bobbie looked puzzled.

"She weren't making much sense, scared as she was. Talked about this Amanda with high heels."

Miss Bobbie frowned. "Might be a new girl on the streets."

Geraldine shrugged. "Might be, or it might just be the beer talking. Queerest thing she did say was about a man called Dickie."

"Do you know any Dickies?" Miss Bobbie asked no one in particular.

"I'll tell you who Melanie said knows him."

"Who?" Peanuts asked.

Geraldine ignored her. "Melanie says he knows Betsy."

"Betsy? That Betsy from Mississippi?" Peanuts asked.

Geraldine shook her head and her eyes shifted toward a far table. Miss Bobbie and Peanuts followed her gaze.

"Our Miss Betsy." Geraldine's voice was even softer. "The volunteer sitting with Sister Anne." She could tell by the expressions on her friends' faces that she had shocked them.

"How does our Betsy know street people?" Peanuts was skeptical.

"Who says that these are street people?"

"And you told this to the Sisters and the police?" Miss Bobbie's eyes were wide. Her scar twitched nervously. "You be crazy, Genie. Who gonna believe you?"

"They musta believed me," Geraldine said with a queasy feeling in her stomach. "They wrote it down. Why would I lie?" She shook her head vehemently. "I don't lie. A liar is worse than a thief."

"Then what happened?" Miss Bobbie prodded. She was fishing for more gossip.

"I asked her to come in," Geraldine said, knowing the best part of the story was over. "I told her I would keep her safe. She knew I could. But she flew down the street like a frightened cat."

At the next table, Crazy Alice must have overheard the word *flew*. It was all she needed.

> "One flew east, one to west,
> One flew over the cuckoo's nest."

She chanted the words over and over in a loud singsong, stopping only long enough to giggle. Miss Bobbie covered her ears. Crazy Alice's nervous high-pitched laughter rose and tumbled and echoed and filled the space until it was the only sound in the large room.

Geraldine felt the goose bumps race up the backs of her arms.

❦❦❦❦

Sister Anne felt as though she were living a dream—no, living a nightmare was more like it. Crazy Alice's incessant giggling made her want to cover her ears as Miss Bobbie was doing and run screaming from the room.

She stiffened in her chair. That would never do. She was the leader. The women looked to her. It was her responsibility to keep calm. Besides, there was no way to escape. How in the world had this happened?

Here she was, sitting at a table in her beloved Refuge while policemen guarded the exits and two Homicide detectives turned the sleeping area into an interrogation room.

She had been ministering at the Refuge for about a year now. During that time, she had to admit that there had been some tense moments and a few altercations among the women. Usually, they involved more name-calling and threats than actions, thank goodness! She had been forced to call the police on two or three occasions. But never had anything come close to murder!

Even with the fan on, the room seemed unbearably hot. Anne felt as if she were bathed in perspiration. She tried not to think of thin, sad Melanie battered, then dumped like yesterday's garbage in a heap by the back door.

She shivered. At last, Crazy Alice was quieting down, chanting, "*Hickory, dickory, dock. Let's all run up the clock.*" Soon she'd stop.

Fortunately, Anne hadn't found the body. She didn't know how she would have reacted. In fact, she hadn't even gone out the back door to see it. Despite the heat, her teeth began to

101

chatter. Thank God Sister Mary Helen had made the grisly discovery.

Anne stole a glance at the older nun sitting across the table from her. Although her wrinkled face was a little paler than usual, she looked quite calm and collected. *How does the old girl do it?* Anne wondered with a twinge of envy.

On the other hand, the volunteer Betsy Dodd, the third person at the table, appeared to be a wreck. Her face had lost all its color, and her hair was a mess. It seemed to be taking all the strength she had to remain in her chair. Was it Anne's imagination or was Betsy even more distraught after she'd called home? She'd spent a long time in the office.

Perhaps it was her husband who had been upset, Anne thought. A lawyer, especially a prominent lawyer who aspires to enter the governor's race, can't be pleased by having his wife involved—even as an innocent bystander—in a murder case.

"Are you all right, Betsy?" Anne asked softly.

Betsy opened her mouth. At first, nothing came out. "I'm fine," she said at last. "Or I'm doing as well as can be expected after what's gone on here this morning."

The words were no sooner out of Betsy's mouth than the door to the sleep room opened and Kate Murphy stepped out.

"Mrs. Dodd." She focused on Betsy. "Can we have a few minutes with you, please?" she asked.

For a second Betsy looked frozen in her chair. Anne was almost positive that she felt the woman trembling. Betsy acted as if she was terrified. *Why,* Anne speculated, *should Betsy Dodd be frightened of the police? She's a big noise in the city. She and her husband both are well thought of and well connected. Of all people, she should be the most blasé.*

Actually I'm the one who should be scared. Our whole operational budget for the Refuge is dependent on the goodwill donations of benefactors. Although many of them suffer from NIMBYism

(Not In My Back Yard), most San Franciscans want the homeless cared for.

With Betsy gone, Anne and Mary Helen were alone at the table. From the looks of things, it would probably be another hour before they could close. No one seemed to be paying much attention to them.

Sister Anne leaned forward. "What did the detectives ask you?" She kept her tone low.

"They asked if I had any ideas about who killed Melanie." Sister Mary Helen adjusted her bifocals on the bridge of her nose and met Anne's gaze.

The inside of Anne's mouth felt furry. "And do you?" she asked.

"Only the names Geraldine gave us. I wrote them on a napkin and handed them over to the inspectors."

Sister Anne thought about the names—Andy, Melanie's pimp; a street person called Olivia—if she had the right woman, Olivia came into the Refuge only occasionally. She was a tall, thin white woman, about Geraldine's age, Anne guessed, with a belligerent attitude.

Peanuts had once remarked, "Sister Anne, she be glad to see Olivia's ass go out the door." Although Anne had not condoned the remark, in truth she couldn't deny it.

Anne had no clue who Amanda might be. And that Dickie who knew Betsy couldn't possibly be her husband, the famous Richard Dodd. Or could it?

"Aren't all those names 'hearsay'?" Anne had heard that expression on one of the television shows about lawyers and courtrooms.

"Hearsay is better than no say," Mary Helen said seriously. "At least, it may give the inspectors a place to begin." Mary Helen took another bite of her muffin.

How could she eat anything? Anne marveled. Her own stomach felt squeamish. Trying not to stare, she studied Mary Helen. Although the old nun's mind seemed to be far away, her face was amazingly serene.

What in the world can she be thinking? Anne felt a little annoyed at the older woman's apparent calm.

How Anne had admired Sister Eileen and Mary Helen when they'd helped the police solve several murders connected with the college! As an onlooker, she had found their adventures exciting and felt a wicked delight in the consternation they'd caused Sister Cecilia and some of the other nuns at the convent.

Now that she herself was in the thick of this adventure, Anne was feeling anything but excited or delighted. At this moment the only emotion that Anne was aware of was the sharp, sickening jab of fear that was heightened when Kate Murphy stepped from the sleep room and called her name.

❦❦❦

Alone now at the table, Sister Mary Helen watched Sister Anne and Betsy Dodd pass each other on their way to and from the sleep area. They exchanged stiff smiles, but that was all.

While she walked across the gathering room, Betsy pulled off her blue volunteer's apron and nervously folded it into a small, neat square. Quickly she made her way to the cupboard where aprons were kept and put it on the shelf.

Like a plane on automatic pilot, Betsy glided back to the table and stood over Mary Helen. Her hazel eyes twitched nervously. "I'm going to leave now, Sister," Betsy said. Her voice was high and strained. "The Homicide detectives said that I can go."

"Are you all right?" Mary Helen asked, then felt foolish. Of course she wasn't all right. Anyone with eyes to see and ears to hear knew that. The woman was distraught!

Betsy gave a quick, uncertain nod. "I'll be fine," she said with a flat smile. "I'm just hungry."

Mary Helen was tempted to offer her another muffin but thought better of it. Betsy's hunger was fueled by a tension that no amount of muffins could satisfy.

"Drive carefully!" Mary Helen called to Betsy's fleeing back. The woman gave her a ragged over-the-shoulder wave as the beefy patrolman pushed open the front entrance to let her out.

Sister Mary Helen surveyed the gathering space. Only a few women remained sitting at tables around the room. Most were silent. A few talked quietly. What a difference from the busy, friendly place she'd entered only a few hours earlier.

She figured it wouldn't be long before the Homicide inspectors completed their interrogations and they'd all be free to go. Her heart jolted at the thought of going back to the convent with this tale. Her only hope was that Anne and she would be able to break the news to the other nuns before anyone else did. At least they wouldn't be on the five o'clock news. Small comfort!

She wondered about the Refugees themselves. After what had happened, how many of them would be back tomorrow? Perhaps it would be better to close the center for a few days. That, of course, was up to Anne. Anne was in charge, she reminded herself. What a relief not to be responsible for the decisions!

Nonetheless, she couldn't help feeling a little responsible for trying to help find Melanie's killer. After all, she was the one who had discovered the poor child's body. And truly she had looked like no more than a child.

Don't do it! a small voice warned her. *Don't get involved. This is none of your business.*

Inspector Gallagher's face loomed large in her mind. Poor

man! When she'd spoken with him, he hadn't looked as if he was feeling too well. No wonder! Doing this job at his age!

Whether or not he appreciated it, Mary Helen would be doing him a favor finding out as much as she could about the murder of Melanie. Actually, it was a matter of charity, aiding the sick.

With that thought firmly planted in her mind, she meandered across the room to the table where Geraldine sat with Miss Bobbie and Peanuts. She knew Geraldine was talking about Melanie's death.

"May I join you?" Mary Helen asked.

Geraldine's face froze. "I be going soon, Sister. I got business," she said, but didn't move.

When neither Peanuts nor Miss Bobbie objected, Mary Helen took a chance and sat down.

"How you doing?" Miss Bobbie asked. "You feeling all right?" The scar around her right eye twitched.

"Fine, thank you," Mary Helen said. "Although it was quite a shock to find poor Melanie like that." Even now Mary Helen's legs felt a little wobbly and she was glad that she was seated.

Peanuts narrowed her dark eyes and studied the old nun. "You ever seen a murdered person before?" she asked.

Sister Mary Helen knew that this was a test, and she wasn't really sure of the correct answer. "The truth is that I've seen several," she said.

Geraldine frowned. She folded her broad hands. "How many exactly?" she asked. Her voice held the challenge.

"Six or seven," Mary Helen answered honestly and waited for a reaction.

After several seconds of electric silence, Miss Bobbie threw back her head and her laugh rose in a deep, hearty chuckle. "You sure got us that time, girlfriend," she said. "Six or seven! Lordy! You had us going!"

The two other women joined in the laughter and set off a torrent of giggles from Crazy Alice.

"*The little dog laughed,*" she chanted, looking around, pleased. "*To see such craft, and the dish ran away with the spoon.*"

"Now, let me ask you ladies something." Mary Helen decided to strike while the mood was light.

"What you want to know?" Peanuts narrowed her eyes. Instantly her whole body was rigid with mistrust.

Miss Bobbie, who was still laughing, quieted down. Geraldine gave Mary Helen a toothless grin. "I can't stay long," she said.

"I just want to ask you about something I heard yesterday." Mary Helen put both hands on the tabletop and leaned forward. The other three women closed around her. Like poppy petals in the wind, she thought crazily.

"It's something I overheard Melanie say when she left the Refuge yesterday morning."

"What she say?" Peanuts demanded.

"She said, or at least I thought I heard her say, that Andy was going to kill her."

"Andy?" Miss Bobbie seemed especially surprised. "He not going to kill her. He her daddy."

"Daddy?" It was Mary Helen's turn to be surprised. "Andy is her father? I thought someone said that he was her pimp."

Geraldine gave her a pitying look. "That what they call they pimps, honey. They calls them Daddy. He take care of her, feed her, give her clothes and a place to live."

Mary Helen nodded. "I see," she said, although she knew she'd never really understand. "And how does a girl get a pimp? Does he choose her?"

"Sure," Peanuts said with a harsh laugh, "after you pay him a choosing fee."

"You pay him to choose you?" Mary Helen hoped she didn't sound too astonished. "How much?"

A look shot among the women. Miss Bobbie spoke. "For Andy—about five hundred dollars," she said.

Sister Mary Helen sucked in her breath. "Do you think he killed her?" She returned to her original question. "He did beat her up pretty badly. I saw her face and her eye."

Miss Bobbie tucked a piece of loose hair back into her tight French braid and seemed to be considering how best to answer the question. "Andy her daddy," she explained. "He whip her to keep her in line, but he don't kill her."

The two other women nodded in agreement. "If he want her dead," Peanuts said, "he'd get a stable sister to do it."

"A stable sister?" Although its meaning was not very hard to guess, Mary Helen had never heard the expression.

Geraldine looked at her as though she were nearly hopeless. "One of his other girls," she explained in the same voice one uses talking to a slow but lovable child.

"And do you think it's possible that he did that? That he asked one of the other girls to kill Melanie?"

"It be possible," Peanuts said.

"Anything be possible, girlfriend," Miss Bobbie added.

"What would be his motive," Mary Helen asked, "his reason for wanting her dead? If she was making money for him, it doesn't make much sense."

Geraldine shrugged her heavy shoulders. "I don't mean no disrespect, Sister," she said, "but the only person it got to make sense to is the killer. Ain't that right?"

"Now, there's the truth," Miss Bobbie added for emphasis.

And Sister Mary Helen couldn't help but agree.

Geraldine stood by the front door of the Refuge and drew in great deep breaths of fresh air. Was that a whiff of salt she smelled? Sure enough!

Although the sky was still cloudless and a well-scrubbed blue, the fog must be starting to pile up at the Golden Gate. Later in the afternoon, it would roll in and slowly cool off the city.

Good! Geraldine thought as an unexpected breeze ruffled her short graying hair. Walking up Ninth Avenue toward Market Street, she ran her tongue over her toothless gums. Geraldine enjoyed the sunny days as much as anybody, but she wanted her nights cool for sleeping.

For some reason today she felt exceptionally tired. Should she ride the Muni home? she wondered, rummaging in her jacket pocket for change. No, exercise would be better for her. She'd had too much sitting and talking with them nuns.

Not that I don't like nuns, Geraldine fussed. *I do. Especially them old ones with the soft, mushy white faces. But they sure can ask a lot of stupid questions. Like that new one. Yes, ma'am! How could anyone live that long,* she wondered, *and not know the ways of the world?*

Geraldine shook her head wearily. And all that business about Miss Betsy knowing Amanda and Dickie—peculiar name for a grown man—where would that all lead?

The crowd thickened as Geraldine drew closer to Market Street. She clutched her purse tight to her side. You can't be too careful.

She was so lost in her own thoughts that she didn't notice Venus until she had nearly bumped into her.

"What you doing, Genie?" Venus asked.

Her voice had a sharpness to it that got on Geraldine's nerves. Not that Venus meant any harm. She didn't. *It weren't her fault,* Geraldine reminded herself, *if her mama didn't raise her right.*

"What you doing, Venus?" Geraldine watched Venus grasp her stomach as though she was in pain. The color drained from the young woman's thin face.

"What's the matter with you, girl? You hungry?" Geraldine asked, wondering if they shouldn't sit down on the curb. She didn't want Venus to fall over right here on the street.

Venus didn't say anything. She just shook her head.

Several people walked around them, never looking directly at them. One woman who did quickened her pace and grabbed her little daughter's hand—as if they might give the child some awful disease.

No wonder, Geraldine thought, studying Venus closely. The girl's greased hair stood up like little black tuffs of broccoli all over her head. And she'd tied a long red scarf around her forehead like a do rag. The ends flowed down and touched her bare shoulder. Her blouse tails, tied in a big knot, left her skinny midriff exposed, and her black leather skirt was short and tight. Oh, Lordy! The heels on her shoes were so high that the calves of her legs were in knots.

Obviously unaware of the other people on the sidewalk, Venus grabbed Geraldine's arm. "What you tell the police that took so long?" she demanded in too loud a voice.

"Stay your nose out of my business," Geraldine wanted to say, but she knew that Venus wouldn't even be insulted. Geraldine set her lips. "I told them the truth."

Venus tightened her grip and moved closer. Geraldine could smell the sour odor of lager on her breath. No telling what Venus would do with a little drink in her. It made her crazy. Geraldine's heart began to thud.

"What the matter with you, girl?" she asked.

"What you tell the police?" Venus's dark eyes were cold.

"The other sisters tell me Melanie gave up some names to you the night before she die."

Geraldine tried to pull away, but Venus's sinewy hand was too tight.

"She didn't make no sense," Geraldine said. "She just rattled off names."

"What names?"

By the time Geraldine finished Melanie's short list, most of the color had returned to Venus's face. She released Geraldine's arm. "She didn't say me?" Venus mumbled with apparent relief.

"Should she be scared of you?" Geraldine asked and immediately knew that she shouldn't have.

Venus stepped so close that Geraldine felt the woman's stinking breath hitting against her cheek. Eyes burning, her thin, dark face twisted into a mean smirk. "Nobody need to be afraid of me, old lady, unless they do me wrong."

Without ever looking back, Venus, her hand on her hip, walked to the corner to look for some business.

Heart still pounding, Geraldine continued toward home. Thank God for Lou. Without him, she might still be on the streets putting up with the likes of Venus! Now she really was tired. Maybe she should take the Muni bus home. She squinted. The nearest bus stop couldn't be too far away. She spotted a sign on the next corner by the Go Go Corner Market.

Who, of all people, was leaning against it eating an apple? Andy! Geraldine's heart fell. Oh, Lordy, she'd had enough for one day!

Even from this distance, Geraldine could tell it was he. Sure enough, his sand-colored Mercedes convertible was parked in the red zone.

Andy stuck out from the rest of the crowd not because he was tall or anything. Actually, he was a short man. What distinguished him was his shiny bald head. The word on the street was that he had shaved it because he thought that made him look like Michael Jordan. Geraldine thought it just made him look silly.

As she approached the corner, Andy pushed himself away from the pole and threw his apple core into the street. As if they weren't dirty enough, she thought. His white silk shirt was open to the waist as if he were from some Caribbean resort instead of from Hunters Point. The split revealed his black, shiny torso. Heavy gold chains hung from his neck, and his one gold front tooth sparkled in the sunlight.

"Hi, Genie. How you doing?" Andy's words dripped with menace, but he didn't scare Geraldine the way that Venus did. He just made her angry. Andy was nothing but a coward, beating on women. She had five or six grown nephews would show him "what for" if he ever tried to touch her. It was not Andy she feared, but those who did his bidding.

"I say, 'Hi, Genie,' " Andy repeated as if she were senile.

"I know what you say," Geraldine snapped back. She wondered what the other people standing at the bus stop were thinking. Most had moved away and were trying to pretend they weren't listening. On the street, several car horns honked at a double-parked UPS truck.

"We need to talk." Andy smiled big, so his ugly gold tooth would twinkle. "Can I give you a ride to your place?"

"Whatever you got to say, you can say here." Geraldine looked around for something to sit on but saw nothing. The store didn't even have a window ledge. Her legs were tired. Maybe she should let him take her home. What harm could it do?

"Then, at least, let's sit in my Mercedes." Andy opened the door on the passenger's side. His face was beginning to tighten. Geraldine knew he was about running out of patience. *Too bad about him*, she thought, but the temptation to sit was too great.

The moment he jumped into the driver's seat, she knew she'd made a mistake. Before she could get out, Andy flipped on the ignition and pulled away from the curb so quickly that her head cracked against the seat back. Geraldine felt fear wash through her like warm water.

"You crazy?" she asked as he pulled into traffic. She felt for the seat belt, but there was none.

Andy leaned toward her and turned up the stereo until the pulse of the music seemed to rock the car. After several blocks, he careened into an alley and braked so fast that Geraldine was thrown against the dashboard.

Turning in his seat, Andy glared at her. Geraldine rubbed her shoulder. Unwanted tears stung her eyes.

"I hear you talking about me to the police." Andy grabbed the back of her neck and forced her to look at him.

"I been talking to the police about Melanie," she said, keeping her voice steady. "What kind of a driver are you, anyhow?" she asked.

Momentarily Andy looked confused. "We talking about the police, old woman!" he shouted.

Geraldine thought for a second that he might slap her. "Watch out what you calls me, if you know what's good for you," she said, her eyes fastened on his. "You just remember Junior Johnson, my little man," she whispered. Even the mention of her nephew Junior frightened most people in the neighborhood. "Junior, he just asked me last week, 'Auntie, could I do something to help you?' I was good to him when he be a little boy," Geraldine said, feeling for the door handle. "But now, he all grown. What goes around comes around, you know."

Andy's eyes grew enormous and he took his hand off her neck. "I didn't kill Melanie. Honest I didn't." He sounded, Geraldine thought, like a whiny child caught in a lie.

"Oh, I know that," Geraldine said. "But I know, too, you could've had it done."

"Why would I do that?"

" 'Cause you be crazy!" With a quick push, Geraldine opened the car door and leaped out. She braced herself, half-expecting to feel the small man's paw on her shoulder, half-hoping that he would hurt her. It would be worth it to have Junior even the score, not only for her but also for Melanie and all the other street sisters that he'd abused.

But even Andy had better sense. A little disappointed, Geraldine turned and slammed the car door as hard as she could. Throwing the convertible into reverse, Andy pulled out of the alley. "Watch your back, old lady!" he shouted as he roared away.

You can count on that, baby, Geraldine thought, hoping the police would question her again. She'd be happy to tell them all that she could about Andy. Slowly she walked to the nearest bus stop. Her legs felt like Jell-O. Fortunately, she spotted the Muni. It was only two blocks away. She hoped it had an empty seat.

🐾🐾

Officers Mark Wong and Brian Dineen decided to start their shift a couple of hours early, hoping to catch sight of Andy. "Giving those Homicide guys a little leg up," Mark said jokingly. But they both knew the real reason. They wanted to find Melanie's killer, and they wanted the pimp to be at the bottom of it.

They had just begun to cruise the area when they spotted a familiar figure weaving up O'Farrell Street.

"Well, look who's back," Dineen said, pointing to a thin woman with bird legs and large, square shoulders.

Immediately Wong recognized the platinum blond hair

teased until it stood out like a helium balloon around her head. "I'll be damned." He whistled softly, "It's good old Olivia, out and about."

"Looks like the streets are back in Sugar," Dineen laughed.

"You mean Candy. If I'm not mistaken, her name is Candy."

Dineen shrugged. "You're right, my man, Milk Chocolate Candy. She's looking a little melted, if you ask me."

With a squeal of tires, Wong pulled the police car over toward the curb. At the sound Olivia began to run. She zig-zagged up the street, bumping shoulders with a woman pushing a shopping cart, knocking a brown paper sack from an old man's hand, and toppling a brimming garbage can.

"She's scared as hell of something," Dineen said, unfolding his large body from the passenger's seat. "She didn't even look to see who it was."

Mark Wong slammed the car door and started up the street after her. "Stop, Olivia!" he shouted. "We just want to ask you a few questions. It's much too hot for this."

His words only made her run faster. *Hell*, he thought, picking up his pace. He watched the platinum hair bobbing through the crowd. They'd catch her eventually. Why did it have to be the hard way?

Olivia darted into the crosswalk against the light. A woman shouted. Truck tires screeched.

"Stop, Olivia, please!" Wong hollered. "This is not worth getting killed over."

Panting now, the woman looked over her shoulder. Before she could turn back, she tripped. Stumbling, she struggled to keep her balance.

Wong winced as he watched her skid headlong onto the concrete. Olivia tried to get up, but the fall had knocked the wind out of her.

"Are you OK?" Wong asked, extending his hand to help her.

Reluctantly she took it, and he pulled her onto her feet. "What the hell do you want?" she asked, examining her skinned knees and the scrapes on the heels of both her hands. "Now look what you made me do. I should sue the whole damn department."

"You need a doctor?" Dineen had caught up to them.

Olivia's brown eyes hardened, and she looked at him with scorn. "I'm a working girl, big guy. I have no time for doctors unless they're paying me."

When she spoke, Wong smelled the sour odor of cheap wine on her breath. In fact, her whole body reeked of it and her clothes smelled musty.

Wong helped her hobble over to the curb. "You want to sit for a minute?" he asked.

"Like some drunk?" Olivia straightened her miniskirt and pulled herself up to her full height. Her head was several inches above Wong's own, and it surprised him. She was so thin that he'd never realized how tall she was.

"What do you want anyway?" Olivia snarled.

"Would you like to sit in the car while we talk?" Wong offered. She must be tired. He was.

"Unless I'm under arrest, how about you ask me what you want to right here?"

A curious crowd was beginning to mill around the trio. "You OK, lady?" a bearded man in a tattered overcoat asked. His hair in dreadlocks, he stared fiercely at the officers.

Chivalry! That's all we need, Wong thought. "We're the police, sir." He showed his badge.

"Then I'd really better keep my eye on the lady," the man slurred. "You think we ain't heard about police brutality?"

"How about a cup of coffee?" Dineen suggested. "We could all use one."

Olivia was trembling now. Whether from the chase or from

116

the fall or from something else entirely Wong wasn't sure. Grudgingly she gave in.

❦❦❦

Sitting in a worn leather booth of a small café, Wong watched Olivia stir six packets of sugar into her coffee. *Poor gal must really have a craving,* he thought.

"What do you want to know?" she asked. "And make it quick. I got places to go."

"To get right to the point," Wong said, cooling his coffee with whatever passed for cream in the silver pitchers at the end of the table, "tell us what you know about Melanie's murder."

Wong watched the color drain from Olivia's face like water from a bathtub. "Nothing!" she shouted angrily. "I know nothing about that little—"

"Ah, ah, it's better not to speak ill of the dead," Dineen cautioned.

"I take it, then, that you didn't like her?" Wong took a sip of the bitter coffee.

"Like her? What's to like? She was a regular little princess, that one. Always whining about something that didn't suit her. Thought she was so cute and so smart. Acted like she was better than the rest of us. But Andy took her down a peg or two. Yes, sirree—" She stopped abruptly as though she'd said too much.

"When did you last see Melanie?" Dineen asked.

"Day before yesterday," Olivia answered nervously.

"Where was that?"

"Here and there," Olivia flip-flopped her skinned hand.

Wong removed some chips of ice from his water glass. "Here, put this on that scrape," he said. "It looks sore."

Olivia's brown eyes narrowed. "Why you being so nice?" she asked.

"We can't help ourselves. We're just nice guys," Dineen said.

Olivia tried not to smile. "Yeah, right," she said, pressing the ice to her hands.

"Can you tell us anything at all about Melanie's death?" Dineen prodded.

Again the color left Olivia's face. Her lips began to tremble. "No!" she shouted. "I don't know nothing."

The waitress behind the counter looked over. "Everything OK?" she asked. Olivia nodded.

Dineen threw a five-dollar bill on the tabletop. "You're not planning to go anywhere soon, are you, Candy?" he asked.

Olivia shook her head. The stiff platinum hair scarcely moved. "Honest, fellas," she whispered, "I don't know nothing." Her voice was earnest, the expression on her face sincere, but her small dark eyes jumped with fear.

❦❦❦❦

"She knows something," Dineen said when the two officers were back in the car.

"She knows lots," Wong agreed, "but who knows about what?" He pulled into the traffic.

"Do you think she knows who killed Melanie?"

Wong shrugged. It was almost impossible to tell. Most prostitutes, especially those who were experienced at it, were very good liars. They needed to be in order to survive. They had to make every john feel special and feed the insatiable egos of their pimps. No matter what.

Once again, Wong felt that tug of sympathy, the one he always felt for prostitutes. In every sense, they were victims, too. Maybe he was in the wrong job.

"You said you talked to Denny Gallagher today?" Dineen interrupted his thoughts.

"Right," Wong said, turning onto Ellis. At the sight of the

police car, an overweight young man in dark glasses walked quickly down the block.

"Drugs or a trick?" Dineen asked, watching the fellow glance nervously over his shoulder.

Mark Wong shrugged. "Maybe both," he said. "Whichever, we spoiled it."

"Anyway, what did Gallagher have to say for himself?"

"Actually, I did most of the talking. I told him about our stopping Melanie last night and about the names she was babbling."

"Yeah?" Dineen took his eyes off the streets. "What do you think about them?"

"I can't get a handle on Amanda, but it's possible that the Betsy-Dick business could have something to do with the Dodds—Elizabeth and Richard."

"*The* Richard Dodd? The governor wannabe?" Dineen laughed aloud. "Did you read this morning's *Chronicle?*"

Wong knew the article to which his partner was referring. It had appeared in this morning's paper, page 1. In it, Dodd was quoted as criticizing the San Francisco Police Department— actually, law enforcement in general—implying that they were soft on crime, even looking the other way. It was a popular position in some quarters, but not, of course, with the city's finest.

"Wouldn't that be something?" Dineen said. "How did Gallagher react?"

"He nearly had a coronary while we were on the phone. You know he's near retirement. Can you imagine what would blow up if the Homicide guys even tried to accuse that particular big political noise of murdering a prostitute? I can hear him hollering, 'Setup!' "

"What would be his motive?" Dineen was thinking aloud, clearly relishing the possibility, however slim.

"Who knows?" Mark said, playing along. "Could be the mysterious Amanda?"

"Wouldn't that beat all! 'Governor Hopeful Murders Woman of the Night.' I can see it on all the tabloids. We'd show him how soft we aren't."

"Couldn't happen to a more deserving guy," Wong said.

His partner was still laughing when a call came in on the radio. The scream of their siren made any more talk impossible.

❧❧❧

When Betsy Dodd pulled her silver Lexus into Presidio Terrace, she was surprised to see her husband's shiny black Jaguar directly in front of her. *He made it home in record time*, she thought, wondering how he was going to attempt to talk himself out of this one.

All the way home she had mentally replayed the telephone conversation with her husband. Usually she'd have ached with shame, guilt, and all those other emotions that tormented her when she found out about his affairs. But not today. Today was different. As the blocks rolled by, taking her from the world of the Refuge to her own upscale world, she felt something out of the ordinary happening. Each time she went over their conversation, instead of the self-hatred she had always felt before, there was a kind of rage. It began like a match flame in the pit of her stomach, then grew and deepened until now her entire insides felt as if they were on fire.

If he only knew what she had planned for him! Betsy pushed a strand of hair back from her forehead. She could hardly wait.

Let him use that smooth innocent act to dig out how much she knew. Well, she knew plenty. She was nobody's fool, despite the fact—or maybe because of the fact—that he treated her like a naive nincompoop.

Her tires squealed as she pulled into the driveway. Thank goodness Rosa's car was gone from the front of the house. The housekeeper, too, had wasted no time in leaving after Betsy had called her from the car phone.

"I hope everything is OK, missus," Rosa had said when she heard the edge on Betsy's voice.

"Everything is fine," Betsy had assured her. *Better than fine*, she thought. With the housekeeper gone there would be nothing or no one to stop her or even to slow her down. She could hardly wait!

The door of their two-car garage opened automatically, and they slid their cars into their respective parking places. Rich was out of the Jaguar first. Sucking on one of those damnable red Tic-tacs, Betsy noticed. Sure sign that, at least, he had the good grace to be nervous. He had no idea!

Without a word he opened her car door and bent in to kiss her. Hoping her face adequately portrayed her disgust, Betsy leaned away from him. "I'm glad you're home," she said coldly. "We need to talk."

Pushing herself off the car's soft seat, she stormed past her husband. "Betsy, baby, please," she heard him whimpering as she walked through their enormous kitchen into the family room and finally into the elaborate formal living room. She hated this room with its pretentious brocade furniture, velvet drapes, ornate crystal-and-gold chandeliers, and expensive art and antiques. It was nothing but an empty show piece. *Just like my husband*, she thought bitterly.

Turning, she faced Rich, who had followed her. A hurt expression played on his strong, honest looking face. He pulled himself up to his full height.

He used to be six-foot-three, Betsy thought cruelly, *but I think he's shrunk.* In the sunlit living room his carefully styled dark hair was scarcely graying, thanks to his expensive hair colorist,

Renee. His deep blue eyes stared at her through contact lenses, and his fine athletic looking tan was the work of the sunlamp.

Everything about Rich was actually for show, Betsy thought with disgust. He and this living room were made for each other. This was the perfect spot for a confrontation.

As he had done so many times before, Rich threw open his arms. "Betsy, sweetheart," he began, but Betsy was ready for him.

"Don't you dare try to sweet-talk me!" she shouted, backing away from him. "And don't you dare try to touch me."

"What is it, sweetheart? What did I do?"

"Oh, please, Rich! Don't play me for a fool. Or should I call you Dickie?" She watched with satisfaction as his tan face took on a yellowish tinge.

"Dickie?" He struggled to sound genuinely curious. "Where did you get Dickie?"

"You know damn well where I got Dickie! That's what that . . . that whore called you!"

Her words ricocheted in the still room. Outside, a dog yipped. Betsy heard a foghorn bleating in the distance. Already whiffs of fog were rolling in from the Golden Gate, sending odd shadows skittering across the Persian rug.

Rich collapsed into one of the brocade chairs, his head bowed as though he had been struck. "Don't, Betsy," he whispered.

She recognized the all-too-familiar act. This was where she was supposed to think she was wrong, to feel sorry for falsely accusing him. No more! She'd had enough.

"Look at me when I'm talking to you!" she shouted, and, grabbing his stiff hair, jerked up his head.

For the first time in a long time, Betsy thought she saw a genuine emotion in her husband's too-blue eyes. Interestingly enough, it was surprise. *Good,* she thought. *Since I have several more surprises in store for you, Dickie-boy.*

She watched, almost amused, as he pulled himself together. It didn't take long. He had this act perfected, and he had confidence. Why not? It had worked on her so many times before.

"What are you talking about?" he asked incredulously.

Ignoring him, Betsy walked to the liquor cabinet and took out two crystal glasses. In each she poured half an inch of Rich's best Scotch, a gift from some grateful client, no doubt. She added ice cubes.

"What are you doing?" he asked as she handed him a glass and a fancy cocktail napkin.

She must do this right. "Here's to us," she said, raising her own glass. "Adios!"

"What do you mean, 'adios'?" He sat up now.

"What's the matter, Dickie? You don't speak any Spanish? That's not what your press releases say. Your Hispanic supporters will be very disappointed." Betsy sipped her drink. The strong, burned taste of the Scotch caught in her throat and almost made her cough.

"What the hell has gotten into you, Betsy?" Rich rose from his chair, towering over her.

She saw the familiar irritation dance across his face. It was a look she knew too well, one she expected, one to which she had become too accustomed. *The act is almost over,* Betsy thought, relieved. Soon they'd get down to the raw truth.

"What's gotten into me, Dickie . . ." She twirled the liquor in her glass.

"Stop that!" he shouted, his face reddening.

"Stop what?" Deliberately she fluttered her eyelids.

"You know exactly what I mean, Betsy. That 'Dickie' crap."

"Sor-ry," she said, pulling out both syllables. "I guess you can only be called Dickie by whores and cute little paralegals named Amanda. Or are they one and the same? Tell me, Dickie, is she thin and blond? Sexy goes without saying, and young enough to be your daughter, naturally. They all are. Have you noticed a pattern, Dickie?" she taunted.

"Don't talk like an ass," Rich snapped.

Betsy laughed. She could feel the effects of the drink. "I've been an ass for years, Dickie bird. Through one, two, three, or is it more like seven affairs? Each time I believed you when you said you were sorry. When you said I was the only one you really loved." Her voice cracked.

Rich seized the moment and tried to put his arms around her.

Without thinking, Betsy threw her drink in his face. He gasped. Giggling, she watched the Scotch drip from his stiff hair and off the end of his patrician nose and run down the collar of his silk shirt.

"You bitch!" he shouted. With his free hand he grabbed for her wrist.

Betsy stepped back before he could touch her.

"You fat, dumb, dumpy bitch!" he shouted, his face flaming. "Did you ever wonder why I'm unfaithful?"

Betsy prepared herself for the awful hurt and self-doubt his cruelty usually caused. But her own fury had taken its place and seemed to protect her heart like a suit of armor. She felt no pain. In fact, she wanted to roar with laughter at the sight of Rich dabbing at his face with a soggy cocktail napkin.

"You're unfaithful because you have no self-control?" she said. "Or maybe because you have a poor self-image and your little sweeties make you think you're important?"

He was seething. She could tell by his blazing eyes and the tight set of his jaw. Now was the time for her final one-two.

"I'm leaving you, Rich. No more chances. No more talk. No more dutiful wife. I simply don't love you anymore, because there's absolutely nothing but an empty shell left to love."

She watched his eyes widen and his lips, the lips she'd once found so irresistible, flap like a beached fish.

"And one other thing." Her voice was steady now and she felt a surge of power. "I told those Homicide detectives, the ones you think are soft on crime, the ones who questioned me today, everything I know about you and about your knowing Melanie and Amanda. And, oh yes, I told them that I was a little late meeting you at the apartment and I have no idea what you were up to before I arrived."

All at once, Betsy saw an odd look cross her husband's face, one she hadn't seen before, one she couldn't really name. He stared at her in disbelief. A chill ran through her entire body. Her heart thudded. Despite the heat in the room, she was shivering. The bile rose in her throat just as it had at the Refuge.

Betsy struggled to keep her voice steady. "And if anyone needs me," she said quickly, "I'm spending the night with my sister Ginger."

❧❧❧

"Let's pack it in, Katie-girl," Inspector Dennis Gallagher mumbled. "I'm bushed."

Kate Murphy nodded. "Me, too, partner," she said. "We've questioned so many people that even *my* tongue is tired."

She ran her fingers through her red hair. It was getting long. Maybe this weekend she'd take the time for a trim. *It must be nice to be bald like Gallagher,* she thought, glancing over at her partner.

Kate was shocked at how pale and drawn his face was. Funny how you could work with someone all day long and never really notice how he looked.

"You feeling OK?" Kate asked, trying not to sound too solicitous. Gallagher had berated her on several occasions for treating him like a four-year-old. Occupational hazard, she thought.

"Considering my age and condition, I'm on top of the world," he joked.

While Gallagher went into the main room of the Refuge to tell the nuns that they were free to go, Kate cleaned up the sleep area. He returned just as she was finishing.

"Let's go," he said. "That young nun will lock up, and your friend looks like she wants to talk."

"Maybe we should let her," Kate said.

"And maybe we should put our heads in the paper shredder, too, but it doesn't sound like a good idea to me."

"I fail to see the connection," Kate said, following him out of the room and out the side door of the building.

Dark stains speckled the corner of the side entrance where Melanie's body had been found. A thick yellow plastic band cordoned off the area, and remnants of powder remained on the door frame where the Forensics team had dusted in hopes of finding fingerprints. Other than that the street was deserted.

There's not a single soul around," Kate said, checking to see that the door closed behind them.

"Look at the time," Gallagher remarked. "Four-thirty. By now most people who hang out in this neighborhood are standing in a dinner line somewhere."

Kate's heart dropped. For the hundredth time that day, she was overwhelmed with her own good fortune. After work she would pick up her son from a kind, loving baby-sitter and when they arrived home Jack would have a nice hot meal in the works. Or, at least, he'd have figured out something. One was never quite sure when it was her husband's turn to cook just how he'd manage. But what she'd heard and seen today made her once again swear she'd never complain again about Chinese takeout.

The police car had been parked in a red zone all day, and the inside was hot and stuffy. It didn't take much to convince

Gallagher to stop at one of the fancy coffee shops that had mushroomed south of Market. Reluctantly he let her talk him into iced cappuccino.

"What's wrong with plain hot coffee?" he groused. "It was good enough for generations of San Franciscans. Remember the old Hills Brothers factory and how good it smelled?"

"My treat," Kate said, knowing he'd complain about the price, too. Slowly she maneuvered the car through the heavy traffic made up almost entirely of commuters heading for the Bay Bridge and their homes in the East Bay.

"Look at that." Gallagher pointed to a sign advertising Luxury Lofts for sale. "Can you imagine paying money to live in one of these old factories?"

"Lots of people are doing it," Kate said. She waited patiently for a group of Japanese tourists to cross in the middle of the street. They were probably on their way to the San Francisco Museum of Modern Art or to one of the discount shopping centers close by.

This whole area south of Market had once been industrial. Recently the district had become known as SoMa and was San Francisco's version of Soho in New York City, with hip galleries, nightclubs, and restaurants.

Kate pulled into the first place she could find with both a coffee sign in its window and a parking lot by its side.

When the waitress served the glass cups, Gallagher picked his up immediately and with a quick, "Cheers," took a large swallow. He seemed to be enjoying it.

"You've got a mustache," Kate said, then stopped herself before she reached over to wipe his mouth. She felt her face flush. It was that occupational hazard of being a four-year-old's mother, again.

Happily, Gallagher seemed not to notice. He took another gulp of his cappuccino. "Not bad," he said, "for cold coffee."

"Do you want to go over it today?" Kate asked. "Or are you too tired?"

"What's all this about being tired?" Gallagher frowned "I'm ready for retirement, all right, but I'm not ready for a retirement home yet."

"Sorry," Kate said quickly. She knew there was no sense reminding him that he was the one who had said he was bushed. "I take it that means you want to talk now?"

"Why not do it while it's fresh?" Gallagher pulled the notebook from his jacket pocket and flipped it open. Then he loosened his tie, a familiar sign to Kate that he was ready to begin.

"First of all, the body." He studied her. "What was your take?"

Kate's stomach jolted at the memory of that frail young woman with her skull crushed, then dumped like garbage in a doorway. "The perp had to be strong to crush her skull with whatever it was—the medical examiner should know by tomorrow."

"A man then, you'd guess?" Gallagher caught the waitress's eye and raised his fingers for another round of iced cappuccino.

"Let's not be gender-biased," Kate said. "It could be a woman who was strong or in the heat of passion."

"Agreed," Gallagher said, sounding like a cop show.

"What did you get from the ladies?" Kate took a sip of the cold coffee.

"Venus," Gallagher checked his notes. "Venus, aka Lois Williams, was highly agitated, but I'd say it was more from a night of heroin than from what she knows about the murder."

"I got the impression that this Andy might be her pimp, too," Kate said.

"Long time ago. Now she runs with Junior Johnson, who she claims, you remember, could make dog food out of our man Andy. Last name Smith."

Gallagher ran his hand over his bald head. "What about the names Geraldine gave us—the one she claims Melanie was spouting?"

"Andy, Olivia, Amanda, Dickie, Betsy." Kate took another swallow of her coffee. "No last names, you noticed."

"And your friend Mary Helen?"

"*Our* friend," Kate corrected.

Gallagher scowled but went on. "She gave us the same names. Of course, she got them from Geraldine."

"Right," Kate agreed.

"What makes me nervous—" Gallagher stopped to take another gulp of his drink. "You know, this stuff is not too bad." He smiled at Kate.

"What makes you nervous?" Kate asked. "Besides all that jolt from the caffeine you're practically inhaling?" she wanted to add.

"Mark Wong from Vice, when I talked to him this morning, he quoted the same names, then made a rather odd connection. For some reason he thought that the Dick and Betsy could be the Dodds."

"You didn't tell me that."

"We've been busy. Besides, I was hoping it might go away." His watery blue eyes locked on hers. "Have you any idea how hot a case that would be? Trying to connect Mr. Big-Time Attorney to a dead prostitute?"

Kate wanted to laugh. "Especially after this morning. Did you have a chance to read the *Chronicle?*"

Gallagher shook his head.

"Mr. Dodd came out with a statement that he thought the SFPD was soft on crime and that the Vice Squad sometimes looked the other way."

Gallagher groaned. "Wong never mentioned that. So if we go after him it looks like we're doing it to retaliate." He ran a finger around the collar of the shirt. "Never mind. I got a feeling it's that pimp, Andy Smith. He is the logical one. And Wong said that they arrested him last night, but he was out in plenty of time to kill Melanie."

"Maybe he thought she fingered him," Kate said.

"Maybe. And let's not forget Olivia and Amanda, whoever the hell they are." Gallagher wiped his mouth with a small napkin. "What did you think of Mrs. Betsy Dodd?" he asked.

Kate Murphy twirled one strand of hair around her index finger. "Mrs. Betsy Dodd." She pictured the slightly overweight woman with her thick black hair and her hurt eyes. "She was hard to read," Kate said. "Something was bothering her. She's probably never been anywhere near a murder scene before. In all fairness, few people have. But there seemed to be something else bothering her, too. Did you notice how vague she was about the time she met her husband last night? It was as if she was deliberately not giving him an alibi. I have a feeling everything is not perfect in paradise."

"I wonder what she's telling him tonight?"

"I'll bet plenty," Kate said. "We're likely to hear from him first thing tomorrow."

Dennis Gallagher moaned. "And I thought this one would solve itself! Pimp for perp—over in twenty-four hours."

"You still might be right," Kate said. "The medical examiner or Forensics might come up with something." She grinned. "What about Sister Anne?"

Gallagher rolled his eyes. "She's no Mary Helen," he said. "Not that I'm complaining. It's nice to find a nun who doesn't try to do your business for you. What I'm afraid of is that she won't stay that way." Gallagher drained his glass.

"Will there be anything else?" the waitress asked.

Gallagher looked at Kate, who shook her head.

Gallagher grabbed the check before Kate could. She cringed

as she watched his cheeks flush. He glared at her. "For crissake, Katie-girl, all we wanted was a couple of cups of cold coffee. I never intended to buy Juan Carlos and his damn mule!"

❧❧❧❧

Richard Dodd felt numb all over. *And why shouldn't I?* he thought, draining his Scotch glass for the fourth time, or was it the fifth? *Whichever,* he sniffed noisily. *I might as well be drunk as the way I am,* he thought, then laughed aloud at the old saw.

Shadows darkened the ornate living room where he still sat. Actually, he hadn't moved at all since Betsy stormed out of the room, except to refill his glass.

He glanced around. The motion made him a little light-headed. *My favorite room,* he gloated, *my showplace.*

Yet in this light the gilt furnishings took on a dull look and the heavy drapes bulged as though intruders might be hiding behind them, waiting to pounce.

The grandfather clock in the hallway struck the half hour, startling him. The deep *bong* echoed in the entry, then fell silent. Quickly the stillness filled the living room, then seemed to spread to the entire house. The only sound Rich heard was the wail of a siren in the far distance. It was eerie.

Rich shivered and heaved himself up from the brocade chair. He had sat there for such a long time because he was trying to figure things out, make a plan. But he couldn't get past the terrible anger that seemed to pump through him and thud in his head.

Weaving his way across the living room, Rich felt the soft carpet under his feet. He leaned against the bar and refilled his glass. One finger, two fingers—without warning the glass slipped from his grasp. It bounced on the Persian rug, spilling out liquor and ice.

131

Swearing, Rich kicked the ice cubes away from the front of the bar and took another glass. Holding it steady, he poured himself a drink.

Rosa can clean that up tomorrow, he thought, making his shaky way back to the chair. *She doesn't do much for her money anyway, if you ask me.* He'd tell Betsy so, too, the moment she came back. *And she will be back*, he thought. *She'll come to her senses.*

Feeling very sorry for himself, Rich took a sip of his drink. The burning taste seemed to rekindle the wrath and it roared back. Good! It felt better than being sad.

And he had every right to be angry, enraged actually. Betsy leaving like that. Oh, she'd be back. He was sure of that. Where would she go? Ginger's was only good for a day or two. She wouldn't want her friends to know. Besides, why wouldn't she come back here? She had it made.

I give her everything she wants, nice clothes, expensive jewelry, fancy vacations, a woman to help with the cleaning, and look at this house! He studied the crystal-and-gold chandelier, which seemed to be spinning. *Just an illusion*, he thought, closing his eyes.

All I ever wanted in return was a little understanding, a little patience, for godssake. He sniffed again. None of this was his fault. If Betsy had been a little more interesting, a little more exciting, a little more provocative, this never would have happened! He slammed his fist against the arm of the chair and watched the dust rise.

That damn Rosa can't even keep my favorite room clean. He wagged his head, then stopped immediately and waited for the room to quit spinning.

What had he got out of this marriage after all he'd brought to it? Not a loving wife, not his needs satisfied, not even a clean house to come home to.

Rich felt the anger gripping his throat and with it a strong, deep coldness. *The nerve of the dumb, fat bitch*, he thought, his jaw tightening. *Pulling my hair, asking me about my self-concept, threatening me with the police. Who does she think she is? Without me she'd be a nobody, a nothing, a zilch! Did she ever think of that, stupid bitch?*

She was lucky he was as faithful as he was. Lots of young, attractive women threw themselves at him. He could have had a dozen more if he wanted.

Like the beautiful, shapely Amanda, he thought. He pictured her in his office this afternoon—her slim waist, her firm breasts, her soft blond hair.

Rich's eyes burned. He closed them and slowly drifted off. At first, he didn't recognize the sound. It took two rings before he realized that it was the front door chime he was hearing.

Aha, he gloated, moving slowly from his chair. Betsy was back. He knew it. Not even gone overnight and back already. *She knows which side her bread is buttered on*, he thought. *And the stupid bitch forgot her key. Just like her. She can't even leave me right.*

Rich swung open the door. "Guess who?" he said, then bit back the rest of the sarcasm. It wasn't Betsy at all. It was Amanda. At the sight of her, panic churned up his insides. But why? He was home alone. His wife had conveniently left him. "Come in, Amanda," he said, running his fingers through his thick hair. He hoped his eyes weren't too bloodshot. "What a nice surprise. I was just having a drink. Let me fix you one, too."

Amanda fit right into the elegance of the living room. Seated comfortably in one of the brocade chairs, her long, shapely legs crossed, she seemed to be studying him.

"What can I get you?" Rich asked. More awake now, he fought down a tickle of apprehension. Why had she come to his home? None of his other lady friends had ever come to his home. What did she want?

"A gin and tonic would be splendid," she said with the demeanor of a queen at court.

Rich felt his shoulders tense as he mixed her drink. While he was up, he might as well freshen his own. What was this all about? Better not to ask. Better to wait until she told him.

It didn't take her long. Amanda raised her glass. "Cheers!" she said and took two deep swallows. Obviously she was watering her courage. She smiled sweetly, but Rich noticed that the smile didn't quite reach those large blue eyes, which suddenly appeared as hard as glass.

"I'll bet you're wondering what I'm doing here," she began playfully.

Rich nodded. For a moment, his head spun.

"I've been giving my position a lot of thought," she said, fluttering her eyelids, "and I think I would be of much more value to the firm if I was given a promotion."

Rich heard the words, but it took a few minutes for their meaning to penetrate his protective Scotch haze. "And just what would you like to be promoted to?" he asked at last.

"Like I said, I've given this a lot of thought." Amanda played with a piece of her long blond hair.

The chill of cold anger gripped Rich's chest. He threw back his drink for warmth, then rose and stepped over to the bar. Slowly, carefully, he poured himself another. He sensed rather than saw Amanda behind him. He smelled a gash of White Linen, her cologne. She put her slender arms around his waist, and he felt her warm breath on his ear.

"I think I'd be perfect as your administrative assistant," she said.

"Administrative assistant!" Rich's laugh sounded like a bark. "I have Catherine."

"Catherine is your secretary, Dickie," Amanda corrected. "I could have a new title. That way we'd always have an excuse to be together and we could still keep Catherine to do the work."

Cunning little bitch, Rich thought, turning to face her. "We need to talk," he said, returning to his chair. His legs felt wobbly.

Amanda stood over him. "We *are* talking, Dickie. At least, I'm talking, and what I want is a promotion." Her tone softened. "You need an administrative assistant. Someone to keep you current. Someone who can talk to the police about things like murders. . . ." She let the last word dangle so that not even a moron could miss her meaning.

"You don't think I—" he stopped, straining now to sound civil. "I had anything to do with that homeless woman's murder, do you? I just wanted to avoid any unnecessary complications." He could hear the wheedling in his own voice and hated her for it.

"Administrative assistants don't think," she said. "They just do what they're paid to do." She gave him a knowing smile.

Scheming bitch, Rich thought furiously. He'd like to reach over and twist the smile from her face, watch those eyes grow rounder with shock and fear.

"What's the matter, Dickie?" she taunted. "Cat got your tongue?" She turned and sauntered toward the bar.

Unable to control himself any longer, Rich launched from his chair. He stumbled and his glass sailed ahead of him and hit like an explosion against the hardwood floor. Ragged shards of glass flew in all directions.

"My leg!" Amanda shrieked.

Rich looked down. Blood spurted from Amanda's calf where a piece of glass had cut her. "Let me get you a wet rag," he said, not knowing exactly where to find one. He probably should take her to the emergency room at St. Mary's Hospital. But there was no telling who would see them there.

"Leave me alone! You've done enough!" Amanda shouted, grabbing a napkin from the bar and pressing it over the bleeding cut.

"Do you think you need stitches?" Rich asked helplessly. "What can I do for you?"

Amanda glared. "A promotion, Dickie-baby! That's what I want. And a substantial raise." She threw the last few words over her shoulder as she ran from the room.

Oddly, Rich was relieved to hear his front door slam. What was happening to him? First Betsy betrayed him, now Amanda. He didn't deserve this. He kicked furiously at the broken glass. This wasn't right! He'd fix it! He'd show them!

"Who do you think you're playing with, sweethearts?" he roared, his words reverberating off the white walls. "You'll be sorry, ladies. You'll be very sorry that you ever messed with Richard Dodd!"

He stumbled back to his chair. He felt the tears forcing their way into his eyes. "Yes, ma'am, you'll be very sorry," he whimpered, "that you ever messed with Dickie."

❧❦❧

When Kate Murphy arrived home with her son, John, thick fog already hung over the Pacific just waiting to roll down Geary Boulevard. *San Francisco's automatic air conditioner*, she thought.

After making an illegal U-turn in the middle of the wide street, she parked in front of their yellow peaked-roof house expecting to see Jack's car. Instead, in front of the house was a familiar blue Ford Escort that belonged to her mother-in-law.

Little John recognized the car immediately. "Nonie, Nonie!" he squealed, eager to run inside to his grandmother.

Kate's heart dropped as she watched her child scamper up

136

the steps. The front door swung open, and he flung himself into the waiting arms of Mama Bassetti.

Although Kate genuinely loved her mother-in-law and appreciated all she did for them, a little of Loretta Bassetti went a long way, especially after a hot, tiring day. Kate took her time locking the car doors, trying to regain her composure.

"Come in! Come in!" Mama Bassetti called. "You look all washed out. I've got your ice and vodka in the glass already. Just need to pour the tonic."

"Where's Jack?" Kate asked, forcing herself to smile. Mounting the front steps, she wondered how many of the neighbors had heard she was about to have a vodka tonic. Would they think that she was such an alcoholic that she couldn't even wait to mix the drink when she went into the house? *Nuts! Who cares what the neighbors think?* she told herself, shutting the door behind her.

The delicious aromas of garlic and onions and of Italian pot roast beef and roasting potatoes filled the house and made Kate's mouth water. Suddenly she was starving.

After giving John a final hug, Mama Bassetti went into the kitchen and came back with Kate's drink, juice for John, and an old-fashioned for herself.

"Let's sit and enjoy," she said, sinking into the front room sofa.

"Jack?" Kate asked again, fighting down the anxiety a policeman's wife can't help but feel when he isn't home on time, especially when the policeman's wife is a policeperson, too.

For a moment Mama Bassetti looked puzzled, as though she couldn't remember exactly who Jack was. "Oh, Jackie," she said with a shrug of her heavy shoulders. "He should be home any minute now. In fact, when I heard the car pull up, I thought it might be him."

"Why isn't he home?" Kate felt a sudden panic. Ever since her husband had been shot by a desperate rapist, she'd had to wrestle with the fear of its happening again.

"Everything is fine," her mother-in-law said quickly. She must have sensed what Kate was thinking. "He was finishing some paperwork when I called him. I asked him whose turn it was to make dinner and it took him a couple of minutes to figure out it was his. Can you imagine?"

Kate could well imagine, although he was getting better.

"Anyway, Jackie said he'd figure out something. Some take-out or another—probably Chinese." She reached over and ran her fingers through John's curly blond hair. "I can't imagine my little angel having another meal out of a cardboard box! I said to him, 'Jackie, I know I raised you better than that. Do you remember me ever serving your papa or you kids dinner from a cardboard box? No. Everything was fresh—good fresh vegetables, meat that went from the butcher shop into the oven. Bread, fresh every day.' "

Loretta Bassetti took a sip of her old-fashioned, fished out the maraschino cherry, and popped it into her mouth. "Anyway, you never know what's in those boxes or how long it's been there. My neighbor, Mrs. Ryan, told me about a friend of hers who's still in the hospital from getting food poisoning at a chicken takeout place. With that fried chicken stuff, I can't even tell which piece is which. If you ask me, Kate, there is something wrong with a chicken when you can't tell its thigh from its breast."

John giggled into his juice. Kate wasn't sure what had struck him funny. It was hard to tell with a four-year-old. "Don't spill," she cautioned him as the juice bubbled up in the glass.

Mama Bassetti smiled lovingly at her only grandchild as though he could do no wrong. And the juice bubbled even higher.

"Anyway," her mother-in-law continued before Kate could say anything else, "they were having a big sale on roast at Twenty-second and Irving. 'Go pick some up,' I say.

" 'Ma,' he says, 'who do you think I am? Superman? I'd have to leap tall buildings to get from the Hall of Justice to Twenty-second and Irving and out to Geary and put the roast in the oven in time for dinner.'

" 'I'm your mother,' I say. 'I know you're not Superman. But I have an idea. Let me go out and pick one up for you. I'll have it on in plenty of time. Thank God I have that emergency key.'

" 'That's for emergencies,' my son says in that tone of voice that made me want to swat him when he was a teenager.

"'What can be more of an emergency than my grandson eating out of a cardboard box?' I ask him.

"He laughs and mumbles something I didn't care to hear, so here I am."

Kate had finished her drink. "Shall I set the table?" she asked.

"It's done." Mama Bassetti looked pleased with herself.

"How about another short one?" Kate walked toward the kitchen, curious to see how many places were set. Only three.

"I've had enough, thanks," Mama Bassetti said.

"Aren't you staying for dinner?" Kate called from the kitchen. She hoped she sounded disappointed. "After all, you did all the work."

"No, thank you." Loretta Bassetti sounded happy to have been asked. "Your little family should be together."

Kate felt her hackles rise. Why did that expression, "little family," rile her so? Was it because it made them sound as if they had not quite arrived yet or they fell short of something?

"You're more than welcome," Kate said, hoping she didn't sound irritated. When she walked back into the living room her mother-in-law was putting on her coat and slipping John a candy bar.

"For dessert," she said, giving him a noisy kiss.

When Jack pulled up in front of the house, the roast was cooked to perfection. The meal was so savory and delicious that Kate and Jack had only good things to say about Mama Bassetti. They even proposed a toast to her with glasses of Chianti.

During dinner little John kept them entertained with stories about his day with Sheila, the baby-sitter, and his pal Jordie, who was disenchanted with his new baby-sister. It seems she cried a lot and spit up carrots all over the place. At least he was off that, "I want a baby, too," kick, Kate thought, relieved, for the time being anyway.

While John watched his favorite program, *Wheel of Fortune*, Kate and Jack cleaned up.

"I hear you found a young prostitute today," Jack said, rinsing the last of the dishes while Kate stacked them in the dishwasher.

"Yeah," she said, "and guess who might be involved? We think Richard Dodd."

Jack stopped scrubbing the roasting pan and stared at her. "You're kidding," he said. "That stuffed shirt was the talk of the Hall today. His statement in this morning's *Chron* has everyone from the chief to Parking up in arms. Wouldn't that be something like poetic justice if our boy was having it on with a hooker!" Jack let out a hoot.

"What's funny, Dad?" John called from the living room.

"Your mother said something funny." Jack looked sheepishly at Kate. "Sorry," he whispered. "You're faster on your feet."

"What did you say, Mom?" He wasn't going to let it go.

"It was a grown-up joke," Kate said, unable to think of anything else.

"Like Nonie saying that she couldn't tell a thigh from a

breast? When Jordie said 'breast' Sheila said it was a grown-up word."

"Kind of like that," Kate said.

Jack stared at her. "What?" he asked.

Kate explained his mother's tirade about the chicken. "What else do you think he's learning at the baby-sitter's?" she asked.

"Beats me," Jack said, "but I'll bet he'll tell us." Wiping his hands on the towel, Jack refilled both their wineglasses. They sat back down at the kitchen table.

"How did Gallagher react to the Dodd connection?" Jack wondered.

"He nearly had a coronary, especially when Mark Wong from Vice suggested the same thing." Kate twirled the stem of her glass. "You know, Jack, I'm a little worried about Denny. At the end of today, when I finally had time to really look at him, his coloring was horrible. I'm afraid there might be something wrong."

"You know, now that you mention it, a couple of other guys at work have said something like that." Jack ran his fingers through his thick dark hair. "I didn't give it much thought. Gallagher seems immortal."

"No one is immortal, pal, and he's getting up there. He can hardly wait until retirement."

"Could you say something to him? Suggest he gets a doctor's appointment? You are his partner as well as his friend. You seem like the logical one."

"Already he thinks I treat him like a four-year-old."

Jack laughed. "Don't tell me you cut his meat."

"I'm not that bad," Kate said, her thoughts still on Dennis Gallagher. His coloring wasn't good, and he looked unusually tired. Jack was right. She was the logical person to suggest that he make a doctor's appointment.

Kate grinned at her husband. "You know, don't you, pal, that suggesting Denny should see a doctor is going to make suggesting Richard Dodd is a murderer seem like a piece of cake?"

They both laughed.

"Mom," little John called from the living room, "are you telling Dad another grown-up joke?"

❧❧❧

"Looks like everyone's gone, at last," Sister Anne sighed and turned off the bank of lights in the gathering room of the Refuge.

Sister Mary Helen rose slowly from her chair. The waning sun shone through the transoms, and specks of dust twirled in its beams. *This must be what they mean when they say "waiting for the dust to settle,"* she thought for no good reason. Mary Helen cleared her throat. This was one of the many times she was glad that people weren't able to read her mind.

With all that had happened today, she should be thinking deep, profound thoughts, but she was too tired. Even her legs felt leaden, and she'd hardly been on them all day. She must be getting old.

"Are we almost ready to go?" she asked, watching Anne check doors and windows and alarms.

"I'm dead!" Anne said in answer to her question.

Suddenly Mary Helen felt better. Perhaps it wasn't age after all. Perhaps it was the stress of the day. Admit it or not, the day had been extremely stressful.

Outside, a cool breeze had started up. As Anne double-checked the front door, Mary Helen looked up and down the nearly deserted sidewalk. Only one man, pushing a double cart full of plastic sacks and aluminum cans, was visible. The street, however, was another story. It was crowded with cars of every

142

make and size rushing down Eighth Street toward an on-ramp to the James Lick Freeway, a feeder to the Bay Bridge. Other cars were undoubtedly on their way to Highway 101, which led to the international airport and to the small cities on the peninsula. Serious bike riders with helmets darted in and out of the traffic.

Mary Helen was glad that Anne and she had only a few miles of city streets to drive to get home. She yawned. Maybe they could get in a short nap before supper. Although what they really needed to do before supper was decide exactly how much of today's adventure they were going to tell at the table.

She handed Anne the keys to the convent car. Thank goodness Anne liked to drive and traffic-crowded streets didn't seem to bother her. Actually, she seemed challenged.

They crossed Market Street and were on Larkin passing the City Hall with its magnificent gold dome before Mary Helen spoke.

"About tonight, at home," she began cautiously, "I don't know how much we should tell—not that we'd lie about anything, if asked directly," she added, unsure of just how delicate Anne's conscience was.

"Funny, I was thinking about the same thing," Anne said brightly. "You know Therese will have a hissy fit if you're involved in another murder." She glanced over at Mary Helen and must have noticed her face flush. "Not that it's your fault," she added quickly.

"Indeed not," Mary Helen said, trying to calm herself. After all, Anne meant well. Age and experience would make her a little more prudent in the way she put things. Not that they had done much for Sister Therese, which was neither here nor there.

Anne was saying something about Sister Patricia.

"Pardon me," Mary Helen said, hoping that Anne wouldn't

think she was losing her hearing. She'd just been too preoccupied to listen.

"I said that we have no idea how Patricia will react. Cecilia, God rest her, used to worry and fret, but when push came to shove, she was always supportive."

"And you don't think Patricia will be?"

"The Queen of Clean Sweep? Who knows?" Anne zipped around a stalled car by Jefferson Square. "What do we say when they ask?" She turned toward Mary Helen.

"Keep your eyes on the road!" Mary Helen wanted to shout. Instead, hoping that Anne wouldn't notice her left foot pressing the floorboard, she pointed her finger straight ahead.

"Well," she said, relieved when Anne took the hint, "I think that if anyone asks, we should look as if it were all terribly confidential. Just say that there was an incident today, but that it's under control."

At least this homicide won't make the five o'clock news, she thought, *thank God for small favors*. There were no reporters at the Refuge, no cameras at the scene. Sadly, it was too routine a homicide to be newsworthy.

"Good one!" Anne giggled and slapped the steering wheel. "An incident that's under control."

Although Mary Helen winced at her exuberance, at least she wasn't vacillating, and there was much to be said for that.

Leaning back against the headrest, Mary Helen closed her eyes, determined to let Anne drive unaided. Drowsily she envisioned a little nap, then sitting at the dining room table looking wise and, if asked, saying as little as possible about the incident.

As it turned out, the convent didn't need a reporter, a camera crew, or the five o'clock news. Sister Therese had a grandniece who was dating a policeman who just happened to hear about it from the black-and-white that had answered the call.

144

"You call murdering a young woman and dumping her battered body at your back door an incident?" Therese asked in a voice two octaves higher than usual when Anne gave the prepared answer.

Her question had silenced every other conversation in the entire Sisters' dining room. Mary Helen wasn't sure that the kitchen crew was talking, either.

Sister Patricia sat up tall. Her head of prematurely white hair bobbed above the other heads at her table. Eyebrows raised, she turned her icy blue eyes toward Therese. "What did you say, Sister?" she asked politely. "Did I hear you say something about a dead body?"

"Of course you did," old Donata said. She had always despised game playing, and age had made her even less patient with it. "Therese's grandniece called about a body being found at the Refuge and we're all dying, excuse the expression, to find out what happened."

"Not I," Therese demurred, but didn't move from her spot at the table.

Donata ignored the interruption. "Dancing around isn't the way to get them to tell us. Or acting shocked." She stared pointedly at Sister Therese. "Anne isn't going to tell us, and knowing Mary Helen as we do"—she smiled broadly—"the best way is to straight-out ask."

With an unexpected feeling of relief, Mary Helen retold the group about her first encounter with Melanie and then about finding the poor thing's body at the side entrance and calling the police. Reluctantly Sister Anne filled in all the details about the other women at the Refuge. Between the two of them, they were able to field all the inquiries, consciously leaving out the names Geraldine had given them. No sense implicating possibly innocent people.

Finally, when Mary Helen thought that they had exhausted

every possible question, Sister Ursula had one more. "Who do you think the murderer is?" she asked bluntly. "Andy, the pimp?"

"I really don't know," Mary Helen admitted, "and I'd rather not guess, but, as I told you, I did hear Melanie say, 'Andy will kill me,' or something to that effect."

"Who's this Randy?" Donata asked, cupping her bad ear.

"Andy," Mary Helen repeated distinctly, turning toward Donata. "He was her pimp."

"That's better," Donata said. "I swear, Mary Helen, you're starting to mumble like the rest of them."

Only Anne laughed heartily, too heartily in Mary Helen's opinion. But youth, like snow, is a problem that goes away if you ignore it long enough.

The kitchen staff had all gone home before the nuns finally left the dining room. Even Donata made the rare admission that their conversation had been more exciting than *Wheel of Fortune*.

"May I see you a moment before you leave?" Sister Patricia sidled up to Mary Helen just before she reached the door.

Uh-oh, here it comes, Mary Helen thought as Sister Patricia led her away from the group. The college president pulled herself to her full height. A strange expression danced on her face, and her mouth twisted. Clearly whatever she was about to say, she was having a difficult time getting out.

"Sister," she began finally, "I understand that you are an avid mystery reader."

Mary Helen nodded. "Yes," she said cautiously. Where in heaven's name was this going?

Patricia's cheeks colored as if she was embarrassed by what she was about to say. "Out with it, girl!" Mary Helen wanted to shout. She held her tongue.

Patricia smiled. "Last night I finished the one I was reading, my last one until I can get to the library. I was wondering if you might have one I could borrow."

"Follow me," Mary Helen said with a grin. Maybe this Patricia wasn't so bad after all!

❧❧❧

After a quick shower, Sister Mary Helen climbed into her bed. She usually showered in the morning, but somehow tonight she felt as if she should wash off all the grime and dirt of the day. With it she hoped to dissolve some of the violence and pain that she had seen. It was difficult to believe all that had happened in just thirteen hours.

Once in bed, she fluffed up her pillows and picked up her latest Linda Grant mystery novel. She was ready to lose herself in Catherine Saylor's adventures. Briefly she wondered if Sister Patricia was doing the same.

She had read only a couple of pages when her eyelids refused to stay open. *Catherine will have to wait until tomorrow,* she thought, flipping off the light and pulling her blanket up around her shoulders.

Thank heaven just enough fog had rolled in to cool the evening. A crisp breeze came through the bedroom window. The convent was silent. Everyone must be in bed. Even the traffic on Turk Street didn't sound as heavy as usual.

Mary Helen turned on her side. Her mattress felt wonderful and she couldn't help wondering about all those women she had met today at the Refuge. Where were they sleeping? Some in shelters; some in dingy hotel rooms or crowded apartments; some in doorways or alleys or in the park or under the freeway. And some, of course, wouldn't sleep at all. They would work all night selling themselves for survival.

She prayed for their safety—for the safety and deliverance of all who were homeless.

Mary Helen turned over in bed. In the distance, a lone dog howled mournfully. She felt sorry for the old mutt. Was he homeless, too?

When had homelessness become such a big problem? Why were so many people without a place to live? Why did they stay that way? Someone should do something about it, that was for sure. When they became better acquainted, maybe she should talk to the women about improving their lives.

And what about Melanie? Her young life had ended so tragically—so quickly. The least Mary Helen could do was help the Homicide inspectors find the perpetrator. Without warning, Inspector Gallagher's face loomed before her, eyes blazing, lips tight, and pale. Mary Helen had noticed his coloring was off. Probably fatigue. She'd be doing him a favor helping out with this homicide.

From the street, she heard brakes squeal. Someone in too big a hurry. *Maybe I'd better put my brakes on, too,* she thought as the words of today's saint, servant of slaves, came flooding back to her. "We must be to them with our hands, before we can speak to them with our lips," Peter Claver had advised.

Mary Helen sighed and felt sleep slowly making her body heavy. How right he was! No one can be helped unless they trust you. Well, tomorrow she'd take his advice. Tomorrow she'd join Anne at the Refuge and serve coffee and doughnuts and pass out shower rolls. All the while, she'd try to bring a little peace and joy into the lives of those who had so much less than she did. As for Melanie, for the time being she'd leave that situation in God's hands.

She could almost swear that she heard God laugh and say, "Any day, old dear, any day!"

Thursday, September 10

❧❧❧

Saint Nicholas of Tolentino, Confessor

On Thursday morning when Sister Mary Helen drove away from Mount St. Francis College, low-hanging fog still shrouded the hill. All across the campus plants dripped from the drizzle. It made a perfect backdrop for her own gray mood. Since she had awakened, nothing seemed to have gone right.

First of all, she had overslept. Impossible as it seemed, she had snoozed through her blaring alarm. She'd arrived in chapel at the end of morning Mass and lingered a few minutes to say a prayer and to catch her breath. She had walked into the Sisters' dining room in time to see Sister Anne hurrying out.

"You take the car," Anne had said breathlessly. "I'll hop the Muni and meet you there."

"I can go with you now," Mary Helen protested. "I'll pick up a doughnut and a cup of coffee at the Refuge. There's no need for you to take the streetcar."

"I'm dying to go where all the action is," Anne said, referring to the donnybrook between the city's commuters and the Municipal Railway that had recently installed an expensive computer system, which seemed to be making things worse instead of better.

"Are you sure?" Mary Helen had asked. "I don't mind going with you." But Anne had already disappeared.

Back in her bedroom, Mary Helen had debated on whether or not to bring a sweater. Downtown San Francisco was always warmer than the college, which was closer to the ocean. It amazed her that a few miles could have such an impact on the weather.

What amazed her even more was that this morning she couldn't remember exactly where she'd left her sweater. After a few minutes' search, she'd decided to go without it. The way things were going for her, it was bound to be freezing downtown.

Fortunately, when she finally did get to the convent Nova, the gasoline tank was full. Maybe her luck was due for a change.

Even as she crossed Divisadero Street, which once had divided the Presidio from the rest of the city, she wished she hadn't spent so much time hunting for her sweater. She really wasn't going to need it. Today was going to be another beautiful Indian summer day. *And a busy one*, she thought, pulling into the parking lot next to the Refuge.

Already several women stood on the sidewalk finishing their cigarettes before they went inside. Sister Mary Helen recognized Peanuts and Miss Bobbie. They were deep in conversation with a woman that Mary Helen hadn't seen before.

"How you doing today, girlfriend?" Miss Bobbie greeted her warmly. "Why you late?"

The question took Mary Helen by surprise. "You don't want to know," she said, realizing how trivial the truth would sound.

150

"Yes, she do," Peanuts said, a twinkle in her dark eyes. "Miss Bobbie, she want to know everybody's business."

The expression on Miss Bobbie's face wasn't hard to read. The scar around her right eye twitched. She glared at her friend.

Time to change the subject, Mary Helen thought, turning to the third woman. "I don't think we've met," she said.

The woman's face stiffened into an ugly sneer. "This be Olivia," Peanuts blurted out before the woman could speak.

Her brown eyes narrow, Olivia stared defiantly at Sister Mary Helen, waiting for something, anything at which to take umbrage.

Itching for a fight, Mary Helen thought, studying the tall woman. Her stiff platinum hair stuck out around her head like thick dandelion fluff, and her broad shoulders showed several homemade tattoos. The leather skirt and elastic tank top grabbed her body and accented her extreme thinness, making her look sick rather than sexy. Her face was gray-white, and she'd made no effort to cover the deep shadows under her eyes—eyes so full of anger that Mary Helen felt a chill run down her backbone.

"How do, Olivia," Mary Helen said politely, then turned away. She'd have enough on her plate today. She could wait to tackle Olivia until later, much later.

Swinging open the door to the Refuge, she was hit by a wall of noise. Although it wasn't even ten o'clock, the gathering room was full and the women were talking in high, loud, excited voices. Everyone in the area must have heard about Melanie's murder and dropped in to add what they knew to the story.

> "Needles, pins, triplets, twins,
> When a man marries, his trouble begins,
> When a man dies, his trouble ends,"

Crazy Alice sang out. Her high giggle rose above the din and gave the room a dreamlike feel.

Flanked by Miss Bobbie and Peanuts, Sister Mary Helen entered the room. If she thought that finding the body would make her a celebrity, she was wrong. Several women waved, but no one stopped her own tale long enough to greet the old nun.

"Don't you pay that Olivia no mind," Peanuts said quietly.

Mary Helen frowned. The clamor and confusion in the gathering room had almost driven Olivia from her mind. "The poor woman looks very unhappy," Mary Helen said in what she figured was a master understatement.

Peanuts nodded. "She always mad about something," she said. "Nothing's right for her. Like I tell you, pay her no mind."

Miss Bobbie pulled out one of the vacant chairs and sank into it. "That Olivia, she gets to my nerves," she said.

Sister Mary Helen was about to ask why Olivia was so angry when Sister Anne rushed by with the tray of day-old doughnuts. "The joint is jumping," she said. "Can you make some more coffee?"

Olivia and her problems will have to wait, Mary Helen thought as she pushed a cart loaded with empty coffeepots to the kitchen to refill them with water.

She was surprised to see Betsy Dodd at the counter measuring coffee into filters. "Look who's here," Mary Helen said, purposely leaving out the *again.*

Betsy jumped then and put her hand to her chest.

"Sorry I startled you." Mary Helen turned on the faucet.

"Not your fault." Betsy gave a halfhearted laugh. "I was a million miles away. Hannibal and his elephants probably could have sneaked up on me." Facing Mary Helen, she gave a forced smile.

It was Mary Helen's turn to be startled, and she hoped it didn't show. After all, no one would purposely look as bad as

Betsy Dodd did. Her round face was pale and drawn, as if lines had been carved into it overnight. Her hazel eyes, usually alive, were flat, and her curly black hair hung limply.

If Mary Helen wasn't mistaken, Betsy wore the same slacks and pink top that she'd had on yesterday. In fact, she recognized the same coffee spot on the front of the top. Although they were surely a designer label, they looked slept in.

According to what Mary Helen had read in the society pages as well as what she herself had noticed in the last few days, Betsy Dodd's appearance was usually impeccable. Strange!

Betsy must have noticed her staring. She wriggled self-consciously. "I thought things might be busy today, what with the"—she hesitated, no doubt groping with the best way to phrase "murder"—"happenings yesterday." The last few words were in a whisper.

Taking a deep, almost painful breath, Betsy put the lid back on the large can of coffee. "It's a good thing I came, too. Today's volunteer had a problem with one of her youngsters. Schoolitis, she thinks. So she couldn't come in. When I got here, Sister Anne was swamped."

The woman must have sensed Mary Helen's curiosity about her clothes or felt she needed to explain. "I spent the night at my sister Ginger's house. Spur-of-the-moment." Betsy Dodd's eyelids blinked rapidly, and the hand holding the coffee scoop trembled ever so slightly. Hesitating, she leveled her eyes at Mary Helen as though trying to decide exactly how much to tell her. The room was unnaturally still, and Mary Helen could almost taste the tension.

Betsy Dodd nibbled her lower lip, presumably building up courage.

"Here you two are!" Sister Anne burst into the room with more coffeepots. "We have a big, hungry crowd out there and Venus and Sonia need shower rolls."

153

All at once, Mary Helen was conscious of the noise drifting back from the gathering room. By the sound of it, the crowd had grown. She loaded up the cart and wheeled it toward the front. Whatever was on Betsy Dodd's mind would have to keep until their coffee break.

❀❧❧❀

Although Betsy Dodd was glad that she'd decided to come to the Refuge, she was having a difficult time keeping her mind on coffee and doughnuts.

Every time there was a lull in the action, which mercifully was rare, her thoughts found their way back to last night's scene in the living room.

The scotch, which she wasn't used to drinking, made part of it a blur. But if she remembered correctly, she had played it well. Acting as if she were afraid to stay in the house with him and letting that fear leak to Ginger was a stroke of genius, if she did say so herself.

Her sister and she had talked half the night. Betsy had told her that Rich was having an affair and that during their married life he had been involved in several others. "This time," she said, "I'm going to leave him."

Although her sister was sympathetic, she had not seemed surprised. Ginger and Rich had never really liked each other. As the evening wore on, Ginger had hinted that over the years Rich had even flirted with her. *The pig!* Betsy thought. Were there no boundaries to his lust?

"Can I have an herbal tea bag?" one of the ladies asked.

Betsy stared at her. Was this the same lady who had asked her for one a few minutes ago? Had she forgotten to give it to her?

Woodenly Betsy went to the kitchen for tea bags. She slipped several into her apron pockets in case there were any more calls for them.

Hands in her pockets, she walked back into the gathering room. The telephone rang and she jumped. *Don't let it be Rich,* she thought, panic rising in her throat. When Anne finally picked up the receiver, Betsy found herself suddenly hoping that it was Rich and that he'd called to beg her to come home. What a pleasure it would be to turn him down.

She gathered up some used coffee mugs from the table and set them on the cart. Mindless work, but it did distract her a little. She couldn't spend another minute with Ginger going over and over what had happened.

Her face had burned when she had told her sister what he had said. To Betsy's surprise, it was from anger rather than from the humiliation and hurt that she usually felt. Was she really becoming immune to his insults? Or was she "beginning to wise up," as Ginger had suggested?

"You feeling OK, Miss Betsy?" Peanuts asked. The tiny woman studied her with such concern that Betsy felt tears rush to her eyes.

"I feel fine, thank you," Betsy answered, too quickly. "I'm just distracted." Her explanation seemed to satisfy Peanuts.

"It's for you," Anne said, pointing to the telephone.

Betsy's stomach churned. "For me? Who is it?" she asked, hoping she sounded calm.

"Someone named Rosa. She says that she's your house-keeper."

"Are you all right, missus?" Rosa asked in a breathy voice.

"Yes, of course," Betsy said, trying to sound as brave as she needed to be and no braver. "What is it, Rosa? Is something the matter?"

"Glass and liquor all over the floor in the company room, the good glasses broken, and you gone," the housekeeper keened. "Dios mio! I thought robbers! What happened, missus?"

"Mr. Dodd? Is he gone, too?" Betsy asked, wondering herself

what had happened. Was the housekeeper exaggerating or had her husband gone on a rampage?

"Nobody is here but me. What you want I should do?"

"Just clean it up the best you can and go home early."

"But what happened?" Rosa insisted.

Pretending not to hear the question, Betsy replaced the receiver. Perfect! Rich had played right into her hands. Rosa had seen the results of his violent outburst, and she wouldn't be likely to forget it. It couldn't be better if Betsy had planned it. She could hardly keep from smiling. Unwittingly he was making her subtle accusations believable. Poor Rich! She almost felt sorry for him. *He thinks he is so clever. He doesn't know he's digging himself a very deep hole.*

Betsy felt perspiration bathe her entire body. Why was it so hot in here? She walked to the front door for some fresh air. What could she possibly give as his reason for murdering the girl? Certainly he didn't care if she found out about his affair— at least, he'd never cared before.

Could it be the governor's race that put him over the top? It made sense. A person like Rich could be that hungry for power.

Betsy wanted to cheer. She had to plant that idea with somebody. The police wouldn't do. She had talked to them already. She didn't want to overdo it. What she needed was someone who could be counted on to keep a confidence until she wanted it revealed. It should be someone objective. Above all, someone who would believe her. But who?

She walked back into the gathering room. "Are you ready for your coffee break?" Betsy heard Mary Helen ask her, and it was as though her question had been answered.

To Betsy's relief, Anne decided to walk around the block for her break. "I need to get some fresh air and quiet," Anne whispered. "Be back in fifteen." With a quick wave she left the center.

"I should probably take a walk, too," Betsy said, setting down a small plate with two glazed doughnuts on it. "It would be much better for my figure than these," she said, as if she cared a nit for her figure.

Mary Helen nodded. "Me, too," she agreed, helping herself to half a doughnut.

Not knowing exactly how to get started without sounding suspicious, Betsy stirred her coffee and folded and unfolded her napkin. She reached for a doughnut, broke off a piece, and slowly chewed it. How does one ask a nearly complete stranger, "Do you think that my husband could possibly be a murderer?"

She looked up to find Mary Helen studying her. Although the old nun's eyes were kind, they were also penetrating. "Is there something bothering you, Betsy?" Mary Helen asked gently.

At first the words caught in Betsy's throat. She made a great show of gathering up her courage. At last, after a few false starts, she began. Then, to her surprise, as though someone had lanced a boil, all her fears and suspicions oozed out, sounding quite natural.

Sister Mary Helen listened without comment as Betsy told of her husband's repeated infidelity, of his short-lived repentances, of his disdain for her, the hypocrisy of their public life together.

Still Mary Helen said nothing, only listened attentively. Betsy told the old nun about the wariness she had felt when Geraldine rattled off the list of names that poor dead Melanie had mentioned. She told of calling Rich's office and finding out that an Amanda did work for her husband.

Finally, tears welling up in her eyes, Betsy told Mary Helen about their terrible scene last night and of her feeling of fear.

"But he wouldn't really murder anyone. I can't believe he'd do such a thing," she said. Betsy paused, scanning Mary Helen's face for a reaction—afraid to hear the words, "I'm sure you're right. An outstanding citizen like your husband would never do such a thing."

Instead Mary Helen said nothing. Her mind seemed to be far away.

"What should I do?" Betsy asked when she could stand the silence no longer.

"If you are really suspicious, there is only one thing to do." Mary Helen paused.

Betsy could hardly wait for what she suspected was coming. Before the old nun told her to go to the police, Betsy couldn't resist laying a little more on. "If my husband is a murderer"—she shivered convincingly—"why won't he kill me, too? Where can I go? And now, by talking so much, have I put you in danger, too?"

All at once the room was stifling. Betsy couldn't breathe. Why was it so hot? She looked around wildly. Why didn't someone open the door? She was smothering in here. How could she get out?

"Miss Betsy, you got any more of that herbal tea?" Peanuts asked in a small voice.

Saved, Betsy thought, rummaging through her apron pockets, ignoring the bags she had put in them before.

"Excuse me, Sister," she said, feeling as if she'd been snatched back from sure death. "I need to get some tea from the kitchen." Without a backward glance, Betsy Dodd hurried away.

❧❧❧

Officer Mark Wong was dead tired. His apartment was quiet and cool, and he had put the sleep mask over his eyes to keep out the light. Yet he could not fall asleep.

It was that murdered prostitute, Melanie, that was on his mind. She wouldn't let him rest. *Such a waste,* he thought, rolling over on his side. Although his partner, Brian Dineen, and he had kept an eye out last night, they had not spotted Andy—which wasn't surprising. Olivia had probably given him the word that they were in the neighborhood asking questions. The pimp would have made himself scarce. They had just busted him the day before. Too many arrests and he'd begin to lose face. His girls counted on him to take care of them. It wouldn't be too cool for him not to be able to take care of himself.

The slimy little creep, Wong thought, wondering if he'd feel better if he ate something. He hated to get up and fix a sandwich—not that he had any bread in the house. There were some stale chocolate-chip cookies in the cupboard and, if he remembered correctly, a quart of milk in the refrigerator.

On his day off, he'd go grocery shopping, a task he hated. No matter what he bought, he always ended up throwing most of it away. The Vice Squad was not conducive to regular meals.

Maybe the coffee he had drunk with Olivia was keeping him awake. Poor Olivia! She was sure terrified of something or someone. Was it Andy that she feared? He didn't blame her. Andy could be a mean bastard, that was for sure. Or was she afraid of someone else? Hard telling, and she wasn't going to be any help.

This is not your case, Wong reminded himself. *It belongs to Gallagher and Murphy. Let them lose sleep over it. You tried to give them a hand, but you drew a blank. It happens,* he thought reasonably, but if he was perfectly honest, he was having trouble being reasonable about anything in this case. It was such a waste of a perfectly good young life.

For no apparent reason, the dog in the neighboring backyard began to howl. The forlorn wail filled Wong's bedroom.

He put his pillow over his head. Why was this happening to him? He needed to sleep. *Dineen is probably snoring by now*, he thought grudgingly.

Wearily Mark Wong put one foot on the floor. First, he'd call Gallagher—put this Olivia business where it belonged. Let Homicide follow-up. Then, he'd sleep.

With some effort, he rolled the rest of the way out of bed. Yawning, he punched in the number for Homicide and took it as a good omen when Dennis Gallagher answered the telephone. Quickly Wong identified himself.

"Did you find out anything we could use?" Gallagher asked.

He sounds tired, too, and he's just starting, Wong thought, and told him about his conversation with Olivia. "She knows something that's scaring her," he said.

Gallagher grunted. "I don't blame her. You can bet that whoever she's playing with is playing for keeps. At least, if that dead prostitute is any indication."

"Did you get any more on the murder weapon?" Wong asked, satisfied that he had brought Gallagher up-to-speed. The next step was his.

"Kate and I were just going over the medical examiner's report. Oddest damn thing! The kid was killed by a hard, round object, probably ceramic, like a vase or a mug. Whoever killed her battered her with the object until her skull was crushed," Gallagher said.

Wong heard the Homicide inspector sigh. "That's a lot of power or a lot of rage," he said quietly.

"Is the ME sure?" Wong asked, wondering if maybe the guy was just tired and in a hurry to go home.

"Seems to be," Gallagher said. "The good news is that he knows that whatever it was, was white, and that if we ever locate it, he can match it to the particles embedded in the girl's skull."

"And the bad news?" Wong asked.

"The bad news is there must be a million white ceramic cups and vases in this city. Every household has to have at least one or two. For crissake, Mrs. G. has about ten herself right in our kitchen cupboard!"

Neither officer spoke. Probably both were contemplating the apparent hopelessness of ever finding the weapon. "Thanks for the tip on Olivia," Gallagher said, at last.

"Oh, yeah. Sure." Wong had almost forgotten why he'd called.

Padding barefoot into his small kitchen, Wong swung open the refrigerator door. The light was out, but even if the room had been dark, too, the milk carton would be easy to find. It was the only thing on the shelf.

He scanned the cupboard for a glass, but there were none. All the glasses must be in the dishwasher, which he had neglected to turn on.

One lone mug hung from the cup tree. He unhooked it and filled it with milk. Then he took the rest of the cookies from the cookie jar and, pushing aside yesterday's paper, sat down at the round kitchen table.

Pensively Wong dunked the cookies into the milk and bit off the soggy sections. Moving his bare feet from the cold floor, he rested them on the table's central pedestal. He studied his mug—white porcelain. *Just like the murder weapon*, he thought uneasily.

Draining the milk, he picked up the mug and he hit it against the palm of his hand. He felt the weight, the rough edge along the bottom. He raised the mug a little higher and brought it down with a little more force. The palm of his hand stung.

So if someone had slammed it down repeatedly with great force, it was possible, Wong conceded, adding his cup to the packed dishwasher. *Then, just put the evidence on the heavy-duty cycle and away it goes. Or would it? Some infinitesimal fragments were bound to adhere,* Wong thought, glad that the problem belonged to Gallagher and Murphy.

Not that he wasn't anxious to nail the perp. There was something sweet about Melanie. She deserved better. At least, she deserved more than to be filed with the city's unsolved homicide cases.

Beginning to feel a little drowsy, Wong settled back in his bed. Who, he wondered, his mind getting fuzzy, would want Melanie dead? Andy, of course, was number one on his list. What reason would the sleezebag have? He'd just have to find the guy and squeeze it out of him. Tonight, first thing, he'd find Andy and go for it.

❧❧❧

Sister Mary Helen sat at the small table, stunned. Betsy Dodd had risen as though her chair were on fire and hurried off to God knows where to get a tea bag for Peanuts.

No wonder! Mary Helen thought. *I as much as told her to report her husband to the police, which she should, if she thinks he's involved. And if she doesn't,* Mary Helen mused, *what is my obligation?*

The doughnut she was chewing suddenly tasted like a lump of sawdust—not that she'd ever tasted sawdust, lumpy or otherwise.

Report what Betsy told you to Kate Murphy and Inspector Gallagher, a small voice within her demanded.

It was confidential and not unlike the Seal of Confession, another voice countered. *Besides, it's only supposition.*

And you could get in a heap of trouble accusing a rich and prominent lawyer of murder, it warned. *Better be a little surer of your facts.*

Best advice yet, Mary Helen thought, swallowing her doughnut at last. *What I probably should do is nose around a little,* she thought—then stopped short. "Nose around?" She found the expression distasteful. "Investigate further," had a much nicer ring to it. *I'll investigate further,* she thought, *just ask a few questions. That seems the most prudent thing to do.*

All at once, she sorely missed her friend Sister Eileen. Mary Helen could just hear Eileen saying in that soft brogue of hers, "Go ahead, old dear; there's no tax on talk."

Mary Helen put her mug on the cart that was already stacked with other used ones and scanned the large room. Many of the tables, she noticed, had been vacated. Was it lunchtime already? She checked her wristwatch. No. Then what had happened?

Even those who remained in the room had become unusually quiet. It seemed as though most of their conversations were whispered.

Sister Anne must have noticed Mary Helen's consternation. Before she knew it, the young nun was next to her. "That last phone call," she said, assuming that Mary Helen had heard the telephone ring, "was from Kate Murphy. She and Inspector Gallagher will be here within the hour." Anne surveyed the room. "Someone must have heard me talking to her. I see most of the women have already cleared out. No one wants to talk to the police."

"I understand," Mary Helen said, her stomach churning. And she actually did understand. She herself didn't want to meet the Homicide inspectors or tell them what Betsy Dodd had confided to her—not, at least, until she had more information. And she'd better get going on it. They'd be here before she knew it.

Frantically she glanced around the room. Peanuts had taken her tea bag and gone. Miss Bobbie, who knew everyone's business, was nowhere to be found. Even Venus and her volcano of pent-up rage had left. The woman Mary Helen had just met—was her name Olivia?—was gone, too. A few women remained, including Crazy Alice, who giggled happily.

Feeling frustrated, Mary Helen pushed the cart of soiled cups toward the kitchen. It jiggled and rattled like her thoughts as she moved down the hall. How could she ask questions when all the women she felt she could ask were gone? What kind of questions could she ask anyway? No one had even established what the murder weapon was or where and when the murder had actually taken place.

What should I do? Mary Helen felt a sense of urgency. Kate and Inspector Gallagher would be arriving any minute now. *Should I tell them what Betsy suspects about her husband or should I ask around a little bit on my own?*

You know how upset that makes them. The small voice was back again.

I thought you had already decided to investigate, came the reply. *Don't tell me you're getting wishy-washy in your old age.*

Mary Helen felt her backbone stiffen. She wasn't sure whether the reference to "old age" or to being "wishy-washy" had caused it. Not that she appreciated either one.

The voice went on undaunted. *Besides, won't it upset them more if you give them false information? Face it; either way Gallagher won't be happy. You might as well be hung for a sheep as a lamb.*

Dear God, she prayed, feeling a little desperate, *I could use a little direction here.*

Still uncertain about what to do, Mary Helen carried yet another tray of doughnuts into the gathering room. She wondered whether any women would drop in to eat them. Just in case, she went back to the kitchen to replenish the supply of paper napkins.

She had just returned and set them on a large table when the front door swung open. Bright sunshine flooded into the room, backlighting a bewildered looking Geraldine.

"Where everybody gone?" she asked, taking in the nearly empty room. "Even Miss Betsy be outside. Only Crazy Alice be in here."

"We're not sure," Mary Helen said, figuring that Geraldine must be the only woman in a radius of a mile who didn't know that any minute the police were scheduled to arrive at the Refuge. "But we think it might be because they overheard that the Homicide inspectors are on their way here."

"You think?" Geraldine said with a sharp laugh. "You be knowing that, for sure!"

Mary Helen waited for Geraldine to bolt. To the nun's surprise, she didn't.

"I needs me a cup of coffee and one of them old-fashioned buttermilk doughnuts," she said, helping herself to two. "Then I'm going to sit for a while. Ouch! My feet are barking."

"Don't you want to avoid the police, too?" Mary Helen asked, curious about Geraldine's attitude.

The deep brown eyes studied her. "Why do I?" she asked. "I ain't done nothing wrong. Maybe I can help find that young girl's killer."

Maybe we both can, Mary Helen thought excitedly. *Thank You, God,* she prayed silently. *This is surely a sign.*

"Hold your horses, old friend," she thought she heard God reply, but then she couldn't be sure.

"How are you today, Geraldine?" Mary Helen asked cheerfully when the two women were finally seated. Actually, Geraldine looked as though she'd been awake all night. Her eyes were bloodshot and the flesh under them looked like dark quarter moons.

Geraldine eyed her cautiously. "Fine, Sister," she said. "I be just fine. And you?"

"Fine, thank you." Mary Helen forced a broad smile. "I thought we might talk."

Geraldine's eyes narrowed. "Talk about what?" she asked.

"About Melanie's death."

Geraldine set her jaw, but she didn't protest. If anything, she looked eager to talk to someone about what she knew. "You know, Sister, I talked to the police. Told them all what I know," Geraldine said.

Mary Helen guessed that the woman's hesitation was more for appearances than anything else.

"You some kind of police?" Geraldine shot the question quickly, and Mary Helen, who wasn't expecting it, felt her face redden.

"Of course not," she said. "I'm just an old woman who hates to see a beautiful young life cruelly taken and the murderer getting away with it."

"Now you're talking my talk!" Geraldine said and began to speak. She told Mary Helen about meeting both Venus and Andy after she'd left the Refuge yesterday.

"Venus?" Mary Helen asked. "That's not one of the names you said Melanie mentioned."

"Maybe she didn't because she didn't know who'd kill her," Geraldine answered reasonably.

"Would this Venus have a motive?" Mary Helen wondered aloud.

"She be crazy when she drinks," Geraldine answered.

"And Andy?" Mary Helen pushed, leading up to her real question.

Geraldine shrugged. "Andy, he be crazy, too, crazy like a fox. Too smart to do his own killing."

"And this Dickie that Melanie mentioned?" Mary Helen tried to keep her voice steady. She didn't want her own anxiety to influence Geraldine's answer. "What are your thoughts on him?"

For several seconds Geraldine pondered the question. "He's not from around this neighborhood," she said finally. "He knows Miss Betsy, so maybe he's somebody important."

Her dark eyes grew round. "Why would anyone important want to kill a little sister like Melanie?" she asked.

Why, indeed? Mary Helen wondered.

❧❧❧

By the time Inspectors Kate Murphy and Dennis Gallagher arrived at the Refuge, the place was literally deserted. Even Crazy Alice had gone. When the detectives swung open the front door, only Sister Mary Helen, Sister Anne, Mrs. Dodd, and an enormous tray of uneaten doughnuts were in evidence.

Kate glanced around the empty gathering room. "Looks as if we were expected," she muttered to her partner, her gaze finally settling on Sister Anne.

Kate watched the young nun's face flush. *You don't suppose Anne announced our coming to the women?* Kate thought, trying to stay calm. *No one is that naive, or is she?*

Not unexpectedly, it was Mary Helen who spoke up. "Someone of the women must have overheard Anne's phone conversation with you. Then, they all seemed to know." She shrugged. "These women are extraordinarily intuitive." Shoving her bifocals up the bridge of her nose, she focused on Kate. "AT&T could learn a lot about communication from our ladies. They don't miss a trick," she said and smiled sweetly.

Look who's talking, Kate thought, smiling back. She turned toward Gallagher, who was next to her, glowering. "Then I guess it's a good thing we did stop for this mug shot of Olivia," she said.

All the way from the Hall of Justice to the Refuge, he had been complaining about the time they were wasting trying to pick up a mug shot of Olivia. The small, fuzzy print gave her name as Olivia Perez, alias Livie Perez, alias Candy Peron and Milk Chocolate Peron.

"Maybe we can spot this Olivia on the streets," Kate said hopefully.

"It doesn't seem like we can do much here," Gallagher said, "unless you want to take a look around for the murder weapon."

The color drained from Sister Anne's face and her slim body seemed to sway. "The murder weapon? Here?" she said in a breathy voice.

"Are you all right, Sister?" Betsy Dodd came quickly with a chair.

"What was the murder weapon?" Mary Helen asked, leaving the caretaking to the volunteer.

Kate Murphy shot Gallagher an angry look. Wasn't he always the one who complained about Sister Mary Helen meddling in their business? Why give her an opening?

Mary Helen's hazel eyes studied Kate eagerly, waiting for an answer. What could she say? "None of your business, Sister"? She cleared her throat. Much as she might like to, she couldn't be rude to the old dear.

"The medical examiner tells us that the young woman—"

"Melanie. The young woman's name was Melanie," Mary Helen interjected.

"Melanie," Kate repeated, "was killed with a heavy, round white ceramic object. Probably a vase or coffee mug."

"A vase or coffee mug," Mary Helen repeated. "This place is full of them—mugs anyway." She pointed to a tray of cups on the serving table waiting to be used.

Kate spotted two white cups on it.

"Follow me," Mary Helen said and led Kate down the narrow hallway to the kitchen. With a flourish, the Sister opened the dishwasher and pulled out the first rack, which was full of soiled cups. Five of them fit the description. Still not saying a word, Mary Helen threw back the cupboard doors to reveal shelves of cups for her to inspect.

"We'll send someone over to bag them," Kate said, doubtful that it would be worthwhile. Whoever the murderer was, he or she had undoubtedly disposed of the murder weapon by now. "You seem to have enough other cups." Kate said.

"We do," Mary Helen said in a tone of voice that Kate recognized. It was the one that meant that she'd be delighted to get involved, no matter how small the scale. Wouldn't Gallagher have a fit, if he heard her. Let him! It was his own fault for bringing up the murder weapon in front of her.

The two women walked back into the gathering room, where a pale Sister Anne still sat on the chair. Betsy Dodd hovered over her. Kate surveyed the room. Her partner seemed to have disappeared. *Where in the world—?* she wondered, then heard a familiar cough. It came from the sleep area, which they had used yesterday as an investigating room. Maybe all that cigar smoking had served some purpose. At least she could find him without really looking.

Excusing herself, Kate walked into the sleep area and shut the door behind her. Gallagher was sitting on a chair, his eyes closed.

"What are you doing in here, Denny?" she asked, fear like a sudden draft running down her spine. "What's wrong?"

Gallagher shrugged "Nothing, really. I just felt like the third wheel on the wagon, that's all. The nun looks like she might pass out any minute, and that Dodd woman seemed to have everything under control. So I decided to come in here and think. Nothing wrong with that."

Kate studied her partner's face. It was the color of dry cement. "You don't feel good, do you?" she demanded.

Dennis Gallagher set his jaw. "Don't you start on me, Katie-girl." He wagged his head miserably.

"Who else has been on you?" Kate asked.

"Who do you think?"

"Mrs. G.?"

"None other than Mrs. Florence Nightingale Gallagher." He looked up at Kate with watery blue eyes. "Like I told her, I'm tired, that's all. The grandkids were over last night. And my son-in-law never knows when to go home. By the time I helped the wife with the cleanup, it must have been after midnight."

"You've looked bad for a while, Denny," Kate interrupted. This was not at all how or when she had planned to bring up the topic, but there was something to be said about striking while the iron was hot. Or, in this case, while the face was pale.

Gallagher moaned and ran the palm of his hand over his bald crown. "Jeez, Kate, that's all I need"—he shook his head—"a second wife. I don't have enough problems with the first one being on my case!" His eyes avoided hers. "You're my partner, for crissake!"

"I am your partner and I'm also your friend. And I'm really starting to worry about you." She stood over him and put her hands on his shoulders. "Denny, as your partner and your friend, I've got to tell you." Kate cleared her throat. "Your color has been bad for a while now, and you've been more tired than usual. This thing is eating at you. Maybe you have an ulcer. Would it hurt you just to see the doctor and get a clean bill of health? Mrs. G. and I will both feel a lot better."

Dennis Gallagher stared up at her. If anything, his face was even more pale. "An ulcer? What are you really thinking, Kate? Are you thinking I've got the big C?"

The directness of his question startled her. If she were perfectly honest, that was exactly what she was afraid of, that her partner had cancer.

Until this moment, when Gallagher had named her fear, it had been a vague one—one that she knew was swimming in some dark pool of her mind, but one that she had never really coaxed into the light.

"Cancer!" she said, trying to sound surprised despite the growing pain in her chest. "What makes you ask that?"

Gallagher loosened his necktie. "Don't try to con me, Katie-girl. I've known you too long. You're afraid it's cancer, aren't you?" He didn't wait for her answer, just looked away. "Well, to be honest, that's what I'm afraid of, too. It runs in my family, you know. My father had it. My grandfather. I've seen what it does to people—strong people." Gallagher gave a short laugh, although he was deadly serious. "I guess I'm like that ostrich fella—if I don't see it, it doesn't exist. Maybe that's why I don't want to go to the doctor."

Her partner rose from the chair, a clear sign that the discussion was over. An uneasy silence filled the small room. Kate wanted to say all those sensible things like "even if it is cancer and you get it early . . . ," or "you have no idea that it is cancer. It could be something quite simple like . . ."—she couldn't think of what. Even if she could, she knew she wouldn't be able to get any words around the block in her throat. Impulsively she threw her arms around her partner, and, surprising them both, she began to sob into his shoulder. The rough wool of his jacket scratched her cheek. The odor of stale cigar smoke assailed her. She cried even harder.

It was Gallagher who recovered first. "What the hell's wrong with you anyway?" he asked, pulling her away. "I'm the one who is supposed to be sick. Besides, this is a helluva way for two Homicide inspectors to carry on. What if one of the nuns saw us?"

Kate noticed that color had returned to his face. Still sniffing, she began to laugh. Denny was right. The two of them would have made quite a picture.

All business now, Gallagher checked his wristwatch. "We got to get cracking, Katie-girl." He cleared his throat. "What do you say we ride around the Tenderloin for a little while seeing if we can spot Miss Olivia?"

"Fine with me," Kate said, "but let's not spend all day at it. We need to look into other leads, much as I know you're dreading it."

Gallagher's neck seemed to stiffen. "I sure as hell am," he said. "Nobody in his right mind wants to put his ass in the meat grinder."

Kate hadn't heard him use that expression in years. He really must be reluctant to question the powerful and prominent Mr. Richard Dodd. It wasn't like Gallagher to avoid a challenge.

"We're not accusing him of anything," Kate said. "We're just going to ask some questions. After all, his name was mentioned in a murder investigation and even his own wife couldn't alibi him."

"Do you have any idea the heat we're going to generate?" Gallagher said. He tightened the knot of his necktie. "They'll hear the fallout clear to the mayor's office."

"Then the sooner, the better," Kate said. "While the mayor has Muni's problems uppermost in his mind."

"Yeah, right," Gallagher said. "I hope we don't live to regret it. Do you know how close I am to retirement? I'd just like to go out peacefully." He pulled his notebook from his jacket pocket and checked Dodd's address.

"Shall we call for an appointment?" Kate wondered aloud.

"Naw, let's take the great man by surprise." Gallagher was clearly beginning to rise to the situation. "Maybe we can give him a little taste of the meat grinder."

"Denny." Kate touched his arm. "Promise me something before we go."

"Yeah, yeah," he said without even looking at her. "I'll call Kaiser and make an appointment with the sawbones for a physical."

Relieved, Kate Murphy followed her partner out of the sleep area into the gathering room. Betsy Dodd and the two nuns were still the only ones there.

"We're on our way," Kate said, hurrying to keep up with Gallagher. "Someone will be here to bag the cups," she added. "We'll be in touch."

She glanced over at the women sitting like three statues at a small table. Was it her imagination or did they all seem suddenly happier when she mentioned that Gallagher and she were on their way out of the Refuge?

❧☙❧☙

Sister Mary Helen watched Kate Murphy and Inspector Gallagher leave the shelter. She felt strangely free. Or was the word *saved*? And she didn't seem to be the only one.

Sister Anne's tight lips began to ease, and her usual high color was returning to her cheeks. "Whew!" she said with a silly grin.

Betsy Dodd bit her bottom lip. During the time that they had sat at the table waiting for something to happen, she had managed to chew off all her lipstick.

"Do you think that we should lock up and go?" she whispered, although at the moment they were the only ones in the place.

Before either Sister Anne or Mary Helen was able to answer, the front door swung open and Venus came in. Then three more women cautiously followed her. Soon the regulars were

173

back—Miss Bobbie, Peanuts, Geraldine, Sonia. Each came through the door determined not to miss any of the action.

London after the blitz, Mary Helen thought crazily, watching the women enter the room. The departure of the police car must have been their all-clear signal.

"Open. Open. Open," Crazy Alice chanted, swinging back the front door. Mary Helen recognized the television commercial but couldn't quite put her finger on what it was selling.

Soon the heavy door was swinging open before it could completely shut and the place was beginning to fill. Quickly the tense quiet was being replaced by animated conversation. Everyone seemed to know something about Melanie's murder and the police investigation. All were eager to tell what they knew.

It was all Sister Anne, Betsy, and Sister Mary Helen could do to keep up with the doughnuts, coffee, sugar, cream, napkins, and clean cups. Actually, though her feet were beginning to hurt, Mary Helen was glad to be busy. She knew once she stopped, she'd start feeling that twinge of guilt about not talking to Kate Murphy.

It was not as though I didn't speak to her on purpose, Mary Helen thought, placing a row of chocolate doughnuts on the tray. *I just didn't have the opportunity. After all,* she justified her actions, *Kate was the one who shut herself in the sleep room with Inspector Gallagher. They must have been on to something, they were in there for such a long time. And when they did come out, they seemed in a hurry to get going. It was definitely not the time to stop them.*

Besides, what do I really know? Only what Betsy Dodd told me about her secret suspicions. Like any secret—what's that old saying? "It's no secret that's known to three." It's undoubtedly better if Betsy does the telling. Yes, indeed, Mary Helen thought, replenishing the supply of napkins. *In this case, much better.*

As she hurried through the large room on her way to and

from the kitchen to the snack table, Mary Helen couldn't help overhearing choppy waves of conversation.

"Yes ma'am, girlfriend," Miss Bobbie was saying loudly, "we all knows who had her killed! It got to be him, Andy. My cousin says he saw him hangin' around like a mad dog, howling for her."

Farther across the room, tiny Peanuts nodded. "The police got to be on to him." Her dark eyes blazed. "Where he be anyway?"

At another table, Venus smiled a toothless smile. "It be a woman who killed her, that for sure. It makes no sense, a man using a cup."

Where in the world did she find out about the cup? Mary Helen wondered, again amazed at the homeless grapevine.

Passing other tables, the old nun heard as many theories as there were conversations. "The police killed her. Who else gonna move a body?" *Curious deduction,* Mary Helen thought. *Why would the police be the only ones to move a body?* She'd have to ask. "Another 'ho' did it." "Lexus, the drug boy, wanted his money." Where was the truth in all of this? Apparently the Refugees were as confused as everyone else about who had killed poor Melanie.

Sister Mary Helen felt her stomach rile as the image of the girl's crushed skull leaped into her mind. She blinked, feeling the tears flash in her eyes. Maybe Richard Dodd was responsible. Secret or no, maybe she should have told Kate Murphy.

She was glad to see Geraldine sitting alone, sipping her coffee. Apparently the other women who had been with her had picked the conversation clean and moved on to another, juicier table. "May I?" Mary Helen asked, motioning to an empty chair.

"Why, sure," Geraldine said with a gracious smile. "You weary?" she asked.

"Just a little," Mary Helen admitted. "As you know, the police were here, and that's always stressful."

Geraldine nodded and the two women sat in comfortable silence. "By the way," Mary Helen began at last. Now was as good a time as any to clear up some of her questions. First, she asked about why someone would think that the police would be the ones who had dropped Melanie's body at the Refuge.

Although she answered politely, Geraldine's look shouted, *How could anyone be so stupid?*

"They got cars," she said. "You can't move no dead body in a shopping cart. Whoever move that girl got a way of doing it."

Interesting, Mary Helen thought, filing the idea away to mull over later.

"Some of the women are saying that another prostitute killed her. Is that possible?"

"Anything possible," Geraldine said and took another sip of her coffee.

"And who is Lexus, the drug boy?"

Geraldine looked puzzled, then let out a short laugh. "You mean Texas, the drug boy."

Mary Helen shrugged. Maybe her hearing was getting bad. If only people wouldn't mumble.

"Texas be possible," Geraldine conceded, "if Melanie owe him money."

"Wouldn't it be better to keep her alive until he's paid?"

"Depends," Geraldine's round face was solemn, "Sometimes it be better to make an example. Scares everybody else."

"And what about Andy, her pimp?" Mary Helen asked. After all, the first time she'd met the girl, Melanie had screamed that Andy was going to kill her. Mary Helen was sure she'd heard that correctly. "Do you think we should try to find him?" Even as she said it, Mary Helen knew it was an insane idea. She and Geraldine, even in the best of times, would be no match for a crazed killer.

Geraldine's heavy shoulders slumped. "What I didn't tell you was that Andy not be feeling too good today," she said.

"Is he sick?" Mary Helen asked.

"Not exactly." Geraldine's dark eyes twinkled. "I just happened to be talking to my nephew Junior Johnson. You've heard of Junior?"

Mary Helen nodded. "Overheard" would be more like it.

"The sweet boy asked me, 'Auntie, I heard on the streets that Andy disrespect you. That true?'

"So I tells him the truth, and poor Andy ain't going to be bothering nobody for a couple weeks, from what I hear." She smiled sweetly. "That Junior always was a loving child. Never could just stand by and let anything bad happen to his mama or to his auntie."

Mary Helen was speechless. This dear little old lady had just made a brutal beating sound like an act of pure charity. Without waiting for her to comment, Geraldine went on.

"Junior say that Andy swears he didn't have her killed, but he could be lying." Geraldine studied Mary Helen. "I hates a liar," she said passionately. "Don't you?"

Mary Helen was glad when one of the women asked for soap and a towel to take a shower. It gave her time to think. Excusing herself, she made her way to the supply cupboard.

When she had finished, she lingered in the small cupboard mulling over the conversations she had overheard, especially her conversations with Geraldine.

"A woman," Venus had declared. Possibly, but which one and why? Melanie had mentioned two women, Olivia and Amanda. Both could use a little looking into. Mary Helen had observed Olivia's anger herself. Amanda worked at Richard Dodd's office. What was his connection to the young prostitute?

And what about Venus herself? Earlier today Geraldine had remarked that drink made her crazy. Was this homicide the work of a crazy person?

Or could Melanie have been murdered as an example? Even as she thought it, Mary Helen felt a chill slide down her spine. An example for the drug boy, or for her pimp, or even for what happens when a person stumbles into the private affairs of one Richard Dodd. She didn't want to think about that and she probably wouldn't have, either, if Betsy Dodd hadn't approached her.

"Sister," Betsy said, leaning through the half-door of the supply cupboard. Her hazel eyes shone with unshed tears. "I'm sorry I cut off our conversation so abruptly this morning. I hope I didn't appear rude."

"No, never rude," Mary Helen said, "but I did wonder why."

Betsy tilted back her head as if she were searching for the answer herself. "To tell you the truth, I was frightened."

"Frightened of what? Going to the police?"

Betsy shook her head. "Not of going to the police. Of going home. If my husband's killed once, why wouldn't he kill again?" she asked sensibly.

Mary Helen felt fear prickle her scalp. Did Betsy really believe her husband was a murderer? Was she afraid for her life? If so, then what she was saying made sense. If Richard Dodd could kill once, what would prevent him from killing again? If he killed once was a big "if," despite what his wife thought. But it seemed foolish to put it to the test.

"You need to get out of your house," Mary Helen said unnecessarily.

"I'm going home right after I finish here, pick up some of my things."

"Where will you go?"

Betsy shrugged. "To a hotel, I guess."

"You'll be alone." Mary Helen was thinking aloud. "He surely could find you in a hotel if he wanted to. All it takes are some phone calls."

"I could go to my sister's house, but that will be the first place he looks." Betsy nervously played with one earring.

Suddenly the idea came to Mary Helen. *Brilliant!* she thought, and the words glided from her mouth like well-trained skaters. "Come to the convent with Sister Anne and me for a few nights. We have plenty of room."

When Betsy hesitated, Mary Helen added, "The other nuns will be delighted to have you."

❧❧❧❧

"You did what?" Sister Anne tried her best to keep her voice low. She must not have succeeded, since Sister Mary Helen was "shushing" her.

"She'll hear you," the old nun whispered. "You don't want that, do you?"

"No, I don't," Anne said softly, "but it is a bit of a surprise, you know. I'm sure that when you explain, I'll understand." She struggled to sound calm and open-minded. "Now, Mary Helen, why did you say that you invited Betsy Dodd to spend the night in the convent when she has a perfectly lovely house in Presidio Terrace and a husband that goes with it?" Sister Anne realized that she sounded a tad sarcastic, but she couldn't help herself. "You know as well as I do that will be the first question Sister Therese will ask. And, as much as I hate to admit it, it's a good one."

Not that having visitors in the convent guest room was unusual. She didn't mean that. What was out of the ordinary was that most guests didn't have their own homes less than a mile away.

Mary Helen pursed her lips. "I didn't say why I invited her.

It's confidential." She must be hoping against all reason that that would be enough said.

"So confide," Anne said and waited. What in the world was going on?

She watched the determined set of Mary Helen's chin relax. Her dimples flashed, once, then twice, as she obviously struggled with herself. Finally she blurted out, "Follow me."

Back straight, Mary Helen led Anne across the busy room. Although some women were beginning to gather up their belongings to leave for the day and find a shelter, a good crowd still remained.

"Be right back!" Anne called as they passed Betsy, who was replenishing the supply of cups. Which reminded Anne that a police officer would undoubtedly be arriving soon to collect the white mugs.

"We can't leave Betsy out here alone," Anne protested.

"She'll be fine for a minute or two, and this won't take long!" Mary Helen threw the words over her shoulder.

Once they were in the privacy of Anne's office, the old nun told her of Betsy Dodd's fear. Suddenly Anne felt as though she couldn't get enough air. *This is impossible! I must be hearing things. A prominent man like Richard Dodd with a lovely wife like Betsy doesn't commit murder! To the world they appear to be the perfect couple. This couldn't be happening!*

"You never know what goes on behind closed doors, do you?" Anne said when she'd recovered her voice. Her grandmother always used that expression, but until this moment Anne never realized how true it could be.

"My point exactly," Mary Helen said crisply. "Our problem, of course, is what are we going to tell the other nuns?" She pushed her bifocals up the bridge of her short nose. Their eyes locked.

"Oh, no, you don't!" Anne said firmly. "This isn't my problem."

At first, Mary Helen looked hurt. "Didn't I say 'we'?" she asked.

"You said 'we,' but that look was a 'you' look," Anne protested.

Even though Mary Helen tried to look puzzled, Anne knew very well that she understood. An uneasy silence filled the small office. Anne could hear the women's voices rising. They'd better settle on a plan and get back outside to rescue Betsy.

"Sorry," Anne said quickly and watched Mary Helen's expression become mollified.

"Me, too," she said so softly that Anne nearly missed it.

"Any ideas?" she asked.

"Several," Mary Helen said, "but only one that isn't a bold-faced lie."

Anne was aware of the women's voices in the gathering room growing ever more strident. "Let's hear it," she said.

"We'll say something is amiss at her home—a private matter—and so we invited her to stay with us."

Anne groaned.

"What's the matter?" Mary Helen sounded insulted. "That is the truth."

"I know. That's not what's bothering me."

"What then?"

"Have you any idea how many questions that kind of a statement will generate?"

Mary Helen smiled. "You're right, but I figure that we can count on everyone to at least be polite and not ask them to her face." She looked to Anne for reassurance.

"How many nights will she be staying?" Anne asked skeptically. She wasn't so sure that everyone could hold back their curiosity indefinitely.

"Not too many. I imagine that Kate and Inspector Gallagher have already begun to run down some suspects."

"You are probably right," Anne said on the off chance that saying something out loud would help it to be true.

"Probably," Mary Helen repeated softly, staring off into middle space.

Oh, no, Sister Anne thought, watching her. That "I'm here, but I'm not here" glaze to her eyes looked dangerous. Anne's mouth was dry. *I don't want to hear that she's getting involved,* she thought. *What's worse, I definitely don't want to hear that she expects me to get involved, too.* She shut her eyes, hoping the whole thing would go away. *I have my plate full just running this place without a murder. Besides, murders are dangerous!* she thought, aware of how ridiculous that would sound if she said it to anyone else. *How did I get into this mess?* she wondered. *How can I get out of it as quickly as possible?*

"Anne?" Mary Helen sounded concerned. She felt the old nun's hand grasp her arm. "Are you all right? Anne?"

Anne's eyes popped open. "Fine, thank you," she said.

"Then we'd better get out there. It sounds as if something is going on."

Something was definitely going on. "I seen you, girl!" Venus shouted. Her angry words quieted the other women in the room.

"Who you talking to?" Olivia faced her, eyes blazing.

"I be talking to you. You better be hearing." Venus circled to the right. "I seen you."

"Seen me what? You talking crazy." Olivia moved toward the snack table and surreptitiously picked up the sharp knife used to cut the cake.

"What's going on in here?" Anne asked in her firmest voice moving slowly toward the woman. Neither one appeared to have heard her. She looked for Betsy. Fortunately, the woman was safely across the room.

"Who you calling crazy?" Venus roared. "I seen you."

"Seen me what? You hear me? Seen me what?" Olivia lowered her platinum head like a charging bull. "You hear me talking to you?"

"I hear you, girl—big mouth like you got." Venus shifted her weight, keeping just out of Olivia's reach.

"Who you saying got a big mouth?"

"You, girl. I seen you shooting off your mouth, sweet as pie, Miss Candy, talking to them police friends of yours—drinking coffee. What else you do for them, 'ho'?" Venus asked viciously.

A sharp slap rang out. Venus grabbed her cheek.

"Stop!" Anne shouted, but it was too late. Olivia hit her again, this time with a closed fist.

Instead of reeling back, Venus sprang forward, knocking over a chair. Lunging, she threaded her fingers through Olivia's hair, gripping tight. With a quick twist, she wrenched Olivia's neck, forcing the woman down on one knee.

Olivia's fists swung out, pummeling the calf of Venus's leg. Venus grunted, bent her other leg, and drew it back, her knee aimed for Olivia's nose.

Olivia saw it coming and bobbed sideways. Then, as quick as a coiled snake, her hand shot out with the cake knife. Blood spurted from Venus's thigh.

Venus bellowed wildly. "You cut me, you 'ho'!" she screeched.

Out of the corner of her eye, Anne saw a figure move. Could it be? It was—Sister Mary Helen. *Oh, no,* Anne thought, her heart thudding in her ears. "Don't!" she called out, but Mary Helen didn't seem to hear.

"You really don't want to do that, do you?" Mary Helen said, her strong voice battered against the tense silence that now filled the room.

Before Anne could stop her, she moved forward and put her stocky body between the two women. Anne sucked in her breath.

"You cut me!" Venus screamed. It was as if her rage blinded her to anyone but Olivia.

Mary Helen held up her hands. "Now, stop!" she repeated, seemingly oblivious of the danger.

Ignoring her, Olivia raised the knife. "Get out of my way, old woman!" she roared, her eyes smoldering.

For a split second it looked as if she might bring the knife down on Mary Helen. Terrified, Anne stood frozen. After what seemed an eternity, it clattered to the floor and Olivia ran from the room.

Shaken, Anne shouted, "Call nine-one-one!" But it wasn't necessary. The front door swung open and the patrolman who had come to collect the cups stood in the entranceway with a bewildered expression on his face. "What's going on?" he asked.

"We've had a little altercation," Anne said, searching for the bleeding Venus. She had disappeared. "But I think it's over."

The patrolman looked relieved. "I've come to pick up some cups," he said.

Anne, somewhat light-headed from the thought of what might have happened, led him to the kitchen, where he put on plastic gloves and began bagging all their white ceramic coffee mugs. The Refuge rapidly emptied out.

He had almost finished when Betsy Dodd, her face a little paler than usual, entered the kitchen with yet another cup. "Here's one," she said. "Somehow it landed on the serving table. Speaking of which, shall I put out some more snacks or shall I clean up?"

"Clean up," Anne said without even looking at her wrist-watch. *Enough is enough!* she thought. "Let's call it a day!"

"It looks as if Rich is out," Betsy Dodd said as the garage door rolled open. She pulled her Lexus into one side of the double garage of her luxurious home, which was set back on a soft green lawn fringed with salmon-colored impatiens.

She sounded relieved and so was Sister Mary Helen. Anne had suggested that while she closed the Refuge the two of them drive to Presidio Terrace to pick up a few things for Betsy. Then the three would meet at the side door of Mount St. Francis Convent.

It had taken Mary Helen the entire ride from the Refuge to Betsy's home to calm herself. Actually, her knees still felt shaky. She hoped she could get out of the car. What she didn't need at this point was another angry confrontation.

She also hoped Betsy hadn't said anything important on the way across town, because she hadn't been listening. Her mind was still at the Refuge. Even she couldn't believe how foolish she had been to step between two angry women, never mind that one of them had a knife. She shuddered to think of what could have happened.

What was it Eileen always said? "There are two things which cannot be cured—death and want of sense." Fortunately, in this case, one had not led to the other.

"I won't be long," Betsy said and turned off the ignition. "Do you want to come in? You look as if you could use a brandy."

Suddenly feeling very tired, Mary Helen shook her head. A brandy was all she needed to put her right to sleep. "I think I'll wait right here," she said. "Take your time. I'll just rest my eyes."

To emphasize her point, she leaned back against the headrest and closed her eyes.

"If you're comfortable there," she heard Betsy say uncertainly. And then, as if it were far away, she heard the door to the house click shut.

A rumbling noise woke her. For a few seconds, Mary Helen could not place the sound. Then she recognized it—the rumble of an electric garage door being raised. Her eyelids felt glued shut. Where was she? She smelled gasoline fumes and heard the soft swish of the car pulling in next to the driver's side.

Eyes still shut, she sat very still. It could only be one person—Richard Dodd. Maybe he wouldn't look over at the passenger side of his wife's car. And if he did, maybe in the dimness of the garage he would miss her.

She heard the car door slam shut. His body hit against the door to the house. "Betsy!" he roared. "Get down here! We need to talk!"

Mary Helen didn't like his tone of voice one little bit. It sounded almost threatening, to her way of thinking. Like it or not, she just might have to get involved after all.

Quietly she let herself out of the Lexus, not bothering to shut the car door. The wooden door leading to the house opened without a squeak into a glassed-in utility porch where a washer and a dryer were lined up next to a large sink. At the far end of the porch an upright freezer hummed. In fact, the hum of the freezer was the only sound Sister Mary Helen heard at first.

Where could the Dodds have gone? she wondered. Obviously, Betsy had not come down. Her husband must have gone upstairs to find her. She strained, listening for noise—any noise. Nothing but quiet.

Warily she tiptoed into the massive kitchen. The white tile countertop was clear except for a toaster oven, a blender, and a brand-new looking cappuccino maker. Every cupboard was neatly closed. Stiff ruffled canary yellow curtains covered the windows. A small glass-topped table and four chairs filled a tiny breakfast nook where French doors opened out onto a Japanese garden. Gleaming pots hung above a granite-topped island that was also home to a state-of-the-art gas stove.

The entire place was immaculately clean. So clean that you would have been hard pressed to believe anyone ever used it. It could have been a model kitchen in a fancy home development. The only sign of human occupancy that Mary Helen saw was a crumpled napkin someone had left on the corner of the island. That is, until she noticed something else.

Right next to the napkin was a wooden knife block full of black-handled knives. She blinked. Well, almost full! One slot was empty. One knife was missing. And it looked as if it was the large carving knife.

Overhead she heard a floor creak. She cocked her head, straining to hear. There it was again. Grabbing a heavy saucepan, just in case, she pushed open the swinging door into the formal dining room. Soundlessly she crossed the room on the thick Persian rug. Still there was no sign of the Dodds. They must be upstairs.

On the other side of the dining room, she found a wide staircase leading to the second floor. Clutching the polished wood banister with one hand and the pot with the other, she slowly made her way up.

Mary Helen had nearly reached the top landing when she heard a savage scream. She felt the hair on her arms prickle. No mistaking, it was Betsy—and it was coming from the second closed door.

Betsy shrieked again. This time it sounded sharper. Without thinking, Mary Helen raced down the hall. Raising the saucepan over her head, she threw open the door. She fully expected to see Richard Dodd wielding the butcher knife over his cowering wife. What she saw instead nearly took her breath away.

Betsy held the handle of the carving knife poised above her head with both hands. Eyes blazing, she roared again and dived at her husband, who was crouched down behind a blue velvet slipper chair.

"Please, Betsy, don't," he begged, his face white. "For godssake, put the knife down, honey, before you really hurt somebody."

But Betsy's fury seemed to have deafened her. With a roar, she struck the chair back, ripping the upholstery.

Terrified, Rich whimpered and covered his face. With frenzied strength she slashed again and again at the fabric on the chair back. Bits of white padding showered the carpet.

"Betsy! Stop! Enough!" Mary Helen shouted, surprised at the strength of her own voice. The startled woman swung toward the door. A lock of hair hung over her forehead. Her cheeks were flushed and her mouth was set in a determined line. She stared at Mary Helen as though she'd never seen her before, her eyes burning with a strange light.

Mary Helen's heart plummeted and she felt a sudden chill. For a terrifying instant she thought she saw madness.

"Sister," Betsy said breathlessly, "I hope I didn't frighten you. I just want to show him"—she pointed to her husband with the tip of the carving knife—"how it feels to be bullied."

Mary Helen's mouth was dry. "I think you've more than made your point," she said finally and tried not to look in Richard Dodd's direction.

For a long time, Richard Dodd sat on the bedroom floor resting his back against the wall, trying to calm his breathing. His entire body was wet with perspiration, and his mouth felt furry from fear. There was only one thing to do about it, he figured, struggling up from the floor, have a good reviving Scotch.

With unsteady legs, he picked his way through the padding from the ruined chair littering the carpet. Then he started down the stairs clutching the banister as if he were an old man. God knows he had aged at least twenty years in the last few minutes. He'd never seen anything like it. It was a Betsy he did not know, slashing at him with the carving knife.

Just thinking of it, his hands began to tremble and his head throbbed all the more. What had happened to her? He'd never seen this side of Betsy before. She'd always seemed so steady, so annoyingly in control of herself.

Rich turned into the formal living room. Obviously Rosa had been there. The place was back in order. He wondered what she'd thought of the mess—not that he really cared. He paid her to clean, not to make judgments. Although he was sure she did. Everything about the housekeeper's demeanor shouted that she considered Betsy an angel and him a bastard.

She should have seen "the angel" in action today, he thought, pouring a generous shot of scotch into a glass. His hand trembled as he brought the drink to his mouth. He savored the burning sensation it made on his tongue.

After a second swallow, Rich settled himself in the brocade chair and closed his eyes. In just a little while his headache would start to feel better. Then he could think more clearly about what to do. And not just about Betsy. He had to think through what to do about Amanda, as well. That little bitch had come—uninvited—to his office first thing this morning again demanding a promotion. She hadn't actually threatened him with anything, but her tone and manner had been very clear. Either she became his administrative assistant or she went to the police and told them about seeing the murdered prostitute when she was with him on Nob Hill.

How the hell could he explain what they were doing up there together? He'd figure out something. It was his word against hers. He'd come up with some plausible reason. Or maybe he'd just deny it.

He had plenty of time to decide. He'd asked Catherine, his secretary, to clear his calendar for today and tomorrow. An odd expression had passed over her earnest face. For a moment, he thought she might ask him the reason, but proper Catherine was far too well trained for that. *Maybe I should have married Catherine instead of Betsy,* he thought, taking another sip of his drink. He could count on Catherine never to lash out at him with a knife.

He'd thought he could count on Amanda, too. She had been so sweet, so flattered by his attention, so empty-headed. Or so he'd thought. Who could have imagined that she'd turn into such a scheming opportunist? *Better position, my ass,* he thought, taking another swallow of Scotch.

Maybe I'm too trusting, he thought, his eyes burning now, *letting myself be taken in. Thinking I could count on anybody. Hell, until today I would have staked my life on Betsy. Until today.*

He ran his fingers through his dark hair. What in hell had gotten into her? She had seemed so ordinary, so like herself, when he bounded into the bedroom. He was furious and she knew it.

"We need to talk, Betsy!" he had shouted at her back. He watched her stiffen. Good. When he shouted she always stiffened, then tried to appease him somehow. The real Betsy hated scenes. He should have realized something was wrong when she didn't turn and face him with that hangdog look on her face.

"Turn around when I'm speaking to you!" he had shouted in frustration and waited, expecting her usual response.

Rich shivered, remembering the shock he had felt when she did turn around—when he saw that she was brandishing the carving knife. He scarcely had time to take it in before she began to slash at him, roaring in that unnatural voice. He felt the air from the flashing blade rush past his face.

Instinctively he had ducked behind the slipper chair, but

that had not stopped her. She had lunged forward, slashing the padded cushions to bits.

He took another swallow of his Scotch and rose to refill the glass. He measured one, two, three fingers. His head was feeling much better already.

What would have happened, he wondered, if that old nun hadn't come in on them? What a sight they must have been—him cowering behind a velvet slipper chair, Betsy slashing madly at him like someone right out of a *Psycho* movie. A fine First Family they'd make. Thank God nobody got that scene on home video—him hiding like a coward while his short, plump wife slashed away.

Rich felt an unexpected laugh rising in his throat. Or was it more like a gagging sensation? No. Leaning back against the chair, he felt the laugh come again, then again and again until he was laughing hysterically—laughing until he couldn't stop. Laughing until he felt as if he would choke.

He tried to get his breath, tried to push up in the chair, tried to swallow. Tears ran down his cheeks. Sweat broke out on his forehead and his whole body began to tremble. His stomach lurched and Richard Dodd scarcely had time to get to the bathroom before he threw up.

For a moment he thought he heard a doorbell ringing. Or was that simply a ringing in his ears?

❧❧❧❧

Inspector Kate Murphy pressed the front door bell of the Dodds' home in Presidio Terrace and listened to the chimes echo through the large house.

"I can hear it ringing," her partner, Dennis Gallagher, said unnecessarily. "Doesn't sound like anyone's home," he added too quickly. "Maybe it was a bum idea, coming out here at this time of day. We should have called first," Gallagher mumbled.

"Wishful thinking," Kate said, knowing that Gallagher was dreading a meeting with Richard Dodd. Which, she thought, was not like him. Usually he welcomed a good fight, especially if his opponent tended to be a pompous lawyer. And there was no doubt about Richard Dodd—he was pomposity personified, plus he had publicly insulted the SFPD in the *Chronicle*. Under ordinary circumstances, he would be first-class grist for Gallagher's mill.

Kate had seen a car pulling onto Arguello as they pulled in. She was hoping that her partner hadn't, as she was almost positive that Betsy Dodd had been driving and that the woman in the passenger's seat was Mary Helen. That was all Gallagher would need to get him going again.

Gallagher stared out at the circle of mansions "Some digs," he said as Kate pressed the bell yet another time. The chimes seemed to reverberate even louder.

"Even if somebody is home, it doesn't look like anybody's going to answer," Gallagher said with a shrug. "Maybe Mrs. Dodd is giving old Richard a lift somewhere."

"Maybe," Kate said. "Are you sure that the secretary said that he was going home?"

"That's what she said." Gallagher turned his back to the door. "God, it's peaceful in here," he said wistfully. Long shadows stretched across the thick green lawns. "I wonder how it feels to come home to this?"

We'll never know, Kate thought, studying the tranquil azure sky turning rose and gold as the sun dipped toward the Pacific, *unless we win the lottery, and even then, we'd have to find one of these homes for sale.* "Let's get back to the Hall," she said, "and see if we can't get this thing moving."

"Right," Gallagher said. He followed her to the car, but Kate could tell that mentally he was still dwelling in the circle of homes in plush Presidio Terrace.

When they arrived at the Homicide Detail in the Hall of Justice the place was empty except for Myrtle, the secretary. Myrtle, who was solidly built and beginning to gray at the temples, was relatively the new kid on the job. She seemed genuinely happy to see them.

"It was getting lonesome in here," she said, "with just me and all these pink slips." She pointed to the stack of telephone messages. Sorting through them, she handed some to Kate.

The top message was from the Chief's office. Someone had offered a $5,000 reward for information leading to those responsible for the death of Melanie Rogers. Fliers would be on their desks before the night shift.

"Did the Chief say who put up the money?" Gallagher asked.

Myrtle shook her head. The phone rang and she raised one finger to indicate that she'd get right back to them. "It's for you," she said. "Mark Wong from Vice."

"Again?" Gallagher said, walking to his desk. He pushed the conference call button so both Kate and he could listen. "What's up, Mark?" Gallagher asked.

"I'm glad you guys are still there. I thought you might hit the road early."

"We did hit the road," Gallagher admitted, "but we didn't go home. We dropped by Richard Dodd's house to see if we could find the guy there. What a joint!" Gallagher said.

"Any luck?" Wong sounded hopeful.

"None at all," Kate answered this time. "What can we do for you?"

"I am on my way to work," Wong said. "I just want you guys to know that I'm looking to find that slimeball Andy tonight."

"Let us know when you get him." Gallagher sounded concerned. "And be careful."

Mark didn't answer.

"Did you know that someone put up five thousand dollars to

find Melanie's killer?" Kate asked. For some reason she thought it might be Mark himself.

"Well, I'll be damned!" Wong said, sounding genuinely surprised. "That ought to make finding Andy easy. Most of these guys would give up their grandmothers for five thousand bucks."

"Be careful," Gallagher repeated, but Wong didn't seem to hear.

"I'll talk to you guys first thing in the morning," he said, and Kate heard the phone go dead.

Gallagher frowned. "Damn hotshots," he mumbled.

Kate studied her partner's face. He looked worried. "What's wrong, Denny?" she asked. "Are you afraid this pimp, Andy, is armed and dangerous?"

"Damn right he's armed and dangerous," Gallagher grumbled, then shrugged. "That is, if you think, like Wong does, that he killed the girl. So, I guess there's no stopping Wong."

She touched her partner's shoulder. "And don't you think the pimp killed her?"

Gallagher had the look of someone whose mind was working overtime. "I don't know what to think," he admitted, "but this whole business just doesn't smell right."

"What do you mean?"

Dennis Gallagher fiddled with a paper clip on his desk. "When a pimp kills a girl, the pimp, the girl, maybe some stable sisters are involved. And the motive is usually pretty straightforward—withholding money, refusing to tow the line. But what had Melanie done?"

He loosened his tie and leaned back in his swivel chair. "Have you ever heard of a fancy lawyer and his wife being involved?"

Kate shook her head.

"And can you remember the last time someone offered a reward to find a hooker's killer?"

Kate shook her head again.

"Who put up the money and why?" Gallagher was almost talking to himself.

"That ought to be easy to find out. Tomorrow, we ask the Chief." Kate checked her watch. "We've done all that we can do for today. Tomorrow things might be clearer. Maybe Forensics will be done examining the cups."

And maybe pigs will fly, Kate thought, making some attempt to clear off the top of her desk.

While she fumbled with papers, Gallagher stared out the window at the crowded James Lick Freeway. "Poor devils," he said, "fighting that mess every night."

"Inspector Gallagher," Myrtle called, "line one for you."

From force of habit, he pushed the conference call button. "Denny," a no-nonsense voice that Kate recognized began. It was Mrs. G., Denny's wife. "I've made an appointment for you at Kaiser. Dr. Little can see you in about an hour."

Before Kate heard any more of the conversation, Gallagher switched off the conference button. "What the hell are you thinking about?" he roared.

Kate knew an exit line when she heard it. She gave her partner a "thumbs up" and with a quick "good night" to Myrtle left the Homicide Detail, feeling as though a burden had been lifted. Rave though he might, Gallagher would be at Kaiser within the hour. Yes, indeed, her partner was in very good hands.

❀❁❁❀

Officer Mark Wong reported in to the Vice Crime Section of the Hall of Justice five minutes before Brian Dineen arrived. The big man lumbered in looking as if he'd just rolled out of bed.

"Howdy, partner," Wong said, glad, once again, that Dineen always tended to be on the early side. A ream of the fliers Gallagher had mentioned were on his desk. Dineen and he could stop by the shelters and distribute them after they located Andy. Locating Andy was Wong's first order of business tonight, and he was eager to get going.

Dineen grunted when Wong peeled their car out of the Hall parking lot. "You a little jumpy or what?" he asked.

"Maybe," Wong admitted. "Didn't sleep so good. It's like Melanie's haunting me."

Turning in his seat, Dineen studied him with bloodshot eyes. "I didn't sleep so good, either, but it wasn't Melanie that kept me up. It was the damn telephone. If it rang once, it rang twenty times."

"Put on the answering machine."

"I did, but that makes noise, too."

"Who was calling you?" Wong asked, turning onto Seventh Street.

"Nobody's calling me. The wife's giving a baby shower. It was the girls RSVPing. Why can't they call at night when I'm gone?"

One of the joys of not being married, Wong thought, although Susie Chang from the Chief's office was a temptation. Turning right again, he went down McAllister toward the Western Addition. That way they'd pass the recently renovated City Hall and see what all the media hype and voter discontent was about. The latest name for the structure was Taj MaWillie, after this city's flamboyant mayor, Willie Brown.

Both officers agreed that the gold-gilded dome was spectacular. "I'm with the taxpayer who said that it's not the Vatican," Dineen groused. "The money could have been better spent, like on giving us a raise."

"Or putting in some bike lanes," Wong said, swerving to avoid a man in a three-piece suit on a ten-speed.

When Wong passed him, the cyclist raised his hand in the universal sign of contempt.

"I ought to pull the bum over," Wong said, "and I would, too, if I wasn't in such a hurry to get to Andy before he leaves for work."

Despite the heavy evening commute, they reached Fulton Street in record time. "There's our boy." Dineen pointed to a short, stocky black man in a gold-colored silk shirt and black leather pants. He was moving slowly, almost painfully, toward the convertible parked at the curb.

"I'd know that shaved head anywhere," Dineen said, opening the car door before Wong had fully stopped. "Police!" he shouted, holding up his badge.

"I know who you are, boy," Andy said without facing the officer. "I just don't know why the hell you want me."

"To ask a few questions about one of your girls—the one who was murdered, smart-ass," Wong said, grabbing Andy's shoulder.

Wong was surprised to feel the man wince, but when Andy turned to face him, he knew why. Somebody had worked the pimp over—good. His powerful torso, at least as much as Wong could see from the open shirt, was bruised. His lip was split, the bridge of his nose cut, and one eye was swollen shut.

"You should have seen the other guy," Andy said with a painful smile. Even his gold tooth was missing.

"Who did this to you?" Wong asked, trying not to sound pleased. It was less than the pimp deserved.

"What you take me for? A crazy man? You think I snitch on a homeboy? Next thing, you find me like my girl."

"Yeah, yeah," Dineen said impatiently. "It's your girl we want to talk to you about. We figure you for her killer."

Andy's face paled, making the bruises even more prominent. "Me?" he said, putting both hands dramatically to his chest. "Me?" he asked again. "Why would I kill a goose that's laying a golden egg?"

"Very literary today, aren't we?" Dineen scoffed. "Maybe because the goose was skimming a little off the top?"

"Never!" Andy looked hurt. "My girls never would."

"Then, there's Olivia—she's one of your girls, isn't she?"

Andy hesitated. "She was, but no more." He motioned as if he were washing his hands. "No, sir, I don't want no responsibility for what that crazy bitch do."

Wong put his face close to Andy's. "Like what does she do?"

"For one thing, she talks crazy, man."

"Could you be more specific?" Dineen asked. Wong could tell by the forced softness of his partner's voice that he was getting a little short on patience.

Apparently so could Andy. His shoulders sagged. "Listen, man." He was almost whining now. "I swear I didn't have nothing to do with Melanie's death."

"You were saying about Olivia?" Wong pressed.

"Olivia be talking crazy—like she think I want her to off Melanie."

"And what would make her think that?" Dineen's voice was so low that it was barely audible.

Andy shrugged and looked away.

"You heard my partner ask you a question, didn't you?" Wong knocked the palms of his hands against Andy's shoulders and watched a wave of pain wash over the pimp's face.

"Yeah, man, I heard you. What makes you think I know what any of them dumb broads think?"

"Take a guess," Dineen insisted.

For several seconds Andy seemed to size up his situation. Apparently he decided that truth was in his best interest. "See, boys, I been having a little stable trouble. You know how women are." His dark eyes searched their faces for understanding. Finding none, he went on. "Well, maybe you don't," he said, "but these 'hos, they get jealous of one another, specially if they think I'm liking one better." He grinned and Wong could see the space where his missing tooth had been. "They do anything to get my attention, be my top babe." Andy's chest puffed out like that of a strutting pigeon.

Wong felt his stomach turn and the bile rising in his throat. He saw Andy through a red haze of rage. *I've been on the job too long*, he thought, fighting down the urge to reach over and knock the man on his cocky ass.

"Like what things would they do?" he heard Dineen ask. "Things like murder for you? Which, of course, makes you an accessory, big-time."

Suddenly Andy seemed to deflate. His dark eyes jumped nervously. "I swear, I never asked her to murder nobody."

"Did you say anything that she could have thought meant that?"

"Like I said, I can't help what that bitch thinks."

"We don't have time for games." Dineen's voice was soft and dangerous. "We need some straight answers."

Andy leaned against the door of the convertible.

"And I'd advise you to give them to us quick," Wong said, finally trusting himself to speak.

Andy's eyes shifted from one officer to the other. *Like a cornered rodent*, Wong thought. Finally, the pimp put the palms of his hands in front of his chest as though he were warding off an attack. "Honest, guys, I didn't tell the bitch to kill Melanie. I just lost my temper. You know how that is." Once again, he looked from face to face for understanding. Once again, he found none.

"Maybe I said some stuff I didn't mean. Stuff like that girl be messing with getting herself dead—stuff like that—but I swear, I never ask nobody to kill her. I love that skinny white girl."

"Why were you so mad at her?" Dineen asked.

Andy's eyes shot open. "Because she messing with a white dude on Nob Hill. She get caught on Nob Hill and we really have the police on our asses."

"What do you mean by 'messing'?" Wong felt his adrenaline rising. Was Richard Dodd really involved in all of this?

"Like I tell you, she saw a white dude she thought she knew up there. Thought she'd try a little freelance."

"Freelancing?" Dineen asked.

"A little money to be quiet about what he was doing. Don't tell nobody she seen him. Know what I mean? With her extra money, she buys herself a little booze." Andy's face darkened. "Drunks be bad for business. 'Sides, I don't want no freelance in my stable. I the main man!

"So." He shrugged. "I lost my cool. It happens."

"And you're saying that Olivia could have misunderstood and thought you'd be happy if she killed Melanie?"

"That what I be saying."

"Then, we better see if we can find Olivia," Wong said.

"That's what you better be doing," Andy said so smugly that it took all of Wong's control not to punch him.

Olivia was not hard to find. Her height and that platinum head of hair made her stand out on the corner of Hyde and Ellis. She was just beginning to negotiate with a pimple-faced young man when the officers came up behind her. "Police," Dineen said.

At the sound of his voice Olivia stiffened. The young man backed away so quickly that Wong thought he might tumble over. Actually, it would serve him right.

"You two, again," Olivia said with bravado.

Coke courage, Wong thought, noticing her glazed eyes.

"Do you know you're costing me business?" She put her hand on her bony hip. "How is a girl supposed to make a living with you two hanging around?"

A small crowd was starting to form around the three of them. "You tell 'em, Candy," a disheveled old man slurred, then held a bottle in a brown paper bag to his lips.

"You better get lost, buddy." Dineen's voice was just loud enough for the man to hear. Wong watched the fellow shuffle away.

"You, Candy, get in the car," Dineen commanded.

Something in his manner must have penetrated the cocaine haze, because Olivia quickly climbed into the backseat.

In silence, Wong drove them to the police substation, where they could question Olivia without an audience. As soon as she realized their destination, Olivia began to whimper. "No," she pleaded. "Don't arrest me. Please! I got nobody to bail me out."

Apparently Andy really had washed his hands of her. "We just want to ask you a few questions," Dineen promised, leading the now-sobbing Olivia into the station.

With the help of two cups of coffee and a box of tissues, Olivia gradually calmed down enough to speak rationally. Yes, she admitted, she had been frightened the other day when they stopped her. Yes, it was because of Andy and Melanie. "But I didn't kill her!" Olivia's eyes searched their faces.

"Why don't you tell us the whole story?" Wong suggested. "From the beginning."

"Why don't I?" Olivia said. Her jaw sagged, adding years to her face. "I'm tired," she said flatly, "and I'm losing my touch."

"What's that got to do with Melanie's murder?" Dineen snapped. His patience was going.

Not enough sleep, Wong thought.

"You said to tell it from the beginning." Olivia sounded hurt.

"You're right; we did," Wong conceded, settling back in his chair. "Go on, please."

Crossing her long, thin legs, Olivia shot Dineen a look of disdain. "Then, he's got to stop being mean to me," she whined.

Dineen clenched his fists. Wong watched his partner's knuckles turn white. "More coffee?" Dineen asked evenly, and Wong was glad when Olivia said that she'd have some. The short walk to the coffeepot would give Dineen a chance to get control.

"What's wrong with him?" Olivia whispered when Dineen was out of earshot.

"He's just tired," Wong said, "and if I were you, I wouldn't push his patience."

"Men! They're such babies," Olivia said, but apparently took Wong's warning to heart. When Dineen returned, she quickly told the officers much the same story as Andy had—adding her own fear of being rejected by him and her jealousy of young, attractive Melanie.

"Then Andy got real mad at her. Something about that uptown guy. I swear he said he'd like to see the bitch dead."

"So, you obliged?" Wong asked, feeling a little sick to his stomach.

Olivia's face turned the color of her platinum hair. Her eyes were wide and frightened. "No, I swear! I just shot off my mouth, said I'd make him happy and do it for him. But I didn't."

"You didn't?" Dineen sounded doubtful. "Then why were you so scared when we talked to you?"

Olivia looked at him as if he were slow-witted but lovable. "I was scared of Andy—scared he would think I killed Melanie. Scared he would kill me. But I'm not scared of him no more."

"Why is that?" Wong asked.

Olivia gave them a great smile. "Junior Johnson! You see what he did to Andy? His Auntie Geraldine is gonna ask Junior to be my man. If Junior Johnson is my man, I ain't scared of nobody."

"Where does this leave us?" Dineen asked when they had released Olivia.

Watching her saunter down the street, Wong mulled over what they had just learned. "At face value, it looks as if both Andy and Olivia are in the clear," he said. "And that leaves only the big mucky-muck white guy from Nob Hill."

"You mean Richard Dodd?" Dineen grinned. "I can hardly wait to hand that piece of info over to Gallagher and Murphy. Let's hope we're not handing Gallagher a heart attack as well."

"At the very least, the old buzzard will get heartburn," Wong said.

Dusk was just beginning to cover the city as the two officers responded to a call in the Tenderloin. The fliers would have to wait.

❦❦❦

Geraldine shivered and bolted the third and final lock on the front door of her apartment. Once again, she was filled with gratitude for Lou and the inheritance he had left her. *God rest his horny little soul*, she prayed and flipped on the front room light. Not even the warmth and brightness of the cozy room seemed able to dispel the fear she felt—the fear she always felt when a prostitute was murdered.

There but for the grace of God, she thought, deciding to light a small vigil candle, the one that smelled like vanilla, for Melanie. She'd let it burn before her statue of the Virgin. She was with Lou when she saw the statue in the window of a pawnshop and admired it. Sweet man had bought it for her.

She turned on the front burner under the kettle and was just putting an enchilada TV dinner in the oven when she heard the buzzer ring. Her heart froze. Who could that be? The buzzer sounded again. Reluctantly Geraldine crossed the room and pressed the intercom speaker. "Who there?" she demanded.

"It's Olivia, Genie. Please let me in."

"I be down," Geraldine said. She thought she recognized Olivia's voice, but it was better to be safe than sorry.

Through the peephole Geraldine spied a tall, thin white woman shivering in her short skirt and see-through top. The full head of platinum hair convinced her that her visitor was Olivia. She cracked open the front door to the apartment.

"Come in, girl," she said, quickly shutting the door behind them. No sense giving someone else the chance to push his way in.

"What you want?" Geraldine asked as soon as she had given Olivia a cup of hot tea. Her dinner was in the oven. Nothing worse than a crisp enchilada, all hard and dry.

"I want Junior Johnson to be my man," Olivia said, then took a sip of her tea.

Bold piece, Geraldine thought, noticing Olivia's eyes. The girl was on crack. No telling what she might do.

"What make you think I can do anything about that, girl-friend?"

" 'Cause you his auntie and you had him beat on Andy."

Geraldine felt the blood drain from her face. "Who you tell that to?" she demanded.

"Nobody," Olivia said coyly, "but I was just talking to Wong and Dineen."

"What those two talking to you about?" Geraldine tried to keep her voice steady. It would never do to let Olivia think she was nervous.

"About Melanie's murder," Olivia said, her voice suddenly weary.

Uh-oh, Geraldine thought. The crack must be wearing off. No telling what kind of attitude it would leave. She'd better get this 'ho' out of her apartment quick! Why had she been so stupid as to let her in?

"Drink your tea," Geraldine insisted. "Don't you got business?"

Olivia's eyes narrowed. "That's why I'm here, old woman. Will Junior be my man?"

"I don't know what Junior do. Or what he say about having a killer in his stable."

Olivia's pale face flushed. Her eyes blazed and Geraldine knew she had hit a nerve. "I tell you, old woman, I didn't kill the bitch!"

"Then your pimp did?" Geraldine would love to see the little bastard in jail. All it would take was an anonymous tip.

Perspiration shone on Olivia's forehead. She shook her head violently. "Andy didn't, neither, but he don't want me no more. Thinks I'm bad luck."

For once, the little fool might be right, Geraldine thought.

"I need someone to protect me," Olivia's voice cracked. "You understand what it's like to get old, Genie." A tear ran down her sallow cheek.

Geraldine felt a pang of sympathy. She remembered vividly when the skeleton of a woman before her had been so sweet and fine that they'd called her Candy. "I know," she said at last and then, against her better judgment, added, "I'll see what Junior say."

After Olivia had gone, Geraldine relocked her front door. The vanilla scent of the small candle mingled with the spicy tang of her dinner. Somehow the odors didn't fight but made her feel cozy.

Geraldine switched on the television and began to eat. She couldn't keep her mind on either the local news or her enchilada. It kept wandering back to her last meeting with Melanie and the names the terrified girl had spewed out. At the time she would have bet that if anyone had her killed, it would be Andy. All the girls knew that he had a short, violent temper and tolerated no messing around. But now, she was not so sure. Nor did she think it was her second guess, Olivia. Not that the crazy 'ho' wouldn't do anything, even kill, to get Andy's attention. Again Geraldine felt the pang of sympathy that usually led to trouble. Maybe she would talk to Junior. Her nephew had a good heart; she knew that. And what harm could one old girl do to his stable? Nothing. And a little kindness never hurt.

Geraldine heard the vigil candle sputtering against its holder. Leaving her dinner, she crossed the room and blew out the dying flame. Staring at the small puddle of sweet-smelling wax, Geraldine was surprised that the tiny candle that had burned so brightly hadn't lasted very long. *Just like tiny bright Melanie*, she thought and felt her throat tighten with sadness. Who had blown out her young life?

If it wasn't Andy or Candy—funny how their names rhymed—it would have to be those fancy uptown people that Melanie was running on about. Dickie or Amanda or Betsy.

All at once, Geraldine felt overwhelmed. What did she know about the goings-on of fancy people? Close as she ever came to fancy was Lou. Sweet Lou! Tomorrow she'd buy another candle and burn it for his soul.

And tomorrow she'd go to the Refuge and talk to the old nun. The poor woman was not too bright about the street, Geraldine knew that, but she'd probably have some smarts about fancy people and she'd seen her talk to the police like they were friends.

That's the way I'll go. I'll talk to the Sister, Geraldine decided and felt as if a burden was lifted.

Full and warm, she settled into her easy chair to watch more news. She must have dozed off, because the front door buzzer startled her awake. *Who now?* she thought, fear gripping her stomach. She pushed the intercom. "Who there?" she demanded.

"Auntie, it be Junior," he answered in a gentle voice that belied his size.

"Come in, sweetheart." Geraldine pressed the front door opener. "Auntie got something to ask you."

❧☙❧☙

Betsy Dodd insisted on driving the Lexus as Mary Helen and she rode from Presidio Terrace to Mount St. Francis College in near-silence. To be perfectly honest, after the scene Mary Helen had witnessed in the Dodds' bedroom, she felt uncharacteristically speechless.

What did one say after watching a wife slashing at her husband with a butcher knife? "Marriage counseling might not be as effective, but it is more acceptable"? Or, "Have you ever thought about becoming a chef?" Or, "The family that slays together stays together"? She felt a giggle rising in her throat—probably a combination of hysteria and fatigue.

Should she call ahead to the college and ask them to hide all the knives? By any standard, this was crazy. Maybe she'd wake up to discover it was all a dream.

Betsy Dodd, for her part, clutched the steering wheel and stared straight ahead. Her round face had lost all of its color, and her jaw was set in a determined bite.

Mary, Mary, quite contrary, Mary Helen thought crazily. She was beginning to feel some sympathy with Crazy Alice.

"Will they mind?" Betsy asked out of the blue.

"Will who mind what, dear?" Mary Helen asked gently.

"The nuns." She spoke as if she were in a tunnel. "Will the nuns mind my coming?"

"Not at all," Mary Helen said, checking the car clock. Most

207

of them would be finishing dinner about now. *Thank God, she thought. With any luck at all, we can feed you and get you to your room without anyone seeing you. You're bound to look better in the morning.*

As planned, Sister Anne was waiting at the side door of the convent when they drove up. "Hello, you two!" she called cheerfully and opened the car door for Betsy. "What took you so long? I was beginning to worry."

If you only knew, Mary Helen thought, getting herself out of the passenger's seat. "Everything always takes longer than you think," she said evasively. She could tell by the expression on Anne's face that the young nun wasn't buying it. She sensed something was wrong. One look at their strained faces and anyone would know that all had not gone well.

Don't ask, Mary Helen urged silently, frowning all the while, in hopes that Anne would get the message.

Apparently Anne did. Without any more questions, she took Betsy's suitcase up the back stairs and put it in the guest room. "You can get settled after dinner," she said when she returned.

Talking cheerfully, Anne led the trio across the campus. On the way, she pointed out the choice views—the Bay Bridge, the East Bay hills. By taking the long way around she was able to show Betsy the Golden Gate, parts of Marin, and, closer to home, the magnificent dome of Temple Emanu-El, which bordered Presidio Terrace.

Although sightseeing was probably the last thing on Betsy's mind, she had the good grace to "ooh" and "aah" at all the right times. She even stopped for a moment at a retaining wall to admire the beauty of the sparkling bay, where tiny white sailboats bobbed.

Hoping for food, a bold blue jay landed on the wall near them. He cocked his head, flicked his long tail, and squawked. Mary Helen had read recently that there were no blue jays in

California, only Steller's jays and scrub jays. Well, it looked like a blue jay to her! Proving, once again, that often things are not what we think they are. Who would ever have thought that this meek, pleasant little woman standing next to her contained such rage? Furtively she studied the round, pudgy face and the troubled hazel eyes.

"We'd better hurry," Anne interrupted her musing. "I don't know what we're having for dinner, but whatever it is, it's better hot!"

When they arrived in the Sisters' dining room, Sister Patricia was just leaving. She paused long enough to greet Betsy Dodd and to assure her that she was most welcome at Mount St. Francis College.

Mary Helen could tell by her generic remarks that Patricia had no idea who Betsy Dodd was or that she lived less than a mile away. Good!

"You'll have to excuse me. I have a meeting in fifteen minutes," Patricia said and was gone.

One more reason to be grateful I left the college, Mary Helen thought, getting three trays. No more night meetings!

Anne led the way through the cafeteria line. Betsy followed as if she were in a daze, past the breaded pork chops, garlic mashed potatoes, hot applesauce for the pork chops, no doubt, and mixed vegetables. Mary Helen brought up the rear, making sure their guest had a decent meal and the silverware with which to eat it.

Mercifully, the Sisters' dining room was nearly empty. Only old Donata remained. Mary Helen's stomach fell. You could never quite be sure what Donata might say. The only one who could be worse was Sister Therese. With her you were sure she'd say something imprudent.

"Well, hello," Donata said, settling down next to Betsy at the table. "Welcome to the college."

There was no doubt in anyone's mind that old Donata knew exactly who Betsy was and was just too polite to ask what in heaven's name she was doing there.

Mary Helen knew that she'd better say something before Donata's curiosity got the best of her manners. "Mrs. Dodd will be staying with us tonight," Mary Helen began.

Donata nodded. So far so good.

Mary Helen stretched for a reason. The one they had planned to use—something amiss at home—was too close to the truth. Betsy looked as if the mere mention of her home might send her into orbit. That would never do.

She glanced toward Anne for help. Anne just looked puzzled. This was when Mary Helen really missed her friend Eileen. Eileen would surely think of something. She cleared her throat, stalling for time. What had Patricia just said? She was going to a meeting. That was as good as anything.

"We are having a little meeting tonight." Mary Helen didn't dare look at either Anne or Betsy. "In the front parlor." At least the room had a door they could close and an extra television set in it. Maybe there was a mystery on KQED or *Masterpiece Theatre*.

"And, in case it runs late, we thought Betsy should stay here—what with her husband away and all. It might not be wise for her to go into an empty house." She was babbling and she knew it.

"The woman lives in Presidio Terrace," Donata said flatly.

"Sometimes the most exclusive neighborhoods can be the most dangerous," Anne piped up. "Where would you go if you were a crook?"

"Where, indeed?" Donata asked. Clearly she was not fooled.

"Why don't you and Betsy go on ahead," Mary Helen suggested to Anne, "while I clear things up?" *In more ways than one*, she thought.

"What's this all about?" Donata asked as soon as they were alone. "And don't give me that baloney about a meeting. Baloney is baloney, no matter how it's served up. And I'm not so old that I can't recognize it."

"Can you keep a secret?" Mary Helen asked.

Old Donata's eyes lit up. There was nothing she liked better than a secret. "At my age, I've a closed mouth and a wise head."

"Sit down then and remember this must go nowhere."

"Nowhere," Donata repeated. The pink tip of her tongue moistened her lips.

"There has been a murder at the Refuge."

Donata looked disappointed. "Tell me something I don't know."

"What you don't know is that the victim mentioned several names before she died."

"And?" Donata prompted.

"One of them might be someone Betsy knows."

Donata blinked. "Like the husband," she said, almost to herself.

"I never said that."

"You didn't have to. Why else would she be staying here? And don't give me that meeting business again. In all the time that Anne has been at the Refuge, she's never had a meeting here."

"It was a good try," Mary Helen said, rising to clear the table.

"Speak up!" Donata said. "What about a good cry?"

"Try," Mary Helen enunciated. She must be on Donata's bad side.

"What were the names the poor woman gave?" Donata asked.

Mary Helen hesitated, although she could think of no reason not to tell her. Everyone at the Refuge knew the names. "Andy, the pimp," she began.

"Candy? Isn't that an odd name for a man?"

"Andy," Mary Helen repeated. "Is your hearing aid turned on?"

Donata reached for her ear and adjusted the small amplifier. "It was too loud during dinner and then Therese was telling a long story." She smiled wickedly. "I plead self-defense. Go on with the names."

"Dickie, Amanda, and Betsy."

"Dickie and Betsy could be the Dodds. Richard and Elizabeth—always in the society pages." Donata pursed her lips. "But who is Amanda?"

"Seems to be someone Richard knows."

"The plot sickens." Donata yawned and checked her wristwatch. "Almost time for *Wheel of Fortune*," she said.

"Not a word to anyone," Mary Helen cautioned.

"Scouts' honor," Donata said, moving slowly from the dining room. She looked as pleased as if she'd just been told how to get through the electronic devices guarding the vaults at Fort Knox.

✿✿✿✿

Sister Anne smiled over at Betsy Dodd sitting on the edge of the overstuffed couch and wondered, once again, how she'd ended up in this mess. The parlor was small and smelled musty and unused—even a bit damp despite the warm September days.

Someone, probably Therese, had dusted recently and put a bouquet of fresh white chrysanthemums on the coffee table. These were the only signs that anyone ever came into the room, which was probably true.

The parlor was a leftover amenity from pre–Vatican Two times, when no one except the nuns, and on rare occasions a priest, doctor, or workman, was allowed inside the cloister. It provided a place to visit with family or friends, although its size and general appearance encouraged short, infrequent meetings.

"Did you have enough to eat?" Anne asked, straining for conversation.

"Yes, thank you. Delicious," Betsy answered like an automaton.

Anne wondered if she asked the woman what they had for dinner whether or not Betsy would be able to answer. She had left her plate nearly untouched.

Anne itched to know what had happened between the time Mary Helen and Betsy left the Refuge and the time they'd met her at the side door of the convent. Something! That was apparent from their faces. On the one hand, Mary Helen's face was dangerously flushed, as if she'd been under a sunlamp. On the other hand, Betsy's face was flat white. Anne had seen marble statues with more color.

Besides, Mary Helen had changed the reason that they planned to give for Betsy's stay at the convent. Something had definitely happened. She wondered how long it would take for her to be told what it was.

Anne bristled. After all, she was in charge of the center. She had every right—actually an obligation—to know what went on down there.

She heard familiar footsteps coming down the hall. Betsy must have heard them, too. Anne saw her stiffen. "It's only Sister Mary Helen," Anne said lightly. "I recognize her footsteps."

Betsy stared at her. Nothing was going to be light tonight.

Sister Mary Helen cracked open the parlor door and quickly closed it behind her. "We didn't fool Donata for one minute," she said softly.

"Did you think you would?" Anne asked, feeling even more put upon since she seemed to be the only one in the dark.

"The good news is we don't have to explain anything to anyone. I just passed the community room and they're watching a video. No one will be around for a good two hours."

"Then, I can go to bed?" This was the first full sentence Betsy had spoken since her arrival at the college. Anne saw that the woman was dangerously close to collapse.

"I'll take her up the back stairs to her room," Anne said, "and then, Mary Helen, you and I can sit in here. No one will know that only two of us are 'meeting.' "

Anne was surprised when Mary Helen had no objections and she went quickly.

When she returned, Mary Helen looked absorbed in *Inspector Morse*. It was a rerun and Anne knew she'd seen it before.

"Can we talk?" Anne said, pushing mute on the remote control.

At first, Mary Helen looked as though she might object, but she must have sensed Anne's frustration. Turning to face her, the old nun pushed her bifocals up the bridge of her nose. Suddenly she looked her age.

"You're wondering what happened at Presidio Terrace, aren't you?" Mary Helen asked. Then, uncharacteristically, she leaned forward and patted Anne's hand. "I was waiting for the opportunity to tell you," she said.

Anne smiled sheepishly, a little ashamed for being annoyed. Presidio Terrace? She had been afraid that whatever happened had happened at her center. That something had gone on at Betsy's home had never occurred to her.

"After we got there, the Dodds had a terrible fight," Mary Helen said, her face grim.

"A verbal fight or a 'fight' fight?" Anne asked, scarcely able to believe her ears.

"A 'fight' fight," Mary Helen said. Her face flushed again

and she seemed reluctant to go into the details. "It was something to behold, and to tell you the truth, I was terrified that I was about to witness another murder." She adjusted her bifocals again and studied Anne's face for several seconds. "To be perfectly candid," she said, "I was fearful that if I went with what we planned—something amiss at home—Betsy might go to pieces. That would never do."

"What did you finally tell Donata?" Anne asked.

"That we were meeting about the names Melanie mentioned before she died."

"She fell for that?"

"She seemed to and she won't tell anyone else, I'm sure. She's given me scouts' honor."

"Scouts' honor?" Anne laughed nervously. "How many years since Donata's been a scout?"

"Once a scout, always a scout," Mary Helen said, "and Sister Patricia was the only other one who saw our guest."

"We're safe then," Anne said. "The whole community will be in bed before she gets home."

Although the pair lapsed into silence, half-watching *Inspector Morse*, Anne could not get the fighting Dodds off her mind. "Fighting?" she asked aloud. "Really fighting?"

Mary Helen nodded.

"Punching each other?"

"No."

"Then, what?"

Mary Helen pushed herself up from the parlor chair. "I've seen this episode," she said, "and I just remembered who the murderer is. So, if you don't mind being alone, I think I'll go to bed, too. It's been quite a day."

"Oh, no, you don't!" Anne complained. "You can't go and leave me wondering. How were the Dodds fighting? Don't tell me they were using karate." The mental picture of proper Betsy throwing her chubby leg at her husband's chest tested Anne's imagination.

Mary Helen hesitated, not knowing how much Anne could handle. "Well, if you must know, one was slashing at the other with a very large, very sharp butcher knife."

Long after Mary Helen left the parlor, Anne sat stunned. Inspector Morse solved his case. During the running of the credits it occurred to Anne that Mary Helen had said that one was slashing. She just assumed it was Richard. *Of course it was,* she thought. *If it were Betsy, she'd surely have told me that. Wouldn't she?*

⚘⚘⚘

Inspector Kate Murphy had just put breaded chicken breasts and sweet potatoes in the oven to bake when she heard her husband's key in the front door.

"Hi, Mom," her small son, John, cried out and ran down the hall to smother her with hugs and kisses.

"How was your day?" Kate asked, holding him close for an extra squeeze.

Wriggling out of her arms, he mumbled, "Fine," then started up the stairs to his bedroom to check on his hamster, who was called just that, Hamster.

"And how was your day, hon?" Jack asked, removing the bullets from his service revolver and storing both the ammunition and the gun on the top shelf of the closet next to hers.

Kate wiped her hands on her apron. "Good news," she said, watching her husband fix her a vodka tonic and bourbon and water for himself.

"Salud!" He raised his glass. "Let's hear it for good news!"

Settling down in the living room while the dinner cooked, Kate told him about Gallagher's appointment with the doctor.

"How did you do it?" Jack was clearly impressed.

"Not me," Kate admitted. "Mrs. G.—she made his appointment."

"How'd he take it?" Jack asked with a grimace.

"How do you think?" Kate laughed, remembering Gallagher's reaction to his wife's phone call. "But the point is, he's there now."

"That was fast."

"That was probably the only way she could get him there. If she'd given him any time to think, he'd have figured an excuse to get out of going. This way he will get some help if he needs it—which I hope and pray he doesn't," she added.

"It is probably something simple," Jack said quietly.

"I know; I know." Kate felt the tears rush to her eyes. She could scarcely stand the thought of the job without Gallagher. Although they often got on each other's nerves, they had been partners for so long that he was like a second self. "He's been looking so pale and washed out," she said miserably.

"But he hasn't lost any weight." Always practical, Jack gave her an encouraging smile

"You're right," Kate conceded. She hadn't thought of that. Although tonight neither of them mentioned the C word, he knew cancer was what Kate feared. As Jack pointed out, it usually involved weight loss and Gallagher still had his very substantial paunch. It hadn't lost an inch, Kate thought happily.

"Did I ever tell you you'd make a fine detective?" Kate joked. She took another sip of her drink. Why did she always anticipate the worst? Maybe it came from being a Homicide detective. Just when you think you've seen it all, you come across something like the young prostitute Melanie Rogers— her face covered with blood, her skull pulverized by a blunt object until tiny pieces of brain clung to her mousy blond hair. She was just a child.

"Are you all right?" Jack sounded concerned.

"Sorry," Kate said. "I was just thinking about the murdered prostitute. Don't ask me how I went from Denny to Melanie, but I did."

"How is that going?" Jackie asked.

"We should get a break soon," Kate said.

"How's that?" Jack rose to fix them a second drink.

"Dinner will be ready in another fifteen minutes," she reminded him.

"A bird can't fly on one wing alone," Jack said.

He said that every time he refreshed their drinks. Kate smiled. It was part of the ritual. They had become an old married couple. The next thing you knew, they'd start looking alike.

"What makes you think you'll break the case soon?" he asked, returning with their glasses.

It always amazed Kate how he could come right back to the point. "Well, for one thing, somebody's posted a five-thousand-dollar reward for information leading to her killer," she said, "and I think Wong and Dineen will distribute some fliers tonight to the homeless shelters. Whether or not they let on, those folks don't miss anything that happens on the streets. And five thousand dollars is a big incentive for them to share their information."

Kate noticed that her husband was unusually silent. "What is it?" she asked.

"Isn't that odd—someone offering a reward to find the perp in the case of the young prostitute? They're usually runaways."

From upstairs she heard their son talking and giggling. He must be chatting with Hamster. How, she wondered, could any mother cope with a runaway youngster? Not knowing where he or she was, worse yet, knowing he or she was on the streets, scarcely surviving. She wouldn't be able to bear it.

"Kate?" Jack's voice interrupted her melancholy thoughts. This case had really gotten to her. Maybe it was because the girl was so young or her murder had been so brutal. "Sorry," she said. "I was just thinking about Melanie again. You're right. It is extremely unusual for someone to offer a reward. That's what makes us think we can break the case quickly. Someone is bound to snitch."

"Who put up the reward money?" Jack was on this reward like a bloodhound on a scent.

"Wants to remain anonymous," Kate admitted.

"Who did she know with that kind of money? And why would that person want the killer found?" Jack was talking to himself now. "Either because the donor feels that he might be a suspect and wants himself cleared before the police arrested him or maybe because he is guilty and wants someone else blamed before suspicion falls on him. A five-thousand-dollar reward in this neighborhood makes fingering the wrong man a distinct possibility. What else do you know about the perp?" Jack asked.

"Not too much," Kate admitted. "That he is strong or, at least, his adrenaline made him strong enough to crush a young woman's skull."

"What else?"

"That the crime wasn't necessarily premeditated. You don't commit premeditated murder with a cup or vase for a weapon."

"Which jibes with your theory that the adrenaline was high. Maybe from fear or, more likely, from anger or frustration."

"With any luck at all, Forensics will have checked out all the cups they collected," Kate said. "We could really get lucky and find the weapon. Which would at least narrow it down to someone who was at the Refuge."

"Or knew somebody who was." Jack was clearly playing the devil's advocate. "The perp could've handed a cup to some woman who was going into the place."

"Right," Kate agreed, "but in a sense, it would narrow it down."

"Anything else about the perp?"

"Nothing very much. He knew the area well enough to drop the body at the Refuge." Kate stopped. "Wait a minute, Jack. Why are we saying 'he'? It could just as well have been a woman. Besides, most of the names that Melanie gave were women. Amanda is really the only one we can't pinpoint."

For several seconds they were both silent. John's laughter floated down the stairs, making them smile. Kate twirled a small lock of hair around her index finger and pushed it into a curl. "Tomorrow we are going to ask the Chief for the name of the anonymous donor."

Jack laughed. "What if it turns out to be Richard Dodd? You'd have to ask him why he was so generous and so concerned. With all the connections he has, that visit will be like walking through a minefield."

"Whether he is the anonymous donor or not, we need to pay Mr. Dodd a visit, and we've avoided it about as long as we can."

Kate heard the timer on the stove go off and John's small, firm footsteps descend the steps. She rose. "Which is another reason I hope Denny gets a clean bill of health," she said. "I can hardly wait to hear his reaction to visiting Attorney Dodd in his fancy office. It should be a classic."

They both laughed.

"Dinner ready?" little John asked. He stood in the doorway. "A classic," he repeated, looking puzzled. "Is that another grown-up joke?"

❧❧

Sister Mary Helen was exhausted. She was so sure she'd fall right to sleep that she didn't even open her Linda Grant mystery. To her surprise, even after a hot bath she lay in bed staring up at her bedroom ceiling. Oddly shaped shadows formed by the headlights on Turk Street danced across the room.

In the distance, foghorns bleated. San Francisco's automatic air-conditioning system was going into action. Tomorrow would be cooler. *Good*, she thought, wondering if she should lower the window. In the end, she was too lazy to get out of bed. A little chill might help her sleep like Betsy.

Before she'd gone to her own room, Mary Helen had checked on Betsy Dodd. From the look of things, the woman was asleep, or at least pretending to be. In either case, she obviously didn't want to be disturbed. Betsy, too, was no doubt exhausted after expending all that physical and emotional energy flailing at her husband.

Mary Helen couldn't block the scene from her mind. If it hadn't been so deadly serious, it would be comical. Pudgy, proper little Betsy shouting and slashing while distinguished looking Richard quailed behind a slipper chair, begging her to stop.

It was macabre! That was the only word for it. What had triggered Betsy's reaction? Mary Helen wondered. At the Refuge and in the car on the way to her home, Betsy had seemed afraid of her husband—frightened that he might hurt her—or so it seemed to Mary Helen. That was why she had invited Betsy to spend tonight at the convent. Actually, Betsy had seemed afraid for her very life.

Mary Helen suspected that was why she had taken the butcher knife from the kitchen upstairs with her. A sure sign that she was terrified of someone.

What had changed? What had Richard said or done to set off such a reaction? Surely something sinister had happened in that bedroom. She shuddered to think how things might have turned out if she hadn't gone upstairs. Would Betsy have actually killed her husband?

Not likely. She seemed too conscientious, too polite, too sweet—yes, too plain and passive—to suddenly kill someone. *No matter what you read in murder mysteries, it just doesn't happen that way in real life*, Mary Helen thought. *Or does it?* Mary Helen felt a little itch of uncertainty. She plumped up her pillow and turned on her side. Should she tell Kate Murphy and Inspector Gallagher what she had witnessed? Absolutely! But would she? She wasn't as positive about that.

She knew how upset Inspector Gallagher could become if he thought she was interfering with one of his cases. *Interfering, indeed! she thought indignantly.* Stepping into that bedroom this afternoon may have actually prevented a homicide.

But would he see it that way? Of course not! Furthermore, when she had seen him today she thought he was looking a little wan, not quite himself. There was no sense adding to his discomfort. Besides, what bearing did a squabble between a husband and wife have on the case he was investigating? None whatsoever. Even she had to admit that it had been considerably more than your ordinary squabble, not that that had any bearing on the situation. If she found it did, she would tell the inspectors immediately.

Sister Mary Helen closed her eyes and tried to think of nothing. What a foolish expression! How could anyone think nothing? Especially with all there was on her mind.

How was she going to explain Betsy's presence to the nuns at breakfast? Quite simply. She'd tell them that they had a late meeting, which they did. "They" being Anne and herself—so it wasn't a bold-faced lie. Probably no one would ask anyway. They'd all be too busy getting their breakfasts and heading off to work.

Mary Helen tried deep breathing. That usually put her to sleep. She wasn't sure whether it was the actual breathing or the fact that she had to concentrate so hard to make her diaphragm expand that she forgot everything else.

Tonight that didn't work, either. The cups popped into her mind. The police had confiscated every white cup in the Refuge. Maybe they'd return them. If they didn't, Anne must have paper cups somewhere for emergencies—not that she'd ever had this kind of emergency before, thank heaven.

Shifting the covers over her shoulder, Mary Helen wondered whether or not the young nun was asleep yet. After a day like today, she hoped so. Should she have suggested hot milk or checked on her, too, as she had on Betsy? *Don't be silly*, she chided herself. *No sense waking someone up to ask if she is asleep.*

Tires screeched on Anza Street, glass shattered, and a dog began to bark furiously. Obviously his sleep was disturbed, too.

And what good was losing sleep doing her? No matter how hard she tried, she couldn't seem to get a handle on this homicide. Was Melanie's world too foreign to her? Or was she stumped because she had no one with whom to bounce around her ideas? All at once, Mary Helen felt a pang of loneliness. She missed her dear friend Eileen.

She glanced over at the illuminated clock on her bed stand. Ten o'clock. Quickly she counted. It was six in the morning in Ireland—entirely too early to call anyone living on the Emerald Isle. She would call tomorrow. By then there might well be something to talk about.

Surrendering any hope of sleeping, Mary Helen decided to let her mind run free, like the psychics on television did. Not that she'd ever been very successful in stopping it. Inanely she wondered if she had that sappy look on her face that the TV seers affected.

For some inexplicable reason, she remembered entering the Refuge on her first day. She saw frail Melanie. Like a frightened animal, Melanie had darted from the place. "Andy is going to kill me," Mary Helen heard her say.

From nowhere, old Donata appeared in her imagination. "Candy?" she asked. "Isn't that an odd name for a man?"

She heard it wrong, Mary Helen thought. As reticent as she was to admit it, her own hearing wasn't all that keen, either. Today she had heard "Lexus, the drug boy," instead of "Texas, the drug boy." Had she heard the name incorrectly? Was that the key to this mystery? Had Melanie actually said "Candy"?

Mary Helen remembered that Candy was a street name, although at the moment she wasn't sure whose. Geraldine would know, or Miss Bobbie. Those ladies knew everything. Maybe Melanie had named her murderer and she had just been deaf to it.

Tomorrow she'd ask her friends at the Refuge, then maybe call Eileen. Tomorrow. It was nearly tomorrow already. She'd better get to sleep. Where had the day gone? Morning Mass seemed so far away. What saint had they commemorated today? It took her a few seconds to remember. Nicholas of Tolentino, a thirteenth-century Italian priest whose eloquent preaching had moved the hearts of hardened sinners.

What would touch the heart of Melanie's killer? she wondered. Her eyes burned and she shut them.

Where do I go from here, Lord? she prayed earnestly.

But the Lord seemed to remain silent. Mary Helen took another deep breath and let it out slowly. *Do You want me to keep trying to figure out this killer? Or is it time for me to let go?*

She swallowed hard. *Because, Lord, if You want me to let go, I will.*

Although she wouldn't swear to it, she thought she heard the Lord say, "Fat chance!"

Friday, September 11

❧❦❦❧

Saints Protus and Hyacinth, Martyrs

S ister Mary Helen had just settled in her pew for morning Mass when Betsy Dodd moved in beside her. For some reason Mary Helen had not expected her up this early. She smiled over at Betsy, who seemed in a deeper fog than that covering the college. The woman stared straight ahead.

Before Mary Helen left her bedroom, she had read an excerpt from *Butler's Lives of the Saints.* Today the Church commemorated Saints Protus and Hyacinth, brothers and slaves, who in the third century had become Christians only to be put to death for their faith.

Betsy's rigid jaw and pallid skin looked as though she were awaiting the same fate. *Saint Protus and Hyacinth, and Betsy,* Mary Helen thought, giddy from lack of sleep. She must tell that one to Eileen when she called her today, and she surely would call her. She was counting up the hours to determine the best time when Father Adams entered the sanctuary. The congregation rose to begin the liturgy.

Breakfast went much as Mary Helen had expected. Sister Anne, looking none the worse for wear, had eaten on the run. "See you at the Refuge," she said in a half-question, half-statement.

Mary Helen checked her wristwatch. "What's the rush?" she'd asked.

Anne leaned closer. "I want to be there if the police call," she whispered, and Betsy's face became almost gray.

By and large, all the other nuns were preoccupied, too, with getting to their ministries. Only Therese seemed to have time to talk. Although Betsy was polite, she was about as communicative as a mummy, so that even Therese gave up trying to start a conversation.

"Did you sleep well?" Mary Helen asked when they were alone.

Betsy nodded. "As well as can be expected," she said. The bruiselike half-moons under her bloodshot eyes betrayed how well that was.

"Maybe you should go back to bed," Mary Helen suggested. Betsy looked in no condition to spend the day at the Refuge. "The convent will be quiet and no one will disturb you."

"No!" Betsy snapped, her eyes haunted. She hugged herself as though she was freezing.

"Suit yourself," Mary Helen said with a shrug. She wished someone would suggest that she go back to bed. She'd be under the covers in a heartbeat.

The ride from Mount St. Francis College to the Refuge was unnaturally quiet. Several times Mary Helen tried to start a conversation. When she realized that it would take the Jaws of Life to get anything but a "yes" or "no" out of Betsy, she decided to let it go.

Instead she stared out the car window. A group of wind-torn Japanese tourists hurried down the Geary Boulevard hill toward the Japan Center with its graceful Peace Pagoda, probably longing for a taste of home. Farther on, a man sat on a fourth-story windowsill of an apartment building washing the glass. Mary Helen shuddered to think of what could happen. Another jaunty fellow in a fishing hat emptied parking meters. She wondered if he was an eccentric official or a very clever crook.

Along the route, she watched commuters, bundled up in coats and hats and scarves, shivering at the bus stop waiting for the crowded Muni. By the time they arrived downtown the sun would probably be shining. Once in a while, a pedestrian caught her eye with a look of envy—probably of the temperature-controlled Lexus. If they only knew the misery that went with it!

Mary Helen stole a glance at her companion. Who would have ever thought that the quiet, well-mannered, affluent woman beside her was capable of such rage? She appeared so self-controlled, which probably should have been Mary Helen's first clue. Proper Betsy was like a dormant volcano. Yesterday afternoon she'd witnessed only a small explosion.

Closing her eyes, Mary Helen tried not to think of the cowering husband, the stuffing all over the floor, the wild slashing with the butcher knife. The butcher knife! What had happened to it? With that thought, Mary Helen's eyes popped open.

Betsy had put her black leather purse on the floor behind the driver seat. If Mary Helen remembered correctly, it was large enough to easily conceal a knife—a whole set of knives, actually.

She gave a quick, wild glance in that direction. There it was! Surely she hadn't put the knife in it. No sensible woman would have. She must have put it back in the knife block in her kitchen. Mary Helen had not been paying much attention.

"What's the matter?" Betsy's voice startled her.

She must have seen Mary Helen craning toward the back-seat. "Nothing, dear," Mary Helen said, hoping her voice was steady. "I must have slept the wrong way, that's all." Closing her eyes, she circled her head as if she had a crick in her neck. Her explanation seemed to satisfy Betsy.

Whew! Mary Helen thought, wondering how long the woman planned to stay at the convent. Now might be an opening to ask. She looked over at Betsy's grim profile and decided against it. Actually, it could wait. Today at the Refuge should be challenge enough.

Even before she opened the front door, Mary Helen could tell that the place was packed. From the outside she heard the noise. Everyone seemed to be talking, and, as far as she could tell, no one was doing much listening.

"Morning, girlfriend!" Miss Bobbie shouted as soon as she stepped inside. "You see this?" Miss Bobbie's dark eyes sparkled as she waved a single sheet of paper toward Mary Helen.

Papers waved from all over the gathering room. Mary Helen grabbed the one that was closest. **Special Bulletin,** it stated in bold red letters next to a colored picture of Melanie Rogers looking terrified.

"That must be her first mug shot," Miss Bobbie explained, "she look so scared."

Quickly Mary Helen scanned the flier. It gave the particulars of Melanie's murder and promised a reward of $5,000 for information leading to the arrest of her killer. The Homicide Detail phone number was listed at the bottom of the page along with the names of both Kate Murphy and Inspector Gallagher.

"Where did these come from?" Mary Helen asked.

Peanuts spoke up in a voice too large for her tiny body. "Last night two Vice police, Wong and Dineen, they come by the shelters. They give one of these out to anybody who wants.

Five thousand dollars!" Her dark eyes danced. "Who got that kind of money?"

Who, indeed? Mary Helen thought. *Someone must want the killer apprehended very badly.* She glanced toward Betsy, who stood in the doorway looking as though she were frozen.

"That be a lot of money," Peanuts said again.

Over the din, Crazy Alice's giggle rang out, making the hair on Mary Helen's arms bristle.

> *"Up and down the City Road,*
> *In and out the Eagle,*
> *That's the way the money goes—*
> *Pop goes the weasel."*

❧❧❧

"I'm so glad you're here," Sister Anne said, hurrying from the kitchen. She was pushing a cart laden with more trays of doughnuts, sugar, cream, and paper napkins. She couldn't remember when so many women had arrived at the Refuge before ten o'clock. There must be at least fifty. And the morning volunteers had both called in sick.

Anne watched Betsy Dodd, head down, make her way across the room straight toward the apron cupboard. *Amazing!* Anne thought. *That Betsy is a real trooper! Imagine being slashed at by your husband*—and a good night's sleep had convinced Anne that Richard had done the slashing—*being driven out of your own home, then showing up to serve the poor as if nothing had happened. You can't help but admire that kind of courage,* Anne thought, smiling at Betsy over a sea of waving reward fliers.

Thank goodness she had come with Mary Helen. The three of them could keep on top of things until the police arrived, whenever that would be.

About fifteen minutes before, Inspector Gallagher had called to say that he and Kate Murphy would be down sometime this morning. He had cautioned Anne to say nothing to anyone. Surely that didn't include Sister Mary Helen. Anne would fill her in the first chance she had. Undoubtedly, the inspector meant the ladies. One whiff that the police were coming and they'd clear out faster than the morning fog.

Unaware, the Refugees were talking long and loud about Melanie's death and especially about the reward. Few prostitutes, either living or dead, had $5,000 offered on their behalf.

Anne heard names bandied about, but the popular favorite seemed to be that of Andy, the pimp. Not that he did the dirty work himself. He'd forced someone to do it for him.

"He a mean one," Peanuts said, shaking her graying head.

"He don't tolerate no messing around." The scar near Miss Bobbie's right eye twitched. "And she be messing!" She nodded her head knowingly.

"Messing around with whom?" Anne wanted to ask, but knew better. The women would stop talking freely the moment they realized that she was listening. And she needed the police to solve this thing so she could get the Refuge back to normal—whenever that was—as quickly as possible. Surely before her donors and volunteers got wind of what had happened. Everyone feels better supporting a place that is safe and successful. It's only human.

She hoped she'd have gleaned some helpful information from the ladies before the Homicide inspectors arrived. Anne stopped in her tracks. She was beginning to sound like, of all people, Mary Helen. *Walk with the lame and you'll soon limp*, she thought with a smile. She could do worse!

"May I have a shower roll?" Venus asked. She grinned wide enough to show her missing front tooth. "I needs to be clean to collect my reward."

"Reward?" Anne bit. "So you know who killed her?"

230

Venus's dark eyes were shrewd. She nodded toward the far side of the room, where Olivia's platinum hair stood out in the crowd.

Olivia's brown eyes, hard as glass, swept the room.

"You got to beat me to the police," Peanuts called out and the whole room exploded with laughter.

Only Crazy Alice was uncharacteristically quiet.

Sister Anne had just made two pots of fresh coffee when Geraldine came through the door looking as if she had bad news.

"How do, Genie!" Miss Bobbie called. Despite the fact that all the seats were occupied, she motioned Geraldine to sit at her table. Without any fuss, one woman moved.

Sister Anne was never quite sure how or why that happened. And, in a sense, she was afraid to find out.

Geraldine, her hair freshly done, sat heavily in the chair. Anne moved closer. Eavesdropping wasn't easy in this noisy room.

"What's wrong?" You could count on Miss Bobbie's directness.

Geraldine recoiled. "What make you think something's wrong?" she asked, although anyone with eyes could see that it was. "Nothing wrong. I just need to take care of my business."

Sister Anne couldn't help but wonder what that was.

Miss Bobbie shrugged. "I know about business," she said and turned slightly in her chair, giving the distinct, if subtle, impression that she was hurt.

When Geraldine didn't seem to notice or care, Miss Bobbie took a different tack. "Did you see the reward paper?" she asked.

"You have to be blind, deaf, and dumb not to," Geraldine said. "They all over the streets." She took a folded flier from her pocket and smoothed it out on the table.

"Word says it be Andy kill her," Miss Bobbie prodded.

Geraldine's nostrils flared. Anne couldn't ever remember seeing her this upset. What was it?

231

"I think the word be wrong," Geraldine's eyes were enormous.

"And how you know?" Miss Bobbie's mouth was a determined line. Her scar twitched.

" 'Cuz I know," Geraldine said. Her voice was gentle, but her eyes were fierce.

"Then who?" Miss Bobbie was not to be deterred.

"How you expect me to know that?" Geraldine asked. She excused herself and went to seek out Sister Mary Helen. *What's that all about?* Anne wondered, and she might have even asked Mary Helen, except that Sonia interrupted her.

"It's my turn in the shower and Venus won't get out," she complained.

Anne went immediately to the showers to sort things out. When she'd finished, she returned to the gathering room to find Mary Helen. By now her curiosity was getting the better of her manners. She scanned the room. The old nun was not there. Neither was Geraldine. Where had they gone?

Something inside her turned over, then sank. *Don't tell me she's gone somewhere with Geraldine. She wouldn't do that without telling me, would she?* The panic began to rise in Anne's throat. *She has no idea how dangerous this neighborhood can be.* Anne rushed into the kitchen, then checked the office and the laundry room. The sleep room was empty, too, as well as the conference room.

Her heart was pounding now. They must have left the Refuge. Desperate, Anne checked the staff bathroom—empty! What should she do? She couldn't leave Betsy here alone. She couldn't leave Mary Helen out there. How would she explain to the other nuns that she'd lost her?

Anne felt the tears flash into her eyes. What should she do? Crazy Alice was staring at her. Her fear must have been showing. She forced herself to smile, to walk slowly toward the entryway.

She had almost reached it when the door swung open and Mary Helen and Geraldine entered together. They had simply stepped outside.

All at once, Anne was angry. "Where were you?" she demanded. Her tone shocked even herself. To her amazement, she sounded like her own mother had when Anne was a teenager.

Pulling herself to her full height, Sister Mary Helen pushed the bifocals up the bridge of her nose. The dimples in her cheeks flashed with anger. She stared at Anne, as though choosing her words very carefully. Slowly, to Anne's relief, the hazel eyes softened. "You were worried, weren't you?" Mary Helen asked softly.

Sister Anne felt the tears burn her eyes.

"You were afraid that I'd gone somewhere with Geraldine?"

Not trusting herself to speak, Anne simply nodded.

"Anne," Mary Helen said gently, "I appreciate your concern, but I'm retired, not senile. Besides, dear, it's best to learn young not to shake hands with the devil until you meet him. And he wasn't even close."

❧❧❧❧

"About time!" Inspector Dennis Gallagher snarled when Kate Murphy walked into the Homicide Detail.

She checked her wristwatch. Actually, she was five minutes early. One look at her partner's jowly face told her it was pointless to mention it. What had happened? She had seen healthier color on a corpse.

"What are you looking at?" he growled.

"You!" Kate said sharply. "What the hell set you off this early in the morning?"

Gallagher pointed toward the coffee room just as Mark Wong emerged, a mug in his hand. "Good morning," Wong said, yawning.

233

"You look more like 'good night,' " Kate said, studying his lined face. Even his eyes were dull with fatigue. "Bad night?"

"So-so," Wong said, taking a sip of the coffee, then making a face.

Kate made a mental note to avoid the coffee at all costs.

Wong set his mug down on the nearest desk. "I just stopped by," he said, "to bring you and your partner, Grumpy Gallagher, up-to-speed on the Melanie Rogers case."

"Don't push your luck with the jokes," Gallagher mumbled. Slumping into his chair, he swiveled toward the windows and stared at the congested James Lick Freeway.

"Like I was telling you before Kate arrived, Dineen and I talked to Andy last night and then to Olivia. You know, the skinny white prostitute with the platinum head. Street name Candy?"

Kate nodded. "And?" she said.

"And both of them claim to be innocent." Wong covered another yawn. "Funny thing, I believe them.

"Last night, we also distributed those reward fliers at the shelters." He pointed to a small pile of papers on Kate's desk. "They must have arrived during the night shift. Someone sure was eager to get them on the streets."

"I know," Gallagher said wearily and skimmed through a stack of pink memo slips. "We must have had fifty calls already," he added. "Do you have any idea how long it will take us to contact all these people? Most of them gave the same phone numbers, which, I imagine, are from the pay phones near the shelters."

Kate was beginning to understand why her partner was crabby.

Wong just shrugged. "Bummer," he said, "but here's something that maybe you can use. I was just in someone's office and I found out from a reliable source that the person offering the reward is none other than Mr. Richard Dodd, attorney-at-law."

"Why would he do that?" Kate asked.

"According to my source"—folding his arms, Wong leaned against the edge of Kate's desk—"Dodd claims it is a humanitarian gesture, helping the downtrodden and underserved, whose lives and deaths are as important as those of the most prominent individuals."

Kate felt that a gagging sound might be appropriate.

"Furthermore," Wong continued, "and I quote, his wife 'works at the Refuge,' and he's 'doing it out of deference to her devotion to the charity.' "

"And what do the Department cynics say?" Kate asked.

"That the guy is somehow involved and wants to throw suspicion in another direction." Wong paused for several seconds. "Or maybe it's his wife." Wong paused.

Kate was taken aback. "Those are the supercynics," she said. "Betsy Dodd is as pure and clean as the driven snow."

"And every bit as boring," Wong said. "Yeah, I know. For whatever it's worth."

Kate Murphy watched Gallagher run the palm of his hand over his bald pate and loosen his necktie. For a minute, he looked as if he might get sick.

"See you guys later," Wong said with a weary wave, "and good luck."

"Who do you think his reliable source is?" Gallagher asked, turning to stare, once again, out the window at the crowded freeway.

"Susie Chang from the Chief's office," Kate said. She had overheard two women on the building elevator saying Wong and Chang were an item. Not that it made the rumor true, but Kate's answer seemed to satisfy Gallagher.

"I guess there is no sense avoiding it any longer," Gallagher said, sounding as if he were referring to a one-way trip to the guillotine. "We've got to question Dodd."

"You bet we do." Kate was beginning to get impatient. "And this isn't a bit like you," she said.

Her partner looked up. Behind his horn-rimmed glasses his blue eyes were rheumy. He had a puzzled expression on his face. "What isn't like me?" he asked flatly.

"To let someone—anyone—intimidate you."

"I'm not intimidated," he growled, straightening his tie.

Kate was glad to hear a hint of the old Gallagher in his voice. "If you're not intimidated, then why are you so hesitant?"

Gallagher stared at her for a full minute. It was almost as if he hadn't seen her before. "To be honest, I'm just tired, Katie-girl," he said. "I'm so near retirement that I can taste it. I don't need no big hassles, no trouble with the Chief, no commissioner chewing my ass, no supervisors or, worse yet, the mayor sticking their noses in where they don't belong. I just want to solve a simple prostitute's homicide by arresting some lowlife perp."

He paused for breath. "If you must know, I'm not feeling up to a high-profile case where I'm taking crap from a smart-ass lawyer who thinks he's the greatest thing since sliced bread. You remember what he said in the *Chron*?"

Kate nodded. "All the more reason to go after him."

Her partner stared at her in disbelief. "All the more reason the bastard will shout police harassment! And if we go after his wife, even my own good wife will be furious! Betsy Dodd is always in the society pages doing good works. We'd sooner go after Mother Teresa, may she rest in peace."

The color had returned to Gallagher's face. It was no wonder, Kate thought, after all that ranting.

"Not that we have any choice." Gallagher wasn't finished yet. "If Dodd or even his wife is involved, then we will go after them." He checked the clock on the Homicide Detail wall. "And the sooner the better."

Abruptly Gallagher stood and pulled up the belt of his

trousers over his paunch. Kate waited for him to check his tie and run his fingers around his fringe of hair. She couldn't help noticing, despite the high color, how worn out he looked. It made her sad and a little frightened. What had Kaiser discovered? Was that what was really bothering him? She was itching to ask, but now didn't seem like a very good time.

They were just about out of the Homicide Detail when the telephone rang. "For you!" Myrtle called out, nodding her head toward Kate.

Picking up the nearest phone, Kate was surprised to hear the medical examiner's voice. "Good news," he said. "We've identified the weapon."

"You identified the weapon," she repeated for Gallagher's benefit. Suddenly he was alert.

"That's right," the medical examiner said. "We found small fragments of the victim's skull and brain on the bottom of a heavy white cup. The size and shape fit the wounds on the victim's skull. In other words, it's a match."

"Where did they find it?" Gallagher asked when she'd hung up.

"Where else? At the Refuge."

"So the perp could be one of those ladies who hangs out there," Gallagher said, sounding relieved. He turned to face her. "Before you came in, I called the place and told the young nun who answered the phone that we'd be stopping by today."

"Why did you do that?" Kate asked.

"Seemed like a good idea just in case the fliers uncovered any new information. And it turned out to be a superior piece of detective work, since now we know that the cup was from there."

"Or, at least, it ended up there," Kate corrected.

While they waited for the elevator, Gallagher was unusually quiet. "With any luck at all, the old nun will have the day off," he said at last.

"She might prove helpful," Kate needled.

Gallagher groaned. "Imagine a man my age taking on both a smart-ass lawyer and a fast-talking nun in the same day! It's enough to give a guy a heart attack."

"Not on my shift, buddy," Kate joked, then wondered if it was a laughing matter.

❧❧❧❧

"Come in, Catherine!" Richard Dodd shouted in response to the knock on his office door. He'd recognize that timid rap anywhere. He glanced down at the list of rescheduled appointments his secretary had left on his desk. Then he checked his Rolex. His client must be early, and Catherine didn't like her schedule thrown off.

There weren't many secretaries like Catherine left—quiet, efficient, deferential. He needed to do something nice for her. *Maybe I'll call the florist and have flowers delivered,* he thought benevolently, waiting for the office door to swing open.

"Mr. Dodd." Catherine was breathless and one look at her long face told him something was terribly wrong.

"What is it?" he asked, his heart thudding.

"I'm sorry, sir," Catherine whispered, her brown eyes frightened, "but two Homicide detectives are here to see you."

Even as the panic flowed through him, Rich forced himself to sound calm. "Homicide detectives for me?" he said, keeping his voice pleasant, almost amused, with just enough genuine curiosity. *Damn, I'm good,* he thought, touching one cuff link as if to straighten it.

"I told them that they needed an appointment, that your schedule is full." She pointed nervously to the paper she had placed on his desk. "But they wouldn't be put off."

"Then we must tell them to come in," Rich said so gra-

238

ciously that Catherine stared at him, a look of astonishment on her equine face.

"Show the inspectors in, Catherine, please." He made sure his *please* lingered long enough to get through the door. The sound of a courteous employer, respectful of his women employees, was an image he wanted to portray. Image was what it was all about.

Head bowed, Catherine ushered the two Homicide detectives into the large office.

To Richard's surprise, one was a woman. He should have expected as much, what with all the Affirmative Action crap. And she was a looker, too. Tall, slim, but not too slim, with even features, not a gorgeous face, but pretty, what his wife would call a "sweet face." Thick auburn hair and deep blue eyes. Rich gave his best "how can I help you?" smile. He noticed that she didn't smile back.

Instead, the policewoman extended her credentials and said crisply, "I'm Inspector Kate Murphy, and this is my partner, Inspector Dennis Gallagher."

Stiffly Gallagher leaned forward, his credentials extended. Rich summed the man up in a glance—typical aging cop, he thought, balding, pleasant, if ordinary, face, a bit of a beer belly, or maybe a doughnut roll, wrinkled suit, lousy coloring—not enough exercise, Rich thought, and watery eyes, which were doing some sizing up of their own.

All at once, an alarm went off in Rich's head. He took another look at the credentials. "Dennis Gallagher," she'd said. Rich swallowed hard. And the woman was Kate Murphy. He'd heard about those two. They'd solved several high-profile murder cases in the city. They were among San Francisco's finest. He'd better watch his step!

Rich felt his heart drop like a plumb bob, then a rush of adrenaline. He loved a challenge! "Sit down, officers," he said, forcing his voice to be friendly, cooperative. "As my secretary must have explained, I have a busy schedule, but if I can help you in a few minutes, I'll be happy to."

Gallagher seemed to be studying the panoramic view behind him.

"Breathtaking, isn't it?" Rich remarked, then swiveled around to look at the city himself.

"Everything seems so tiny from here," Gallagher said, pointing to the Palace of Fine Arts dwarfed in the distance. "Must make you feel a little like God."

Rich laughed jovially, studying the man. He seemed sincere enough. Yet Rich wasn't going near that one. "I'm sure you're not here about the view," he said.

"No, sir, we're not." Gallagher sounded reluctant to get to the real business at hand.

Although Rich wasn't sure exactly what angle the detectives were coming from, he felt sure they'd end up at the death of the young prostitute. He'd bide his time, follow their lead, not offer any more information than was requested.

"We understand, sir, that you offered a reward for the apprehension of the killer of a young woman. We were wondering why. Did you know her, Mr. Dodd?" The direct questions came from the woman. Her mouth was set in a narrow, no-nonsense line. He should have known. Those sweet-faced broads were the worst kind.

"Why did I offer a reward?" He was surprised at how quickly the information had leaked. He had figured it would eventually and that when it did it would make him look good. But this quickly? He might as well spread it on thick. This might be his only chance.

"As I told your Chief," he paused to let the word *Chief* sink in, "I didn't want to let a young woman die without someone caring who killed her—besides the police, of course," he added diplomatically. "But primarily, I offered the reward because my wife does volunteer work at the Refuge, where the woman was found. She was quite upset about it." He paused for several seconds as he often did in the courtroom, giving the impression that he was feeling another person's pain. What he was really feeling was the urge to laugh. He was really on a roll!

"I see." The redhead sounded skeptical. Rich was disappointed. "Did you know the young woman?" she asked.

Rich raised his eyebrows, clearly shocked. He had that expression down to an art. He gave a snort of disbelief. "Know Melanie Rogers?" he asked, letting just enough sarcasm drip into his question. "Hardly. We weren't in the same social circles. Why do you ask?" Rich knew this was a dangerous question. "Excuse me, officers. Where are my manners?" he said. He must not let down his guard. "May I have Catherine bring you a cup of coffee? A cold drink?"

"No, thank you," the police broad answered for the both of them. She was coldly professional now, Rich noticed. *Good,* he thought, ignoring a tunnel of fear.

"We were asking you if you knew Melanie Rogers because, sir, your name was mentioned in connection with this case."

"Mentioned by whom?" Rich asked, forcing himself to sound patiently amused. "One of the street people my wife is so fond of?"

"Who said it doesn't matter, Mr. Dodd." At last, the old cop spoke up. *About time,* Rich thought. *It's so much easier to deal with another man. Men know how business is done.*

"The question is," Gallagher began. Rich watched the detective's eyes shift toward him in a flat stare. "Did you know Melanie Rogers?"

"Of course I didn't know her, Inspector." He showed a bit of temper now—more like righteous indignation. His timing was impeccable. "How would I know a woman of her caliber?"

At first, Gallagher didn't say anything, simply continued to stare. "Have you any idea why your name would be mentioned?" he asked softly.

Careful, now! Rich warned himself. *Don't blow it!* He pretended to consider Gallagher's question. "As far as I can figure, Inspector, whoever mentioned my name may be someone I've gone up against in court." No harm reminding them that he was a prominent lawyer. "Someone holding a grudge and wanting to get back at me."

"That's possible," Gallagher agreed, to Rich's relief. He was right. The old cop was going to be easier to deal with. Feeling a rush of confidence, he decided to be even more helpful.

"Depending on who you heard my name from, and I respect your obligation to keep it confidential," he said with a dash of largesse. It always sweetened the pot. "Someone could have seen my name in the paper or heard it on the TV. Someone who hates people who get notoriety," he said, hoping he sounded modest enough.

"Or"—it was time to muddy the waters—"someone who is jealous of my wife and wants to hurt her through me."

A slight crease in Gallagher's brow told Rich that he had struck home with the mention of his wife. It would serve her right, hysterical bitch. *Let Betsy see if she can go after a policeman with a butcher knife when he confronts her.*

Frustrated, Richard Dodd ran his fingers through his thick dark hair. When was his five thousand bucks going to pay off? How long before someone desperate for a fix would turn in an enemy or even a friend?

Until it happened, Betsy would make a perfect diversion. Rich wondered how far he should push the insinuation. *Restraint,* he thought. It was better in the beginning. There would be time to let a little more slip in if this went any further.

"One more thing, sir." Gallagher fumbled in his jacket

pocket for his notebook and opened it, ready to write. "Can you tell us where you were last Tuesday night?"

Rich made a great pretense of checking the appointment calendar on his desktop. "I had a dinner business meeting, and then I met my wife and we went to a cocktail party at the Blacks' and from there home."

Gallagher wrote. "Can anyone verify that, sir?"

"Of course. The person I was doing business with"—Rich sounded slightly befuddled—"the other guests at the party, and, of course, my wife."

"May we have that business associate's name?" Murphy was back in the game.

Reluctantly looking up Amanda's home address, Rich scribbled it, plus her home phone number, on a piece of notepaper. Forcing a cooperative smile, he handed the paper to Gallagher. "Here you are, Inspector," he said, wondering just how Amanda would respond. *It's still her word against mine,* he thought, watching the two detectives leave his office.

Richard Dodd swiveled toward the window and the magnificent view of the city. Except for some small whiffs of fog hovering atop the Bay Bridge, the sun was bright, glinting off the windows of the tall buildings. What had the old cop said? "Must make you feel a little like God." Well, actually, at this moment, he felt a lot like God, moving everything according to his will and pleasure.

Hot damn! He had surely conned those two cops—San Francisco's finest, big deal! And it was a stroke of genius, pulling in Betsy's name. That ought to keep them busy. For all their notoriety in solving cases, underneath they were nothing but a pair of dumb flatfoots. He'd made mincemeat of their lame insinuation that he might be involved. Did they have any idea who they were dealing with?

Puffed up by his victory, Rich dialed Amanda's work number.

From the sound of her first "hello," he realized that she was not going to be as easy to deal with as the two cops.

❧❧❧

Inspectors Kate Murphy and Dennis Gallagher rode the empty express elevator down in silence. One look at her partner's face and Kate knew that he was fighting a losing battle with his temper—a battle, experience had taught her, it was best to let him fight alone.

But she couldn't help saying, excitedly, "Amanda is one of the names Sister Mary Helen mentioned."

He seemed not to hear. They were seated in their car, buckling the seat belts, before Gallagher trusted himself to speak. "Did you ever hear so much colossal bullshit in your life?" He asked fiercely. "Made me feel like I was watching some goddamn lawyer show on TV. And about that anonymous reward. He wanted to be as anonymous as a billboard."

"And what did you think about that subtle mention of the Chief?" Kate laughed. "It was supposed to scare us, I guess. I didn't notice you shaking, for all you said before we got there. What happened?"

Gallagher looked over at her, his eyes sharp. "What happened," he said, "is simple. The guy made me damn mad, that's all." He hit the steering wheel with the heel of his hand. "Imagine him trying to bring his wife into it! What he doesn't know is that she already told us that she was late meeting him. He expects her to lie and give him an alibi. Poor gal is probably a saint for living with him. And if she did kill anybody, it would most likely be him, for which, in my opinion, she should be given a medal."

"He really did make you mad, didn't he?" Kate said, eying Gallagher's red neck and flushed cheeks. "What do you think? Is he our man?"

Her partner hesitated, then shook his head. "Much as I'd like him to be, we have no real proof that he is involved in anything illegal. It's only my nose that tells me he's guilty of something. I'm not sure what, but something. And noses, as you know, aren't admissible evidence in court. How about you?"

Kate stared out the car window at the yuppie types rushing down California Street, expensive briefcases swinging. She held her breath as a bike messenger nearly hit a Yellow Cab. All they didn't need this morning was to be witnesses at the scene of an accident.

Gallagher turned the key in the ignition. "Kate," he said, "did I lose you? What do you think?"

"I think you're right, Denny. He is hiding something. Why else would he put on that elaborate charade? And who do you think this Amanda Cribbs is, really? He made her sound like some big client."

"Or another damn lawyer," Gallagher put in, his face slowly returning to its normal color. "My guess is she's some kind of high-priced call girl."

Kate laughed. "That's just wishful thinking, Denny. Big shots like Dodd don't get involved with call girls. They don't have to. Guys as powerful as he is have affairs. Any number of young women would be happy to have an *affaire d'amour*."

"Fancy name for the same thing, if you ask me," Gallagher mumbled and Kate laughed again.

We need to check with Sister again, Kate said. "See how we can find out the last name of the Amanda she mentioned."

Gallagher groaned. "That's all we need today, that old nun meddling in our case." He was straining the words through his teeth.

"Asking her a few questions scarcely constitutes letting her meddle," Kate said. She didn't know why she always felt obliged to defend Sister Mary Helen. She suspected that it was because Gallagher expected her to and would probably be disappointed if she didn't. Anyway, over the years it had become their own private ritual.

Her partner turned on Bryant Street, obviously heading toward the Hall of Justice. "Didn't you tell Sister Anne that we'd drop by the Refuge this morning?" Kate reminded him. She checked her wristwatch.

"First I thought we'd go back to the Detail," he explained. "We can run through the phone messages. See if any real leads were called in. And I want to phone this Amanda Cribbs. Find out if she can back up our Mr. Dodd's story. After that we'll head over to the Refuge."

At the Homicide Detail, the pile of pink slips on Gallagher's desk had mounted. Myrtle must have added thirty since they left.

"Who's the most popular team of all?" Myrtle chanted as she handed Kate two more memos.

Kate began to read through the stack as her partner dialed Amanda's home phone number. "You are just dying to have him be guilty, aren't you?" she said.

"*Dying*, Katie-girl, may be a little too strong a word," Gallagher quipped with a crooked grin.

To Kate's surprise, the phone was answered. After Gallagher identified himself and asked to speak to Amanda Cribbs, he hit the button for the speakerphone.

"I'm sorry, Inspector. Amanda is not at home. She's at work." It was an older woman's voice.

"Who am I speaking with, ma'am?" Gallagher asked.

"I'm her mother. I just dropped by to leave her some homemade soup. She's so busy. Is anything wrong?"

"No, ma'am. We'd just like to ask her a few questions."

"Well, I'm sure she'd be happy to answer anything." Uneasiness had crept into her voice. Too many TV cop shows, Gallagher thought. "She works for Dodd, Roach, Crosby, and Chin. They're lawyers, you know, and my Amanda is a paralegal for the firm."

"Thank you, ma'am," Gallagher said politely and replaced the receiver in the cradle.

"Bastard!" he shouted and loosened his tie. "Phony bastard, sending us on a wild-goose chase!" His neck was red again, and the color was quickly spreading over his jaw and cheeks like spilled paint. "He never counted on Mama dropping off soup. What say we go right over to that fancy law firm and raise hell?"

"What say before we do that we calm down," Kate suggested, "have a cup of coffee, go through these messages, then stop by the Refuge as we planned, see if anyone remembers anything about a cup?"

"What the hell would make one cup stand out among the hundreds they use every day?" Gallagher snapped.

Kate shrugged. "Just dumb luck, I guess."

"Even your friend Sister Mary Helen isn't that lucky," Gallagher grumbled.

"You never can tell," Kate taunted, knowing he was right. What she was really interested in was what else the old nun had observed. There was no doubt about it, the woman had an uncanny way of ferreting out the truth. "*Our* friend," she said, emphasizing the "*our,*" "has strange powers."

Gallagher raised his bushy eyebrows. "What about this Amanda lady?" He was like a bulldog with a bone.

"Are you calm enough to talk to her yet?"

Gallagher nodded.

"How about calling and making an appointment this afternoon?" Kate's suggestion seemed to satisfy her partner. He called the offices of Dodd, Roach, Crosby, and Chin.

"Amanda Cribbs, please," he said.

After a moment, he slammed down the receiver. "Stepped away from her desk!" he shouted. "I'd bet my pension she's in

Dodd's office this minute getting instructions on what to tell us. I've a good mind to go right over there and catch him in the act."

"Down, boy," Kate said and, grabbing up both their mugs, went to the coffee pot. Fortunately, Myrtle had just made some fresh coffee.

When Kate returned, Gallagher was thumbing through the stack of messages, reading about every third one. Obviously, he was taking her advice and trying to calm down. Suddenly Kate saw all the color blanch from his face. He stared at the pink paper as if he could not believe it.

"What is it, Denny?" she asked, setting down his mug. Over his shoulder she read the slip. "Call Dr. Little at Kaiser," Myrtle had written in her clean, straight hand. "Test results are in."

Kate's stomach lurched. Fear wrapped her body like a chill. She put her arm around her partner's shoulder. "Do you want to use a private line? We could go to a phone booth."

Gallagher shook his head. He dialed the number and, identifying himself, asked for the doctor.

Please, God, please, God, Kate prayed over and over, never taking her eyes off her partner. *Please make it good news!* She watched his jaw set as he hung up the phone.

"The guy's had an emergency," Gallagher said hoarsely. "They don't expect him back until late this afternoon."

Kate felt as if they had just been given a stay of execution.

❀❀❀

"Meet me . . . office . . . ten minutes," Sister Anne whispered as she passed Sister Mary Helen, who was hurrying from the kitchen with more paper napkins.

At first, Mary Helen wasn't sure that she'd heard correctly. One look, however, at Anne holding up ten fingers convinced her that she had. *What in the world is going on?* she wondered, feeling as if she were living a scene right out of a spy movie.

"Come in, quick!" Anne said, ten minutes later. She closed the door part way. To close it completely would raise suspicion.

"What is it?" Mary Helen felt her heart thudding as she tried to keep her voice even.

"Inspector Gallagher called before you and Betsy arrived this morning. He and Kate Murphy are going to drop by, but they don't want any of the women to know. He's afraid they'll scatter, and the inspectors want to be able to question some of them."

"On the contrary," Mary Helen said, peeking out at the gathering room, which was becoming increasingly packed with women waving fliers. "If you ask me, they're more liable to be mobbed by reward seekers." Of course, no one was asking her.

"Oh, dear." Anne's hazel eyes clouded with concern. "Do you think one of our women might have done it?"

"I did until Geraldine spoke to me," Mary Helen said. "Now I don't know what to think." She pushed her bifocals up the bridge of her nose. *One of these days, I'll take the time to get the blasted things adjusted,* Mary Helen thought, waiting for Anne's next question.

But Anne just stared anxiously. *The poor kid is too well mannered to ask outright what Geraldine said,* Mary Helen thought. She sat down in the desk chair. Might as well save her feet. This was going to be a long day!

"According to Geraldine," she began, "Melanie's murderer is not a street person."

The color left Anne's face. "How can she know that?"

"If you ask me, Geraldine seems to be very knowledgeable about what happens on the streets. Although she asked me not to tell the police how she knows, it seems that the information came from Junior Johnson."

Sister Anne nodded as if she were in a daze. "Junior Johnson is her nephew."

"She mentioned that," Mary Helen said, "claims he's 'the man,' whatever that means."

"You don't want to know," Anne muttered.

"Anyway, this nephew was talking to Jungle Jumbo, who was trying to work the corner when Melanie left. Well, anyway, Mr. Jumbo saw Melanie come back to California Street and approach a parked car. She got into the backseat, and then he saw what looked to him like a fight. He got scared and took off before someone called the police."

"Why doesn't this Jungle Jumbo contact the police for the reward?"

"Geraldine says that he's afraid he'll end up being blamed. It seemed to make sense to her."

Anne had a hard time getting her tongue around her next question. "Has she any idea who was in the car?"

"Geraldine suspects that Richard Dodd may have something to do with it."

Sister Anne gasped.

"Or a woman named Amanda. Maybe the police will have some information on who she might be. Or . . ." Mary Helen hesitated, trying to think of how best to tell Anne Geraldine's third suspect. She decided that the best way was quickly. "She also mentioned Betsy Dodd!" she blurted out.

For a moment, Anne looked as if she might be sick. "Betsy!" she whispered. Then, regardless of what it would raise, she closed the office door. "How could anyone suspect that lovely woman? Why, it's . . . it's just insane to think that she'd be capable of such a thing."

Mary Helen was about to tell Anne just how insane things could get when she heard a commotion in the gathering room.

"I'll bet it's Inspector Gallagher and Kate," Anne said. She was right.

The two Homicide detectives came uninvited into the

small office. Mary Helen could tell by the grim looks on their faces that things weren't good, although she had no idea what these things could possibly be. She didn't have to wait long to find out.

"Sisters." Gallagher acknowledged them with a curt nod. "We have found the murder weapon," he said with no preliminary remarks.

"The cups," Anne breathed.

Gallagher's watery blue eyes turned on her. "Yes, we found it here, Sister," he said.

Feeling sorry for Anne, Mary Helen slowly rose from her chair. "Which means what, Inspector?" she asked, trying not to sound too take-charge.

Gallagher faced her, still looking peaked, Mary Helen thought. "It means that you have a murderer in your midst," he snapped.

Anne cringed as though she'd been struck.

"Or, perhaps, a clever killer who planted it here to make you think that one of our ladies was guilty." Mary Helen had read dozens of mysteries where this was the case. Surely it must happen once in a while in real life.

"Besides," she continued turning toward Kate, who seemed unusually quiet, "I had it on good authority that Melanie's murderer was not a street person." From the expression on Kate's face, Mary Helen was sure that this came as no shock.

"And who is this good authority?" Gallagher interrupted.

"I'm not free to reveal my source," Mary Helen said.

"Then I hope you're free to spend some time in jail, Sister," he snapped.

Not trusting herself to reply, Mary Helen clamped her lips shut. This morning Inspector Gallagher was especially cranky even for Inspector Gallagher, she thought, looking to Kate for support.

Although Kate's blue eyes were sympathetic, at first she said nothing. "Can we all sit down and talk about this calmly?" she asked, sounding worn-out.

It isn't even noon, Mary Helen thought. *Something else must be going on.* "That seems like an excellent idea," she said. One look at Gallagher's face and she wished she hadn't. He liked it much better when he thought he was calling the shots. Too bad about him!

After Sister Anne had been excused to tell Betsy Dodd that they would be tied up for a few minutes, the four of them sat at a small table in the corner of the office.

"Let's start over again at the beginning," Kate suggested.

"That's fine with me," Mary Helen conceded, still a little put out at Gallagher's bullying. Put her in jail, indeed!

"You start." Gallagher pointed at her.

Although she didn't like his tone one little bit, she did. Without mentioning Geraldine's name, Mary Helen told the Homicide inspectors about the woman's meeting with Andy, then about Olivia, whose street name was Candy.

"I thought that I may have heard incorrectly." She pointed to her ears. "That can happen when you get older."

Gallagher looked puzzled. "Run that by me again."

"Please," Kate added quickly.

"Certainly," Mary Helen said, wondering why they were both so thick this morning. "The first time I saw Melanie she said, 'Andy is going to kill me,' or, at least, that's what I thought I heard. Perhaps what she really said was, 'Candy is going to kill me'—Candy is Olivia's street name—and I heard her incorrectly. Old Sister Donata does it all the time."

She paused to see if the detectives were following her line of reasoning. They seemed to be. Only poor Anne looked confused.

"It doesn't matter, dear." Mary Helen patted the young nun's hand. "Neither of them is guilty."

"And how the hell—excuse me—heck, do you know that?" Gallagher exploded.

Mary Helen refused to be rattled by bad temper. "Because my source told me that Melanie was not murdered by a street person," she said. "And I believe it." Gallagher let his breath out slowly.

"Your anonymous source?" he said with a touch of sarcasm that Mary Helen chose to ignore. She hoped she wasn't being as foolish as he made her sound.

"I'd suggest that you look into this Amanda, whoever she may be. Or, God help us, the Dodds."

Beside her she heard Anne suck in her breath. "What about the cup?" Anne asked.

"What about it?" Gallagher turned on her.

"You said it came from here. Were there any fingerprints?"

Inspector Gallagher narrowed his eyes and stared at her. "Don't tell me we've got another detective on our hands," he said.

Anne flushed.

"No clear prints," Kate said before Mary Helen had a chance to jump in. "Only some small fragments of skull and traces of blood and brain clinging to the cup's rough bottom."

Sister Anne shuddered. "To think it was in our kitchen," she said softly.

Kate nodded. "The question, of course, is how did it get there?"

How, indeed, Mary Helen wondered, feeling as if there was something she needed to remember but couldn't—not unlike an itch that can't be reached to scratch. Was it true what they said about the brain? Was everything you'd ever seen or heard recorded there? Was it all a matter of being able to call it up? What was buried somewhere deep in a wrinkle of her brain?

A gentle rap on the door stopped any further mulling. Betsy Dodd, her face drawn, peeked into the room. "Several women want to talk to you about the reward, Inspectors," she said. "They are getting a little unruly."

"And you could use some help," Anne added.

Although she didn't answer, Betsy looked relieved.

"You can set up your office in this sleep room, again," Anne offered. She was back in charge.

Thank goodness, Mary Helen thought, hurrying to help Betsy. For now, she'd leave her brain to sort things out, as she knew it would, in its own good time.

❧❧❧❧

"This is a road to nowhere," Inspector Kate Murphy admitted after she and her partner had interviewed about ten women.

Dennis Gallagher loosened his tie. "More like a colossal pain in the neck," he said, running his thick finger around the collar of his shirt.

"Speaking of pains in the neck"—Kate pointed to the flaming red line circling his—"are you putting on a little weight?"

"In the neck?" Gallagher stared at her. "People don't put on weight in the neck. It's the damn starch that the laundry puts in the shirt collars."

If that's the case, Kate wanted to ask him, why didn't he just tell the laundry to stop? But she decided against it. Today Gallagher was in no mood to accept simple solutions to his problems.

"What do you think we should do about continuing these interviews?" she asked. "I haven't uncovered one piece of real information that could lead anywhere. Which makes me think they really don't know anything."

Gallagher let out a sigh. "And if these gals don't know, nobody knows," he agreed. "Besides, I'm dying to get back to that double-talking Dodd guy. Can you beat the nerve of that smart-ass telling us that Amanda is a business associate when

254

the gal actually is one of his employees? How long did he figure it would take us to find out?"

"A lot longer than it did," Kate said, "if her mother hadn't stopped by with soup."

Dennis Gallagher smiled for the first time that day. "I can't wait to see the look on the guy's picture-perfect face when we tell him we know that Amanda works for him. I'll bet he'll give an Oscar performance.

"You know, Katie-girl, if you ask me, that's what he was keeping from us—that he's banging an employee." He shrugged. "After work, during work, who knows? Anyway, banging her before he goes home to his mansion and his wife."

"You don't know that," Kate said, although she suspected the same thing.

While Gallagher went to get their car, Kate found Sister Anne and told her that they'd be back later. The women in the gathering room didn't miss a syllable. Several groaned.

"I never had my turn to try for the reward," a thin young woman complained.

That was just what this morning had been, Kate realized—a giant guessing game, a desperate try to get the prize, to collect $5,000 reward.

As Gallagher had predicted, Richard Dodd's act when he saw the two detectives reappear was something to behold. Kate wished they had it on film. He began with a friendly handshake. "What can I do for you, officers?" he asked.

When Gallagher asked him why he didn't tell them that Amanda Cribbs worked for him he looked shocked, then amused—as if it all had been a silly oversight. "Well, you didn't ask me that, Inspector," he said smugly.

When Kate questioned their personal relationship, Dodd had swollen with indignation. "We have none!" he bellowed. "We are simply colleagues."

255

Despite his bombast, Kate could tell that Richard Dodd knew he wasn't convincing anyone, not even himself. In the end, although he didn't apologize or even admit guilt, he invited them to use one of the firm's conference rooms and sent for Amanda Cribbs.

"Look at the view from this window," Gallagher said. "You can see nearly to Ocean Beach. This has got to be as good as the twirling restaurant at the top of the Hyatt Regency."

"And a heck of a lot cheaper." Kate joined him at the window. "What do they call it anyway?"

"The Equinox." The soft female voice startled them. A young woman with a thick mane of blond hair had slipped into the conference room. "I'm Amanda Cribbs," she said.

Quickly both Kate and Gallagher introduced themselves and showed her their badges. "Why don't you sit down, Miss Cribbs?" Gallagher said gruffly. "We need to ask you a few questions."

While Amanda settled herself in the chair, Kate studied her. At first glance, Amanda Cribbs looked like the stereotypical dumb blonde. Not that she could help her long legs and her model-like figure, which her form-fitting blue sheath dress showcased to perfection. *Talk about dressing for success,* Kate thought sarcastically.

"I'll be happy to answer any questions I can," Amanda said, sounding like an airhead.

Maybe that's what she is, just plain dumb, Kate thought, *an airhead who is out of her depth and whose mother brings her soup.* Oops! That didn't sit right. Jack's mother provided them with dinner all the time. It didn't make them dumb, just lucky.

"We are investigating a murder case," Kate heard Gallagher say. It was then that Kate noticed a subtle change in Amanda's large blue eyes. There was something there—a cunning, shrewdness, and intelligence that didn't jive with the facade. Amanda blinked innocently at the two detectives. *Miss Amanda Cribbs isn't as dumb as she'd like us to believe,* Kate thought. In fact, Kate was banking on it.

Gallagher cleared his throat. "We need you to answer our questions as completely and as honestly as possible."

Kate noticed a slight tremor run through Amanda's body. She still blinked innocently.

"First of all, where were you last Tuesday night?"

"I was at a dinner meeting with Mr. Dodd," she said, too quickly.

For the next thirty minutes Gallagher continued to ask and to re-ask questions about the night of Melanie's murder. Kate watched Amanda stiffen in her chair. She watched the perspiration form on the woman's forehead and upper lip. The questions went on and on. Kate waited until Amanda's hands were squeezed into tight fists and her knuckles turned white before she took what she hoped was a lucky jab.

"Why don't we cut out all this questioning, Amanda, and you just tell us what is really going on here?"

Amanda Cribbs studied her. Kate could almost see her calculating what was her best move. All at once, her shoulders slumped and she seemed shorter and even thinner than she actually was. The phony blinking stopped and Kate felt almost as if another person was emerging.

"Richard Dodd and I are having an affair," she admitted flatly. "He says he's unhappy with his wife, yet he doesn't want to leave her. The guy wants to be governor!" She gave a half-laugh that sounded almost like a bark. "Can you beat that?" She stared at Kate. "He says he loves me and that someday it will all work out. Big deal! Someday isn't good enough."

"And how do you feel?"

Amanda sighed. "At first, his attention was flattering. I felt wonderful. But to tell you the truth, the more I get to know him, the less I even like him, let alone love him."

"Why don't you break it off?" Kate asked.

That look clouded Amanda's eyes again. "Because I need my job," she shrugged, "and besides, he takes me to nice places, buys me expensive gifts. I was even hoping he'd make me his administrative assistant. I'd be good at that. But the old fart refused to do it. He raised his voice and pounded on his desk." Fear shone in her blue eyes. "Called me awful names. Said terrible things. I actually cried. Still, he wants me to alibi him for the night of the murder."

Kate's hopes rose. Excitement ran down her backbone like an electric shock. Was Richard Dodd their murderer after all? Could they go right across the hall and collar the guy? How would that sit with the district attorney? Next to her she felt Gallagher shift anxiously. Undoubtedly he was having the same thoughts.

"And can you?" Kate asked, wishing for the right answer.

"Unfortunately," Amanda said, sounding disappointed, "I can."

A sullen silence filled the room. Amanda Cribbs looked from one inspector to the other as though trying to figure out what she had said wrong. "I was with him until about five minutes before his wife was scheduled to arrive," she said. "I don't know if she was on time or late."

Suddenly those large blue eyes focused on Kate. "If I were you," Amanda said, "I'd take a good look at the wife. She's as off-the-wall as he is."

❧❧❧

"The wife again," Gallagher said when they were both back in the express elevator. "You think that's a coincidence or do you think there's something to it?"

Kate twisted a few strands of hair around her index finger. "Hard to tell," she said finally, "but since we keep running into brick walls, why don't we give Mrs. Elizabeth Dodd a go? It can't hurt anything."

"I was hoping it would help," Gallagher said, once again running his finger along the collar of his shirt. "You want to grab a bite to eat, then head back to the Refuge?"

"Sounds like a plan." Kate checked her wristwatch. It was after one o'clock. "But first why don't we go back to the Hall and you can call your doctor? His emergency must be over by now."

"I can call from the restaurant," her partner said, his voice much too unconcerned to ring true.

Kate Murphy pointed out a small sandwich shop on New Montgomery Street that looked clean and fairly uncrowded, and Gallagher pulled the car into a no-parking zone. While Kate studied the menu board, Gallagher counted out his change. "Order me corned beef," he said, "and a diet anything."

"That makes a lot of sense," Kate mumbled, but Gallagher was already dropping coins into the public telephone on the wall.

Anyone who noticed her would think that Kate was trying to make a decision. Her full attention, however, was riveted on Gallagher and the telephone. Thank goodness that most of the lunch crowd was clearing out and that he had a loud voice. Now if only the dishwasher would go on the drying cycle.

"Can I help you, miss?" the counterman asked, wiping his hands on his apron.

"Give me a few minutes, please. I'm still trying to decide."

"Who's next?" the man called out, moving to the only other customer at the counter.

Above the splashing of the dishwasher, Kate heard Gallagher identify himself. She stepped back as if she were having a difficult time seeing the entire menu and strained to hear. But there was only a long silence, punctuated by several "yesses" and several "I sees."

"Good-bye, and thank you, Doc," Kate heard finally. The voice sounded upbeat enough, but he could be putting on a brave front. Did she dare look at him? One glance at Gallagher's face and she'd know without a doubt whether the doctor's news was good or bad.

Please, please, please, God, she prayed. Fingers crossed, she slowly turned to face her partner. *Please let it be good news!* What she saw sent a tingle down her spine. Although Gallagher's watery blue eyes glistened, his round face shone like a cherub's and his shoulders looked as if boulders had been lifted from them.

"It's just anemia!" he spoke as though it was an accomplishment. "I'm just anemic. All I need is a few iron pills."

Of course, Kate thought, light with relief—his fatigue, his pale coloring, his lack of energy. Why had she thought cancer? Why did she always think the worst? She'd have to stop it.

"I'm going to give Mrs. G. a buzz," he said, fishing in his pocket for more coins. "She was kind of worried about the test results. I'll put her mind at rest."

"I'll bet she was," Kate said, watching him head back to the phone, a spring now in his step. *Maybe our luck is about to change,* she thought.

"Have you decided yet, lady?" The counter man was back; this time there was a touch of long-suffering in his tone.

"Yes, I have," Kate said. Suddenly she was starving.

"What can I get you then?" He wiped off the counter while he listened.

"I'll have a Caesar salad," Kate said, "with a French roll and for my friend corned beef—no, scratch that—a large spinach salad with a side order of raisins."

❧❧❧

Betsy Dodd's head was pounding as she rushed from the kitchen to the gathering room at the Refuge. With every step she felt the thud. If one more woman asked her for one more thing she thought her skull would explode and her brain would fly out in little pieces all over the rug.

"You all right, Miss Betsy?" Geraldine asked.

What do you care about how I'm feeling? Betsy thought savagely. *What does anyone care? All I am to people is a reliable old workhorse.* Betsy fought with herself to answer evenly.

"I'm fine, thank you," she said with a deliberate smile.

"Can I have a shower roll, please?" Peanuts asked.

Betsy hurried to the supply closet and handed the tiny woman a towel. Her face burned. Was it hot in here? She could hardly breathe. She looked around the small space. She needed air. She needed to get out of here, out of this place, before she was torn to pieces. Everyone wanted a little bite of her. If they didn't all stop asking her questions, making demands, wanting, waiting, she'd be as tiny as the woman who was staring up at her with puzzled brown eyes.

"You OK?" Peanuts asked.

This time Betsy just nodded. She didn't trust herself to speak. If she opened her mouth a scream might easily escape. All over her body her nerves prickled as if she were crawling with fire ants. She needed to go outside into the street and scream and scream until all the tingling had been screamed away and all the heat extinguished.

Pressing her temples, Betsy stared at nothing. Even the nuns had let her down this morning, treating her as if she were nothing but a convenience—leaving her alone to cope with all these women while they talked to the police. Well, the police, all business, were talking to the wrong people. *If they only knew what I know,* Betsy thought. Oddly, it struck her as funny. All at once, she felt like laughing out loud. She bit her lip, afraid to start. Laughing might be like screaming—once she started she might not be able to stop. Like old Laughing

Sal, the mechanical fat lady that used to be at Playland-at-the-Beach. And no one paid much attention to Sal, either, until she was gone. Then they said they missed her.

If only her head would stop pounding. She closed her eyes just for a minute and leaned against the wall, enjoying the darkness.

"We're back," Sister Anne announced, walking quickly toward the kitchen with the empty sugar bowl.

Betsy was startled. She hadn't noticed the Sisters coming out of the office. Nor had she seen the police leave. Why not? How could she have missed them? She must have been in the supply cupboard. Or maybe they wanted her to miss them. Maybe the nuns were sneaking by on purpose—spying, seeing what she was doing. Well, she was too smart for them, too smart for the police, too smart for Rich, too.

Rich—just the thought of him and she felt suffocated. Was there no fresh air in this place? He disgusted her. Who did he think he was fooling? She'd seen him going into the firm's apartment building with his blond paramour. Actually, he looked more as if he should be the girl's father rather than her lover. He'd been so sure of himself that he hadn't even spotted her sitting in the car drinking a cup of coffee and watching. She'd tied her hair in a scarf and brought along sunglasses, but it wasn't necessary. Only the young prostitute was aware of her. Rick was so cockeyed sure of himself that he hadn't even noticed her presence.

It hadn't surprised her. Rick had noticed nothing about her for a long time now—not how she was feeling, what she was thinking, what her hopes were. Tears flooded her eyes. One thing that he did notice was her appearance. The disdain on his face when he looked at her told her what he thought about it. Damn him! She wiped her eyes with the end of her apron.

Well, she sure had his attention last night. He was focused on her every move. She still could hear his voice demanding in that loud, authoritarian way of his that she look at him. Well, she had looked at him, that was for sure, and the next thing she remembered was the acrid smell of fear. And him squatting behind the slipper chair for protection. Poor slipper chair! She'd have to find an upholsterer to re-cover it. Maybe this time in rose brocade. The rose color might cheer her up. It couldn't hurt.

Here comes that old nun, Betsy thought, watching Sister Mary Helen cross the room. She seemed to be stopping to chat with everyone. What was she saying? What were they telling her? It was so hot in here. Couldn't they get more air?

Was the Sister heading toward her? Was she going to start to pick, pick, pick at her like that Melanie had? Betsy felt sorry about Melanie. She was so young, but she shouldn't have started making demands, asking for things, pushing.

When would her head stop throbbing? She felt nauseated. She wanted to go home, to lie down on cool sheets and drift off to sleep. But she couldn't. She wasn't up to explaining to Rosa what had happened to the chair. She pressed her hand against her pulsing forehead, hoping to keep her head from splitting. She felt its dampness.

Eventually Rich would come home. She knew that. He'd go at her again. They'd have another horrible scene, and frankly, she could not be responsible for what she might do. He demanded too much—demanded until she lost track of herself, until she felt as if a bellows were fanning the white heat that consumed her entire body.

Betsy looked up. Sister Mary Helen was approaching her, smiling. *She's completely unaware,* Betsy thought, her head beating a constant rhythm. *Unaware that I feel torn—torn and tired. That I can't take it anymore. That I'm ready to explode. Here she comes, smiling like a simpleton, smiling as though nothing is wrong.*

Betsy's eyes burned as she watched unblinking. The roaring

in her ears blotted out all the other noises in the room. Sister Mary Helen came toward her as if she were a character in a dream. Closer and closer she came, no longer smiling, now frowning with concern.

"Betsy," she heard the nun say in a faraway voice, "are you all right? You're so pale. Don't you feel well?"

Burning with an inextinguishable fire, Betsy didn't trust herself to speak. *Please, Sister, don't push; don't claw; don't demand*, she pleaded with her thoughts.

To her relief, the old nun must have understood. When she spoke she simply said, "Why don't you sit down, Betsy? You must be exhausted. Let me get you a cup of hot coffee."

❧❧❧

Poor Betsy, Sister Mary Helen thought as she poured two mugs of coffee. *She looks as if she's had it. And no wonder. After the scene last night with her husband, she couldn't have slept very well—and in a strange bed besides. I hope she's not coming down with something. Maybe I ought to take her back to the convent where she can rest.*

Mary Helen was so deep in her own thoughts that she was unaware of Miss Bobbie sidling up to her. "What wrong with Miss Betsy?" she whispered.

"I think she's worn out," Mary Helen whispered back. "What makes you ask?"

Miss Bobbie stared at her in amazement. "You got to ask me that, girlfriend? You got eyes. Look at her. She don't even look like herself. And all morning she got an attitude."

"An attitude about what?" Mary Helen was curious.

"You know. About everything. You asks her for something and she just looks like she don't hear you. Or else she snaps back. She just ain't herself." Having that off her chest, Miss Bobbie rejoined her group at the table.

By now the gathering room was clear of most of the flier-waving reward seekers. Having given up hope of the $5,000 when the Homicide inspectors left, the crowd had followed soon after. Only the regulars remained, and just a handful of them.

Geraldine seemed to be holding court at one of the tables, with everyone paying very close attention. As Mary Helen passed the table carrying the coffee mugs, she caught only a snippet of the conversation, which seemed to center around the name of Junior Johnson, Geraldine's nephew, who, as Mary Helen remembered, was "the man," whatever that meant.

Venus laughed uproariously at whatever Geraldine was relating. "I wish I could have seen Andy when Junior cornered him!" she shouted and laughed again.

Mary Helen noticed Betsy wince at the sharp sound. *Miss Bobbie is right. She's not herself*, Mary Helen thought, putting a mug on the table in front of Betsy. "Would you like a dough-nut to go with that?" she asked.

Betsy shook her head.

"Half a doughnut?" Mary Helen coaxed.

When Betsy made no reply, Mary Helen decided to drop the offer. The two women sipped their coffee in silence. Sitting this close, Betsy Dodd looked even worse than she had from a dis-tance. Her face was pasty white except for the two fiery balls that had formed high on her cheeks. Her hair, hanging helter-skelter over her forehead, could have used a good brushing. Her mouth was pulled tight, and one hand lay limply on the tabletop.

But her hazel eyes held the real tale. They had a look about them—it took Mary Helen several seconds to think of the right word. *Haunted!* That was it. They had a haunted look about them, and there was something else.

Suddenly they focused on Sister Mary Helen. "What did the police want?"

The question startled her. It was uncharacteristic of Betsy to be so direct, almost rude. Mary Helen hesitated a moment, wondering how much she should reveal, then tucked her reservations away. This was Betsy Dodd she was talking to—reliable, thoroughly dependable, true-blue Betsy Dodd. She lowered her voice to a near-whisper. "They told us that they'd found the murder weapon in here," she said and waited for Betsy's reaction.

To Mary Helen's amazement, there was none. Betsy simply gave a supercilious smile and took another sip of her coffee.

There's that funny look in her eye again, Mary Helen thought, watching some of the natural color returning to the woman's face. *Good! The coffee must be helping.*

"How did it get here?" Betsy asked.

A shrill giggle rose from Crazy Alice, who was holding a lively conversation with an imaginary friend. Betsy recoiled and covered her ears.

> *"See no evil.*
> *Hear no evil.*
> *Speak no evil,"*

Crazy Alice chanted and giggled again.

"What did you ask me?" Sister Mary Helen was distracted.

"The cup," Betsy demanded impatiently.

Mary Helen shrugged. "Who knows? The police found no clear fingerprints on it. They only know that it's the murder weapon because the bottom ridge held some bone and scalp fragments."

"No one knows how it got here?" Betsy seemed to be checking.

"Of course someone must know," Mary Helen said. She wondered what Betsy was getting at. "But I have no idea."

Did Betsy see something she was reluctant to tell? Maybe she is actually afraid. And why not? If a person killed once, what was to stop him—or her—from killing again? Where is this going? she wondered as the woman across from her fell silent again. *Wherever this is going, it is going slowly*, Mary Helen thought. Should she help Betsy along by asking a few direct questions? Or should she wait it out?

She was debating which approach to take when Peanuts emerged, fresh and clean, from the shower. "What's really going on here?" she asked as she passed their table.

"What did she mean by that?" Betsy's face paled again. The spots on her cheeks burned brightly.

"It's just an expression. Anyway, I don't think she was talking to us," Mary Helen said, watching Peanuts pull up a chair to Miss Bobbie's table. Quickly she joined in the gossip. Venus let out another, "Whoop!"

Betsy Dodd frowned into her coffee cup. She seemed to be far away, wrestling some private devil. *Whatever she knows is really bothering her*, Mary Helen thought. *She'd feel so much better if she could talk about it. Often naming a fear dispels it.* In the old nun's opinion, Betsy Dodd needed to tell someone what was bothering her. And after last night, it surely couldn't be her husband.

Mary Helen sat up straight in her chair and drew in a deep breath. She might as well take the plunge. What did she have to lose? "Betsy," she said, "what's bothering you?"

The woman looked up and shook her head.

"Do you know anything about the cup or how it got here?"

In the profound silence that followed, Betsy's face seemed to shut down, then hardened. Mary Helen noticed her hazel eyes glazing over. It was as if the woman had retreated into the deepest part of herself and was no longer here. Mary Helen studied her with growing anxiety. Perhaps talking about it hadn't been the best idea after all. It was hard to know.

She was glad to see Sister Anne come into the room at this moment carrying two pots of water for the coffeemaker. Any distraction was welcome.

"Fresh coffee?" Anne called out cheerfully.

"Not for me," Mary Helen said. Her nerves were already on edge. She didn't need another shot of caffeine.

"I'll have some." Betsy's words sounded hollow as she went toward the coffeepot.

Mary Helen turned to watch Betsy making her way back, steam rising from the cup in her hand. Without warning, something touched the correct wrinkle in her brain. A vision opened up as easily as the right key opens a lock—Betsy Dodd entering the kitchen with a stray cup. And handing it to a patrolman. Where had the cup come from? Who had given it to her? Whoever it was, that person was undoubtedly Melanie's killer!

Mary Helen could hardly contain herself. As soon as Betsy sat down again, the old nun pressed her. She couldn't help herself. "Do you remember the day the patrolman came to pick up our cups?"

Betsy nodded and sipped her hot coffee.

"And you came in with a stray one?"

Again, Betsy nodded, that peculiar glint in her eye.

"Do you remember who gave it to you?"

Suddenly Betsy blanched. She looked as if she might be sick. "I want to go home," she said, rising so quickly from her chair that it fell backward with a thud.

At the sound, a tense silence covered the room. Even Crazy Alice was quiet. Betsy hurried to the office.

"What's happening?" Geraldine asked, sounding loud in the stillness. All eyes were upon her.

"Nothing, ladies." Mary Helen struggled to keep her voice calm. "Our volunteer just isn't feeling well."

Betsy emerged from the office clutching her purse. Her face was ashen except for the fire spot on each cheek. Mary Helen approached her. "Don't be afraid," she said quietly. "Just tell the police who gave you the cup. They'll make sure you're safe."

Slowly Betsy Dodd raised her head until her eyes locked with Mary Helen's. In that instant, Mary Helen recognized the strange glint in Betsy's hazel eyes for what it really was. Her heart turned over and sank. *Of course,* she thought numbly. *How could I have been so stupid?* The look was the look of absolute madness. The cup belonged to Betsy Dodd herself.

With a savage roar, Betsy reached into her purse. She pulled out her hand. It brandished the butcher knife. Mary Helen's mouth went dry. Raising her hands, she slowly backed away. Away from the sticky heat of Betsy's body.

"You couldn't stop!" Betsy screamed, her eyes pinning Mary Helen. She raised the knife above her head. "You had to keep it up, keep it up." She made one sweeping arc with the knife. Reflexes alone made Mary Helen twist to her right. She felt a rush of air as the blade narrowly missed her.

The room was silent. No one moved. The only sound Mary Helen heard was that of her own heart pounding. She took a wild glance behind her.

Betsy steadied the knife in her right hand. Her fingers clutched the handle. "You had to keep asking and asking. Tearing at me. Clawing me to pieces." She slashed again. The blow was too wide. Frustrated, she lunged toward Mary Helen, lashing out, missing her by inches.

"Neither you nor that Melanie person knows when to stop!" Betsy's eyes blazed. "Pushing, pushing. Well, I'll stop you, old woman, for good!"

Mary Helen backed up farther. She knew the wall was behind her. *Dear Lord,* she thought crazily, *what an unusual way for a nun to go!*

Head lowered, Betsy gripped the handle of the knife with both her hands, ready to slam forward. Mary Helen tensed herself for the blow.

"Enough now!" The words rang out, startling Betsy. Geraldine had found her voice.

"She getting on my nerves, girlfriend," Miss Bobbie said, deftly grabbing Betsy Dodd's arms from behind.

Betsy struggled, pulling against her, screeching obscenities, but Venus was too quick for her. She knocked the butcher knife to the ground, where Peanuts scooped it up.

"Now what?" Anne said. Mary Helen hadn't realized that she was even in the room.

Before anyone could answer, the front door slammed open and Inspectors Dennis Gallagher and Kate Murphy entered. "What's going on in here?" Gallagher roared, reaching for his gun.

Crazy Alice giggled and began to chant:

> "There was a little girl,
> Who had a little curl,
> Right in the middle of her forehead.
> When she was good,
> She was very, very good,
> And when she was bad,
> She was horrid."

❤❤❤❤

It was nearly four o'clock in the afternoon before the Homicide inspectors had sorted everything out. It took Sister Mary Helen about that long to start breathing normally again.

Betsy Dodd had, indeed, confessed to killing Melanie Rogers. The young prostitute had approached her while she sat in her car. Melanie had hoped that Betsy could be blackmailed into protecting her husband's good name. Instead, her insistence had pushed Betsy into murder.

"Poor kid! Looks like she was no better at blackmail than

she was at anything else," Inspector Gallagher commented. And Mary Helen had to agree.

In fact, to her amazement, Inspector Gallagher and she got along quite well all afternoon. Mary Helen had expected him to go into his usual tirade about knowing her place—whatever that meant—and staying in it. Leaving police work to the police and praying to the nuns.

Something good must have happened to the inspector since she'd last seen him this morning. Thank goodness! When last encountered the man was about to give new depth to the meaning of the word *cranky*.

Despite her protests that she was just fine, Mary Helen was still shaken by Betsy's violent outburst. How could such a thoroughly nice woman snap so completely? What circumstances had pushed her into madness? No doubt her husband's neglect and verbal abuse played a big role. Yet she was not so mad that she didn't know her own mind. She had refused to call him and stated quite clearly that she would rather hang than have him for her attorney. The thing that seemed to be upsetting her the most was the failure of her plan to implicate him in the murder. "He is guilty, you know," she said again and again.

Having been read her rights, Betsy Dodd, handcuffed and pale, was about to be taken in on murder charges when the front door of the Refuge swung open. Officers Mark Wong and Brian Dineen walked into the nearly empty room.

"What are you guys doing here?" Kate Murphy asked.

"We're just starting our shift," Dineen explained, "and we wondered if the reward fliers paid off."

Wong stared openly at Betsy Dodd. "Looks like you're busy," he said.

"Just finishing up," Gallagher announced. "We have a pretty good idea of what happened to Melanie."

"And about the reward," Kate said with a wink in Mary

Helen's direction, "I think it should go to the Sisters for the Refuge. If it weren't for them and this place"—she shrugged—"who knows if we'd ever have solved this one."

Even Gallagher didn't object.

Sister Anne, who was just beginning to get her voice back after the shock of watching her prize volunteer slash at her favorite old nun, forced a smile. "Thank you," she said graciously, although Mary Helen knew she had mixed emotions.

As much as Anne wanted Melanie's killer found and appreciated the reward money, she never could have imagined that it would be Betsy Dodd. Who could?

Exhausted now, Mary Helen waited at the front door until Inspector Gallagher and Kate Murphy drove away with Betsy Dodd. She watched the two Vice officers speed off in the opposite direction. Sister Anne and she were alone.

"Are you sure you're all right?" Anne asked.

Mary Helen nodded. "And you?"

"I'll never get used to this," Anne said. Tears glinted in her hazel eyes.

"Who does?" Mary Helen countered.

Anne shrugged. "You came very close to being seriously hurt." Her watery eyes widened with concern. "Sister Eileen would never forgive me if anything happened to you."

"None of this was your fault," Mary Helen said. *Or mine, either,* she thought a little defensively. "How can you possibly be blamed for Betsy Dodd's madness?"

Anne brightened. "Why don't you call Eileen? Then we'd better plan on how to break the news to the nuns at the college convent."

Mary Helen checked her watch. *Unless the evening news does it for us,* she thought. "In Ireland it's one o'clock in the morning," she protested weakly. This was the first time she had been involved in a murder investigation without Eileen, and she missed her. If the truth be known, she was dying to call her old friend and tell her all that had happened.

"Oh, go ahead," Anne said. It was all the urging Mary Helen needed.

The telephone rang only once before Eileen picked it up. Despite the time, she sounded delighted, if surprised, to hear Mary Helen's voice. "Is everything all right?" she asked.

"Fine. But you'll never believe what's happened."

"Let me guess, old dear," Eileen said. "Another murder?"

Mary Helen was taken aback. "How in heaven's name did you know that?" she asked.

Over the miles, she heard Eileen's familiar chuckle. "Just a lucky guess. As they say here at home, 'What is in the marrow is hard to take out of the bone.' "

❧❧❧

Sister Mary Helen thought she'd be asleep the moment her head hit the pillow. But she was wrong. Tonight her mind refused to shut off. It kept playing and replaying the events of her first week at the Refuge. And what a week it had been!

A bright autumn moon shone through her window, lighting up her bedroom, while a cool breeze off the Golden Gate ruffled the curtains. It was perfect sleeping weather, but she couldn't seem to doze off. Were there loose ends that needed to be tied up? She didn't think so.

Clearly, Betsy Dodd had murdered Melanie Rogers. Apparently the young prostitute had viewed her accidental meeting with Richard Dodd and Amanda Cribbs as a stroke of luck, especially when she saw Betsy Dodd in the car watching them.

Mary Helen could understand how Melanie might think Betsy would pay to keep her husband's indiscretions quiet. Her husband's political ambitions frequently were hinted at on the

273

evening news. Melanie was young but not stupid. She survived by her wits.

What the poor girl had underestimated was the fragile state of poor, dear Betsy's mind. Melanie never suspected that her demands for money might be the final blow to Betsy's sanity. For that matter, neither had Mary Helen realized how delicate the balance was. She shuddered to think what might have happened today at the Refuge if the women hadn't jumped to her assistance. There was no telling how much longer it would have taken for Betsy to actually stab her.

Mary Helen was a little chagrined at her own reaction to the prospect of dying. Imagine being worried about how it would look when she should have been praying. Though she hated to admit it, when it was all over, the only prayer that came to her was, "Bless us, O Lord, in these, thy gifts." It took her a minute to realize that she was starting Grace before Meals. *Odd how the mind works*, she mused. *Thank heaven God reads the heart.*

She had surely been off on this homicide. She would have bet it was Andy or maybe Candy and that she had just misunderstood the name. She would have to have her ears checked. A hearing aid wasn't the worst thing that could happen to a person.

Although she didn't have any trouble at all hearing Richard Dodd when he'd called the convent tonight demanding to know what had happened to his wife.

Her reply had shocked him into silence. *Wait until he finds out that she doesn't want anything to do with him,* Mary Helen thought. *Maybe this will be the thing that makes him reexamine his life*—although she rather doubted it. Pompous fool that he was, he'd probably never even realize the part he played in his wife's downfall.

She rose up on one elbow and fluffed her down pillow. Maybe that would help. With her head resting on it she couldn't help but wonder how Betsy was sleeping on her first night in custody. For her sake Mary Helen hoped the woman had not come back to reality. The guilt she would feel about brutally bludgeoning a young woman to death and then attacking a nun could be overwhelming.

It seemed impossible that Betsy had coldly stuffed the dead body into the trunk of her Lexus and driven to the Refuge, then met her husband and gone to a cocktail party. The thought of riding with Betsy in that same car made the hairs on Mary Helen's arms stand up. Forensics would have a field day examining that trunk.

In the distance she heard a toilet flush. Someone else was awake. She suspected it was Sister Anne. She, too, must be reliving the day.

In retrospect, Mary Helen felt that Anne and she had done a good job telling the nuns at the convent about Betsy Dodd before the news media had broken the story. By the eleven o'clock news, everyone would know. Therese's niece's boyfriend must not be on duty.

After much discussion, they had agreed to leave out the part about Betsy Dodd slashing at Mary Helen with the butcher knife. "Nothing can be served by their knowing that," Mary Helen said.

"But it's the truth," Anne said defensively. She liked the part when the Refugees rescued Mary Helen.

"Well, we're not going to lie about it," Mary Helen assured her. "Remember we're just relating an incident. We're not going to confession. We don't have to tell the entire truth."

Anne seemed to be mulling that over while Mary Helen waited impatiently. *Youth is something she'll soon get over*, Mary Helen reminded herself.

The nuns naturally were shocked. "Why did the volunteer kill the girl?" Sister Patricia asked. Although Mary Helen suspected that the college president had a meeting to attend, she stayed around to hear the reason. *Once you love a mystery, you can't help yourself*, Mary Helen thought.

"Because she had a touch of madness," Mary Helen explained, "and when Melanie pressed her for money, Betsy felt trapped, suffocated, unable to do anything but lash out."

"She was such a wonderful woman, a saint," Sister Therese said, "so generous and hardworking."

"And so angry about it," old Donata added. "Whoever heard of an angry saint?" she insisted.

Therese simply rolled her eyes.

"To think she slept under our roof." Ursula looked secretly pleased. That story would be good at family gatherings for months.

"I still think she acted like a saint," Therese insisted, out of Donata's hearing, of course.

For once, Mary Helen had to agree with Therese. This very morning hadn't she thought at Mass, *Saints Protus, Hyacinth, and Betsy?* Was that not even twenty-four hours ago? How had everything changed so quickly? How was a woman who in many ways was genuinely good able to harbor such vicious madness? It was a mystery.

Mary Helen turned over on her side. *So much of life is a mystery to be lived and accepted,* she thought, not to be figured out. *Figuring out who's to blame and who's culpable belongs to God.* "And good luck to You, Lord," she said, her head beginning to ache with fatigue.

What was that Eileen always said? "God is not as severe as He's made out to be." *How could He be,* she wondered dreamily, *when He loves us so unconditionally?*

"Poor press," she heard God answer. Then He laughed. "Grace before Meals! Only you, old friend, only you!"